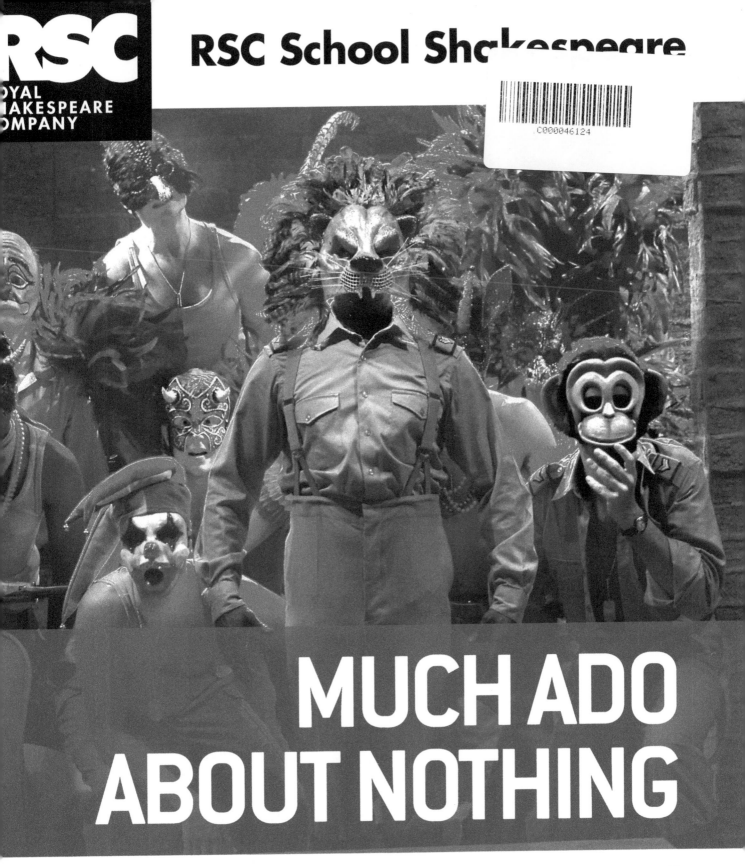

RSC
ROYAL SHAKESPEARE COMPANY

RSC School Shakespeare

C000046124

MUCH ADO ABOUT NOTHING

TEACHER GUIDE

OXFORD

UNIVERSITY PRESS

Great Clarendon Street, Oxford, OX2 6DP, United Kingdom

Oxford University Press is a department of the University of Oxford.

It furthers the University's objective of excellence in research, scholarship, and education by publishing worldwide. Oxford is a registered trade mark of Oxford University Press in the UK and in certain other countries

British Library Cataloguing in Publication Data

Data available

ISBN 978-019-836924-0

10 9 8 7 6 5 4 3

Printed in Great Britain by Ashford Print and Publishing Services, Gosport

Acknowledgements

Cover and performance images © Royal Shakespeare Company 2016

Much Ado About Nothing photographs by Simon Annand (2006) and Manuel Harlan (2014).

Contents

Celebrating with a dance, *Much Ado About Nothing*, 2014

Introduction

'*You do not understand Shakespeare fully until you have spoken the text aloud. This is because there is something in the physicality of the language which is not only an intrinsic part of the rhythm and form of the writing, but also of the underlying motive and reasoning of the characters involved. And I believe young people of whatever academic ability, given the right opportunity to speak the language, latch on to this in a remarkable way and I know it excites them and makes them want more.*'

Cicely Berry, RSC Voice Director

The classroom as rehearsal room

All the work of RSC Education is underpinned by the artistic practice of the Royal Shakespeare Company (RSC). In particular, we make very strong connections between the rehearsal rooms in which our actors and directors work and the classrooms in which you and your students work. Rehearsal rooms are essentially places of exploration and shared discovery, in which a company of actors and their director work together to bring Shakespeare's plays to life. To do this successfully, they need to have a deep understanding of the text, to get the language 'in the body', to speak it as if it is 'fresh-minted', and to be open to a range of interpretive possibilities and choices. The ways in which they do this are both active and playful, connecting mind, voice and body. They are also approaches that young people take to readily, allowing them to explore complex language confidently and openly.

Becoming a company

To do this we begin by deliberately building a spirit of one group with a shared purpose – this is about *us* rather than *me*. We often do this with games that warm up our brains, voices and bodies, and we continue to build this spirit through a scheme of work by shared, collaborative tasks that depend on and value everyone's contributions. The ways in which we work encourage young people to discuss, speculate and question – there is rarely one right answer. This process requires and develops critical thinking.

Making the world of the play

In rehearsals at the RSC, we explore the whole world of the play: we tackle the language, characters and motivation, setting, plot and themes, but we do that through a collective act of imagination, in which we bring to life the human experiences the play contains. Every member of the company is implicated, contributing their ideas and skills, so they become fully invested. In our rehearsal-based classrooms, a similar investment can take place. By 'standing in the shoes' of the characters and inhabiting the world of the play, students are implicated and engaged with their whole selves: head, eyes, ears, hands, bodies and hearts are involved in actively interpreting the play. In grappling with scenes and speeches, students are also actively grappling with the themes and ideas in the play, experiencing them from the point of view of the characters. Students should have the opportunity to identify themes as they arise from exploring the action, and make their understanding of those themes specific by relating them to their experiences of the world of the play.

The text is central to our discoveries

At the heart of this pedagogy is the idea of young people encountering Shakespeare as fellow artists. Working with his language in the same ways that actors do, they can create outcomes that offer real insight into the text, in which they can take great pride and which are often genuinely beautiful. For the actor in the rehearsal room, there is little distinction between play and work; they make plays for a living. The playful approaches we ask students to commit to and take seriously are real work in the real world.

We place the text at the core of everything we do. Whatever the abilities of the young people you teach, active, playful approaches can make Shakespeare's language vivid, accessible and enjoyable. His words have the power to excite and delight all of us.

Pushing back the desks

In the rehearsal room, the RSC uses social and historical contexts in order to deepen understanding of the world of the play. The company is engaged in a 'conversation across time', inviting audiences to consider what a play means to us now and what it meant to us then. We hope that the activities in this resource will offer your students an opportunity to join that conversation.

You will not need any specialist training in the fields of Shakespeare or drama to teach using this resource. All of the activities can be done in a normal English classroom, although occasionally you might push back the desks. The pedagogy you will find in these pages has been developed with teachers who work in a wide variety of classroom settings with students of all abilities and backgrounds. The activities require close, critical reading and encourage students to make informed interpretive choices about language, character and motivation, themes and plot. Often, the activities invite an intuitive, spontaneous response which is developed through questioning. The work is rooted in speaking and listening to Shakespeare's words and to each other's ideas. This way of working can produce sophisticated analytical responses, both oral and written, challenging the most able learners as well as motivating the most reluctant.

Building a classroom culture that values and celebrates this pedagogy takes time. For many young people, it may make demands on them that are unfamiliar, even uncomfortable to begin with. But persist and the rewards can be great, as students grow in confidence, embracing and unlocking this extraordinary literary inheritance.

Using *RSC School Shakespeare*

This resource will support you to teach Shakespeare using the pedagogy of the RSC rehearsal room. As you open each spread, you will see the complete script of the play on the right hand page. Accompanying the script, on the left hand page, are a series of features which we hope will enable you to work actively in your classroom. Those features are:

Summary
At the top of every page is a summary of what happens on the facing page. This is provided so that students can efficiently and easily contextualise the text and understand the action.

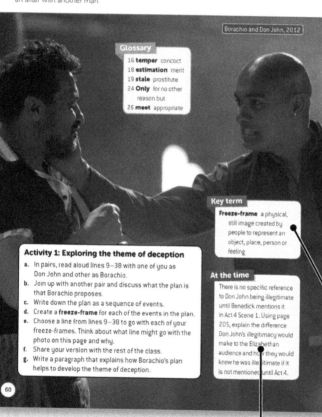

Borachio proposes a plan to Don John that will ruin Don Pedro's plans for Claudio and Hero. He suggests that they make Claudio and Don Pedro believe that Hero is having an affair with another man.

[Borachio and Don John, 2012]

Glossary
16 **temper** concoct
18 **estimation** merit
19 **stale** prostitute
24 **Only** for no other reason but
25 **meet** appropriate

Key term
Freeze-frame a physical, still image created by people to represent an object, place, person or feeling

Activity 1: Exploring the theme of deception
a. In pairs, read aloud lines 9–38 with one of you as Don John and other as Borachio.
b. Join up with another pair and discuss what the plan is that Borachio proposes.
c. Write down the plan as a sequence of events.
d. Create a **freeze-frame** for each of the events in the plan.
e. Choose a line from lines 9–38 to go with each of your freeze-frames. Think about what line might go with the photo on this page and why.
f. Share your version with the rest of the class.
g. Write a paragraph that explains how Borachio's plan helps to develop the theme of deception.

At the time
There is no specific reference to Don John being illegitimate until Benedick mentions it in Act 4 Scene 1. Using page 205, explain the difference Don John's illegitimacy would make to the Elizabethan audience and how they would know he was illegitimate if it is not mentioned until Act 4.

60

Act 2 | Scene 2

Enter Don John and Borachio

Don John It is so. The Count Claudio shall marry the daughter of Leonato.

Borachio Yea, my lord, but I can cross it.

Don John Any bar, any cross, any impediment will be medicinable to me. I am sick in displeasure to him, and whatsoever comes athwart his affection ranges evenly with mine. How canst thou cross this marriage? 5

Borachio Not honestly, my lord, but so covertly that no dishonesty shall appear in me.

Don John Show me briefly how.

Borachio I think I told your lordship a year since how much I am in the favour of Margaret, the waiting gentlewoman to Hero. 10

Don John I remember.

Borachio I can, at any unseasonable instant of the night appoint her to look out at her lady's chamber window.

Don John What life is in that to be the death of this marriage? 15

Borachio The poison of that lies in you to temper. Go you to the Prince your brother. Spare not to tell him that he hath wronged his honour in marrying the renowned Claudio – whose estimation do you mightily hold up – to a contaminated stale, such a one as Hero. 20

Don John What proof shall I make of that?

Borachio Proof enough to misuse the Prince, to vex Claudio, to undo Hero and kill Leonato. Look you for any other issue?

Don John Only to despite them, I will endeavour anything.

Borachio Go then. Find me a meet hour to draw Don Pedro and the 25

61

At the time
There are simple social and historical research tasks, so that students can use knowledge from the time the play was written to help them interpret the script. The social and historical information can be found towards the front of the edition of the play.

Key terms
Where needed, there is an explanation of any key terms used, literary or theatrical.

Did you know?

For every scene, we have provided insight into RSC rehearsal practice, so that students can link the work they are doing in the classroom to the work that is done by actors, directors and designers at the RSC. We hope that students will see themselves as fellow artists, working alongside the professionals, exploring the play in a similar way.

For your teaching needs, you may choose to work on key scenes. However, if you work through the whole play from beginning to end, using the activities on each page, you will be taking your students on a progressive learning journey. Their journey parallels the journey which the RSC follows in rehearsal for a production: a collaborative, cumulative exploration. Some activities may feel more comfortable for your teaching style or environment than others, and you may, of course, choose to use the activities alongside your own classroom approaches.

Glossary

Where needed, there is a glossary which explains those words which may be unfamiliar to students and cannot be worked out in context.

Don Pedro, Claudio and Leonato leave Benedick alone. He shares with the audience his thoughts and feelings about Beatrice, and decides that he loves her. Beatrice comes in and tells him it is dinner time.

Did you know?

Actors often physically explore the punctuation in a speech to help them connect with the way their character is thinking and feeling.

Glossary

182–183 **no such matter** there will be nothing in it
184 **a dumb show** speechless
185 **sadly** seriously
187 **full bent** fully stretched (like an archer's bow)
196 **horribly** totally
201–202 **career of his humour** pursuit of his mood

Activity 7: Exploring punctuation

a. Read lines 185–205. As you read aloud, stand up on the first full stop, sit down on the next one and then continue standing up or sitting down every time you come to a full stop. Treat the question marks in the same way. When you come to a comma, stamp your foot.

b. Join up with a partner and discuss what impact the use of punctuation has in this speech. The punctuation is an indicator of a character moving from one thought to another. What state of mind would you say Benedick is in? How do you think he is feeling during this speech? Why might that be?

c. Write a paragraph or two explaining what you think Benedick's state of mind is at this stage in the play. Use evidence from lines 185–205 in your writing.

Benedick, 2014

76

Leonato My lord, will you walk? Dinner is ready.

Claudio (Aside) If he do not dote on her upon this, I will never trust my expectation.

Don Pedro (Aside) Let there be the same net spread for her, and that must your daughter and her gentlewomen carry. The sport will be when they hold one an opinion of another's dotage, and no such matter. That's the scene that I would see, which will be merely a dumb show. Let us send her to call him in to dinner.   180

Exeunt Don Pedro, Claudio and Leonato

Benedick This can be no trick. The conference was sadly borne. They have the truth of this from Hero. They seem to pity the lady. It seems her affections have their full bent. Love me? Why, it must be requited. I hear how I am censured. They say I will bear myself proudly if I perceive the love come from her. They say too that she will rather die than give any sign of affection. I did never think to marry. I must not seem proud. Happy are they that hear their detractions and can put them to mending. They say the lady is fair. 'Tis a truth, I can bear them witness. And virtuous. 'Tis so, I cannot reprove it. And wise, but for loving me. By my troth, it is no addition to her wit, nor no great argument of her folly, for I will be horribly in love with her. I may chance have some odd quirks and remnants of wit broken on me because I have railed so long against marriage, but doth not the appetite alter? A man loves the meat in his youth that he cannot endure in his age. Shall quips and sentences and these paper bullets of the brain awe a man from the career of his humour? No. The world must be peopled. When I said I would die a bachelor, I did not think I should live till I were married. Here comes Beatrice. By this day, she's a fair lady. I do spy some marks of love in her.   205

  185

  190

  195

  200

Enter Beatrice

Beatrice Against my will I am sent to bid you come in to dinner.

Benedick Fair Beatrice, I thank you for your pains.

77

Activity

Every page includes at least one classroom activity which is inspired by RSC rehearsal room practice.

RSC production photographs

Every page includes at least one photograph from an RSC production of the play. Some of the activities make direct use of the production photographs. The photographs illustrate the action, bringing to life the text on the page. They also include a caption that identifies the characters or event, together with the date of the RSC production.

Editing choices

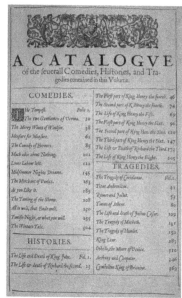

A list of the plays contained in the First Folio of William Shakespeare 1623

Following his death in 1616, two of Shakespeare's friends and colleagues, John Heminges and Henry Condell, put together a collection of his plays which was published in1623, known as the First Folio, and this edition of the play is based on the First Folio text.

Punctuation

Our text has been edited for punctuation, and choices based on clarity have been made where wording and lineation vary between Folio and Quarto★. Fashions in punctuation change but its purpose is always to support the reader's understanding. In this edition, our motive has been to keep the punctuation as simple and clear as possible but to avoid influencing students' choices. Exclamation marks, for example, are rarely used in the First Folio whereas today's fashion is to use them more liberally. In this edition, they have been used only when they appear in the First Folio or when it is clear an exclamation is required, such as calling out a greeting. In most cases, sentences end in full stops, allowing the students to decide the tone of a line and whether they feel it should be spoken as an exclamation, a statement or a question.

Stage directions

Similarly, there are very few stage directions in the First Folio but those that do exist most probably reflect the stage business as originally performed. Where these stage directions do exist, we have kept them so that students can choose to follow them or not. Generally, Shakespeare gives us important stage directions in the text; for example entrances are often marked by 'Here comes…'. Students are encouraged in the activities to discover directions for action written in the text and to add their own choices about actions and movements appropriate for the scene.

★ The Quarto was a smaller format of publication. As with the larger Folio editions, many versions of the Quarto were produced with variations in editorial decisions

Dogberry, Verges and the Watch, *Much Ado About Nothing*, 2014

Working collaboratively

When a new group of actors and their director come together to rehearse at the RSC, time is spent on the practical, playful process of building a company. This is partly achieved by 'warming up' through a series of physical and vocal games and exercises, before exploring together whichever scenes and speeches are in the rehearsal schedule for that day.

Starter activities

In the classroom, the equivalent to the 'warm up' would be the 'starter' activity, which scaffolds the main activity of the lesson. In a rehearsal-based classroom, starter activities should build physical and vocal confidence, communication skills and positive relationships, as well as introducing any new knowledge required for the lesson. For example, if you are going to ask your students to work in pairs to explore a dialogue, you might start the lesson with a game. If the dialogue you are going to be exploring is full of conflict, the game you choose might be one in which your students can score points against their partner. Or, if you want the focus to be on the quality of the relationship between the two characters, you might ask pairs to make a freeze-frame which shows their initial interpretation of that relationship, before going on to explore the dialogue in more detail.

Grouping

We have left grouping as open as possible, so that you can use the activities flexibly. While some of them can be done as individuals, we recommend that you enable your students to collaborate wherever possible. Interpretation in rehearsal always comes from sharing and valuing each other's ideas, questioning assumptions and speculating possibilities, which we can only do with others. Often the number of characters in a scene will lead naturally to grouping in your classroom. If a scene has four characters, a group of four should explore it. If you don't have the right number of students to make equal sized groups, there is a benefit in having an 'extra' group member who can either bring in another point of view as a non-speaking character (for example, as a servant in a court scene) or fulfil a directorial function, acting as an outside eye for the rest of their group as they decide how to interpret a scene together.

> **Examples of flexible grouping activities include:**
> - Act 1: page 16, 24, 28
> - Act 2: page 38, 46, 70, 74
> - Act 3: page 90
> - Act 4: page 122
> - Act 5: page 152, 154, 160, 182

Antonio, Balthasar, Hero, Leonato and Beatrice, *Much Ado About Nothing*, 2014

Questioning

Good questioning is crucial both in encouraging students to experiment with ideas and in leading their reflections after each activity. Students will often have found an embodied understanding through the activities, but without time spent articulating that understanding it can easily dissipate.

Using open questions

Open questions are often defined as questions to which you cannot respond with one 'right' answer or with a simple yes or no. The questions we offer in these activities are framed to avoid yes/no answers and encourage students to reflect more deeply on the understanding they have gained actively. These questions are far from exhaustive and we would urge you to ask others.

Making personal connections

One successful approach is to ask questions that encourage students to link the emotions and situations of the play with emotions and situations they can relate to from their own experiences and imaginations. Opening questions you can always ask are:

- How did that exercise make you feel?
- What discoveries did you make by speaking the text in that way?

Some students need more time to think and process their thoughts than others. Paired or group reflections are very useful in giving each student more opportunity to express and develop their responses in dialogue with each other. This can be followed by a whole class plenary in which more students can be encouraged to take part because they have had time to formulate their ideas.

Many teachers have found that asking students to record their thoughts and ideas in journals as they work through their study of the play is hugely beneficial and provides personalised notes to return to when completing assessments.

> **Open questions appear on every page but examples of activities with more open questions include:**
> - Act 1: pages 16, 20, 28, 30, 34
> - Act 2: pages 42, 56, 62, 78
> - Act 3: pages 90, 92, 96, 106, 110, 114
> - Act 4: pages 120, 124, 126, 136, 142
> - Act 5: pages 154, 158, 162, 164, 172, 176, 186, 190

Leonato and Antonio, *Much Ado About Nothing*, 2006

Creating a character

Character motivation

In order for an actor to play a character, they must first understand what motivates their character. The questions that actors and their director ask about the characters in a scene are often deceptively simple: 'Who are they?', 'In what time period and time of day is the scene taking place?', 'Where are they?', 'What are they doing?', 'What are they trying to achieve?', 'Why are they doing that?' It is through these basic questions that the company begin to bring the play to life. By asking these questions of themselves and each other, the company have to search for clues in the text which help them to decide what is motivating the characters.

Developing the 'given circumstances'

Actors pay attention to the 'given circumstances' of a scene, or those things that we know from the text. For example, in asking 'Where are they?', the company might know from the text that a scene is set in 'a room in the castle', but which room? What are the values, social customs and atmosphere of the place? In asking 'Who are they?', the company might know that the characters are father and daughter, but they must work out what the exact nature of the relationship is and how it evolves, the shifting status of the characters, their 'backstory' (or what has happened between them before the play starts), and what has happened in the play thus far to affect the characters and their actions. Character motivation is discovered by actively exploring the evidence in the text to make informed interpretations.

The activities in this resource are designed to help students answer the basic questions about character for themselves: Who? What? Where? When? Why? so that they can work out character motivation. A company of actors rehearsing a play at the RSC ask each other questions all the time, and we recommend that you encourage students to ask each other these questions as they work. Using the activities will offer your students plenty of opportunities to do just that.

> **Examples of activities requiring students to ask questions about characters include:**
> - Act 1: pages 16, 20, 22, 28, 34
> - Act 2: pages 40, 46, 50, 52, 70, 74, 76
> - Act 3: pages 84, 90, 92, 104, 112
> - Act 4: pages 120, 124, 136, 138, 140, 142
> - Act 5: pages 152, 154, 158, 160, 168, 182, 184, 190

Margaret and Hero, *Much Ado About Nothing*, 2006

Layering

In rehearsal, actors and their director explore the same part of the text in different ways, with the aim of developing a deep understanding of that part of the action. It is a cumulative, layered process, in which multiple possibilities for interpretation are explored. Then, the company make mutually agreed, informed interpretive choices based on the evidence in the text.

Extending learning opportunities

In order to emulate this rehearsal process in the classroom, we recommend offering a series of short activities, which build on each other but explore a different aspect of the text each time. This can enable close reading and active engagement, but avoid students getting bored working on the same part of the text. In this resource, we have usually offered a single activity for exploring the text on each page, for the sake of clarity. But, as you work through the activities with your class, you will notice strategies which could easily be transferred to use with a different part of the text. If there is a particular scene which you want your students to focus on more fully, we hope you will consider transferring some of the activities from other pages to enable a deeper understanding of your focus scene. In this way, we can layer and extend the learning opportunities for our students.

Repeating activities

In the rehearsal room, it is common practice for the company to explore each new scene or speech in a play using familiar activities. A shared set of approaches is deliberately developed. Because the strategies are applied to different parts of the text, they feel fresh each time. Similarly, in the rehearsal-based classroom, we deliberately apply the same strategies to different parts of the text so that our students have the opportunity to become familiar and more confident with those activities. In so doing, we build layers of understanding and engagement. As you explore this resource, you will notice strategies that are repeated. We hope you will also notice how the same activities can produce widely differentiated outcomes, simply because they are applied to a different part of the text.

One of the outcomes of using this layered approach can be to highlight the structure of a play. In the many plays where Shakespeare offers a parallel or 'sub' plot alongside the main action, using the same active strategies to explore parallel events in the play can enable our students to see the similarities (and differences) between them.

> **Examples of activities which use several strategies to layer understanding in this way include:**
> - Act 1: pages 24 and 30
> - Act 2: pages 54 and 64
> - Act 3: page 102
> - Act 4: pages 126 and 136
> - Act 5: pages 154, 156 and 182

> **Examples of activities highlighting structure include:**
> - Act 2: page 30
> - Act 3: page 90
> - Act 4: page 124
> - Act 5: page 158

Creative constraints

In order to test the relationships between characters in an RSC rehearsal room, actors often find it useful to try exercises that put some kind of limitation on how they respond. By applying this limitation, actors make discoveries about what the lines could mean and about their relationship with other characters. Using the same exercises, students can experiment with different ways to interpret a scene and can discuss what feels right for them in expressing the relationship between their characters and why.

Movement choices

In some activities students are asked to choose between simple movements. Giving students simple but specific choices to make removes the fear of 'acting' but also means they can't just stand still and speak because standing still becomes a choice, not a default. In making these simple choices, students find intuitive responses led by the words their own character speaks or the words that are spoken to them. These exercises are also useful for thinking about characters present in a scene who have no, or few, lines. These characters are still required to make the choices about movement and other characters have to respond to what they do.

> **Examples of activities exploring movement choices include:**
> - Act 2: page 30
> - Act 3: page 90
> - Act 4: page 124
> - Act 5: page 158

Speaking choices

In other activities, students are given constraints about how they speak. For example, they can compare how whispering lines and then speaking them loudly brings out different qualities of expression; how reading aloud and swapping reader on each punctuation mark can clarify sense but also express whether a character is feeling calm or agitated; how speaking to achieve a simple objective, like getting another character to look at you, brings language alive by giving a character a reason to speak.

> **Examples of activities exploring speaking choices include:**
> - Act 1: page 30
> - Act 4: page 136
> - Act 5: page 182

Claudio and Hero, *Much Ado About Nothing*, 2006

Speaking text aloud

Unlike many of the other texts we tackle with our students, a play text is intended to be shared aloud, between characters on stage and with the audience. The text is not simply black marks on a piece of paper, but words that are meant to be expressed and received orally and aurally. In the RSC rehearsal room, the company of actors and their director use the text as a script, to be shared. One of the challenges of working with a play which is four hundred years old is that it has been done many times before. Nevertheless, each new company which tackles the play will go through the process of speaking and listening to the words, negotiating meaning until a unique, new version of the play is discovered. We can offer the same opportunity to our students, in a speaking and listening process which can lead to highly engaged and personalised responses to the text.

Making meaning

A word on the page may appear to have a fixed meaning, but when that word is spoken, the meaning of the word is dependent on the intention of the speaker. Consider for a moment the word 'yes'. We all know the dictionary definition of that word. However, when the word 'yes' is spoken as if the speaker is doubtful, it means something entirely different than when the same word, 'yes', is spoken as if the speaker is excited. Tone, pitch, volume and pace are essential to the meaning of the spoken word. So, in rehearsal, meaning is negotiated by speaking the text aloud, exploring and experimenting until a consensus is reached. The activities in this resource offer students the opportunity to follow the same process.

> **Examples of activities making meaning include:**
> - Act 1: page 18
> - Act 2: pages 48 and 54
> - Act 3: page 102
> - Act 4: page 136
> - Act 5: pages 156 and 182

Getting the language 'in the body'

Actors and directors at the RSC refer to 'getting the language in the body', by which they mean doing exercises which connect them with the sound and rhythm of the words. The phonic and poetic quality of the language is as important as the literal meaning of the words. Sound and rhythm are deeply affective, experienced on an instinctive level. By voicing and hearing the words, actors can experience the effect of the language. We can offer the same opportunity to our students by encouraging them to speak and listen to the words through the activities in this resource.

> **Examples of getting the language 'in the body' include:**
> - Act 1: page 30
> - Act 2: pages 42 and 76
> - Act 3: page 110
> - Act 4: pages 122, 128 and 130
> - Act 5: page 164

Embodying text

Embodying the text is an actor's job. A fundamental aspect of exploring the plays as plays is being on your feet, stepping into the shoes of the characters, experiencing what it is like to be Beatrice or Juliet, Shylock or Banquo, and able to express your thoughts and feelings as articulately as they do. Working with play texts provides excellent opportunities for developing every student's inbuilt facility for communication skills. Just as most of us naturally and easily learn to speak as very young children, we naturally and easily learn to read body language. Students with English as an Additional Language (EAL) and less confident readers often thrive with this work because they can use their understanding of gesture and tone.

Examples of activities for embodying text:
- Act 1: pages 16 and 24
- Act 2: page 54
- Act 3: pages 102 and 94
- Act 4: page 144
- Act 5: pages 152 and 154

Freeze-frames

Freeze-frames are frequently suggested in our activities because they can quickly tap into the key themes in the plays or physically summarise a relationship. For example, a freeze-frame of 'a royal leader and his subjects' created by the students themselves enables a kinaesthetic, imaginative understanding of abstract notions like status and hierarchy to deconstruct through questioning. Freeze-frames of 'brothers' or 'father and daughter' can provide a spectrum of attitudes: love, happiness, fear, disappointment, resentment. Acknowledging these different possibilities can provide a quick and easy insight into the complexity of family relationships. Discussion of these images can lead us into the world of the play by making it relevant to our own worlds. Asking students to create a freeze-frame from a line of text, or asking students to adjust a freeze-frame to reflect or include a line of text are ways to deepen connections between our physical, emotional and intellectual understanding of the text.

Examples of activities using freeze-frames include:
- Act 1: page 22
- Act 2: page 52
- Act 3: page 100
- Act 4: page 126
- Act 5: pages 160 and 178

Gestures

Other activities ask students to find 'gestures' for key words. In a similar way to working with freeze-frames, these activities support an intellectual understanding of the text through physical associations. For example, creating gestures for the rich imagery of the oppositional elements in antithesis can support appreciation of the internal conflicts a character feels.

Examples of activities exploring gesture include:
- Act 1: pages 18, 20 and 32
- Act 2: page 48
- Act 3: page 92
- Act 4: page 134
- Act 5: pages 156 and 188

Rhythm

Working with the rhythms of the text can give an actor important understanding of how a character might be feeling. You will notice that activities ask students to engage physically with rhythm through galloping, clapping or tapping. This physical approach makes it very clear when there are variations or disturbances to the rhythm so that students can consider what the variations might suggest about a character's state of mind, and how Shakespeare crafts his writing around unfolding rhythms.

Examples of activities exploring rhythm include:
- Act 1: page 26
- Act 3: page 88
- Act 4: page 132
- Act 5: page 166

Glossary

Adjective a word that describes a noun, e.g. blue, happy, big

Antithesis bringing two opposing concepts or ideas together, e.g. hot and cold, love and hate, loud and quiet

Backstory what happened to any of the characters before the start of the play

Blocking the movements agreed for staging a scene

Body language how we communicate feelings to each other using our bodies (including facial expressions) rather than words

Courtship a period of time where a couple develop a romantic relationship

Dialogue a discussion between two or more people

Director the person who enables the practical and creative interpretation of a dramatic script, and ultimately brings together everybody's ideas in a way that engages the audience with the play

Dramatic climax the most intense or important point in the action of a play

Dramatic irony when the audience knows something that some characters in the play do not

Dramatic tension the anticipation of an outcome on stage, keeping the audience in suspense

Emphasis stress given to words when speaking

Epitaph something written or said in memory of a dead person

Explicit clear and open

Extended metaphor describing something by comparing it to something else over several lines

Falling action the part of a play, before the very end, in which the consequences of the dramatic climax become clear

Freeze-frame a physical, still image created by people to represent an object, place, person or feeling

Gesture a movement, often using the hands or head, to express a feeling or idea

Iambic pentameter the rhythm Shakespeare uses to write his plays. Each line in this rhythm contains approximately ten syllables. 'Iambic' means putting the stress on the second syllable of each beat. 'Pentameter' means five beats with two syllables in each beat

Imagery visually descriptive language

Improvise make up in the moment

Malapropism mistaken use of a word that sounds like another word but has a very different meaning

Monologue a long speech in which a character expresses their thoughts. Other characters may be present

Motivation a person's reason for doing something

Objective what a character wants to get or achieve in a scene

Obstacle what is in the way of a character getting what they want

Pace the speed at which someone speaks

Paraphrase put a line or section of text into your own words

Parody an imitation of a style of writing, with deliberate exaggeration to make it funny

Pronoun a word (such as I, he, she, you, it, we or they) that is used instead of a noun

Prop an object used in the play, e.g. a dagger

Pun a play on words

Rhyming couplet two lines of verse where the last words of each line rhyme

Soliloquy a speech in which a character is alone on stage and expresses their thoughts and feelings aloud to the audience

Stage business activity onstage

Stage direction an instruction in the text of a play, e.g. indicating which characters enter and exit a scene

Staging the process of selecting, adapting and developing the stage space in which a play will be performed

Statue like a freeze-frame but usually of a single character

Subtext the underlying meaning in the script

Syllable part of a word that is one sound, e.g. 'highness' has two syllables – 'high' and 'ness'

Symbol a thing that represents or stands for something else

Tactics the methods a character uses to get what they want

Theme the main ideas explored in a piece of literature, e.g. the themes of love and marriage, male and female relationships, deception, loyalty and honour might be considered key themes of Much Ado About Nothing

Tone as in 'tone of voice'; expressing an attitude through how you say something

Vowels the letters a, e, i, o, u

Woo to try to make someone fall in love with you so that they will agree to marry you

JOURNAL CONTENT

Shalom !

Thank you for choosing this notebook to discover and practice the Hebrew alphabet.

Hebrew is more than just a language; it is also the reflect of an ancient and rich culture.

Learning this culture comes with learning the alphabet – the *aleph bet*.

This notebook is perfect for kids, teenagers and adults interested in learning and

practicing the Hebrew letters. Please note that this journal contains only the letters

and the sofits, not the vowels/ niqquds.

This journal shows, for each letter, both the handwriting and the printing versions

(this last one being the one Israeli kids learn at school). Each letter is in dot so that you

can practice the writing.

Good practice ! Thank you – Toda

ALEPH

א

Hand-writing

2

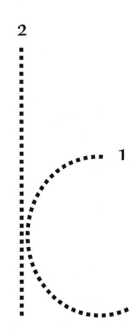

1

Printing

1

2

3

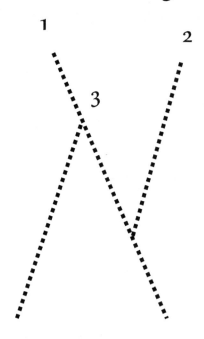

Draw line starting at 1

Draw line starting at 2

Draw line starting at 1

Draw line starting at 2

Draw line starting at 3

Practice

BET

Hand-writing

Printing

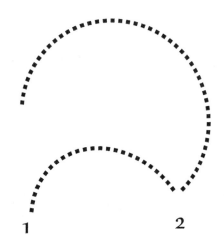

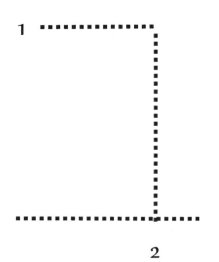

Draw line starting at 1

(Draw curve clockwise)

Draw line starting at 2

(Draw curve counter-clockwise)

Draw line starting at 1

(Right, down)

Draw line starting at 2 (left)

Practice

GIMEL

Hand-writing	**Printing**

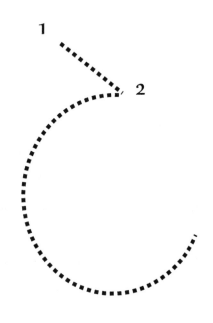

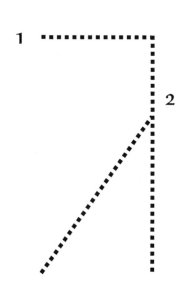

Draw line starting at 1

Draw line starting at 1

(Right, down)

Draw line starting at 2

Draw line starting at 2

Practice

DALET

Hand-writing

Printing

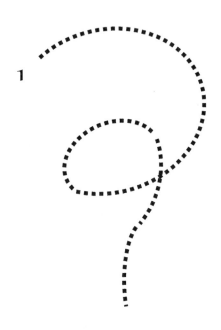

1

1   2

Draw line starting at 1

Draw line starting at 1

Draw line starting at 2

Practice

HE

ה

Hand-writing

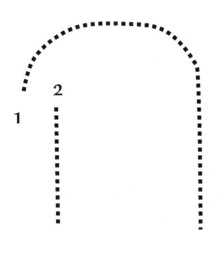

Printing

Draw line starting at 1

Draw line starting at 2

(Down)

Draw line starting at 1

(Right, down)

Draw line starting at 2 (Down)

Practice

....

....

....

....

....

....

....

....

....

....

....

....

....

....

....

....

....

....

VAV

ן

Hand-writing	Printing
1	1
Draw line starting at 1	Draw line starting at 1 (Right, down)

Practice

ZAYIN

Hand-writing

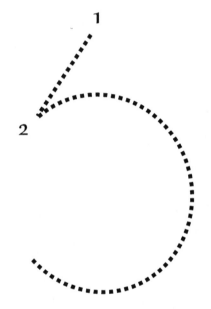

Printing

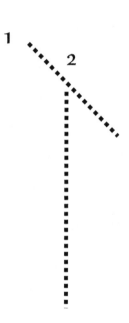

Draw line starting at 1

Draw line starting at 1

Draw line starting at 2
(Draw curve clockwise)

Draw line starting at 2 (Down)

Practice

....

....

....

....

....

....

....

....

....

....

....

....

....

....

....

....

....

CHEIT

ח

Hand-writing

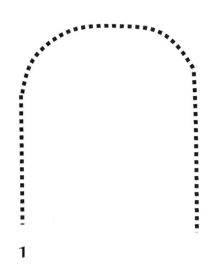

Draw line starting at 1

Printing

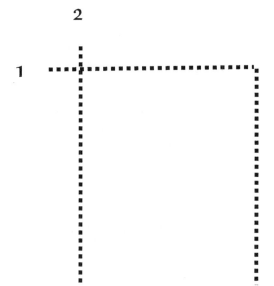

**Draw line starting at 1
(Right, down)**

Draw line starting at 2

Practice

TEIT

ט

Hand-writing

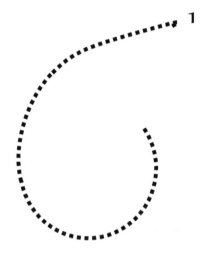

Draw line starting at 1

Printing

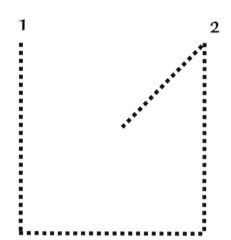

Draw line starting at 1
(Down, right, up)

Draw line starting at 2

Practice

YOD

י

Hand-writing

Printing

Draw line starting at 1

Draw line starting at 1
(Right, down)

Yod is a letter placed in the upper right side

of the letter frame

Practice

KHAF

Hand-writing	Printing

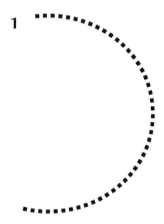

Draw line starting at 1

Draw line starting at 1 (Right, down, left)

Practice

KHAF sofit
ך

Hand-writing   **Printing**

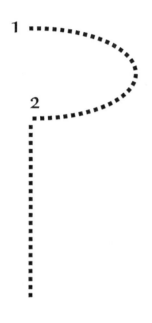

Draw line starting at 1   Draw line starting at 1
                                 (Right, down)

Draw line starting at 2

Khaf is written like this when it is at the end of a word

Practice

LAMED

ל

Hand-writing

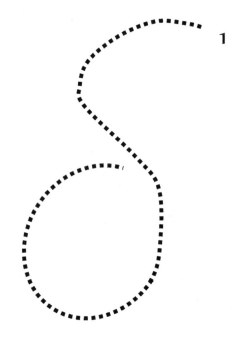

1

Draw line starting at 1

Printing

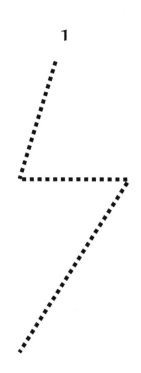

1

Draw line starting at 1
(Down, Right, Down)

Practice

MEM

מ

Hand-writing	Printing

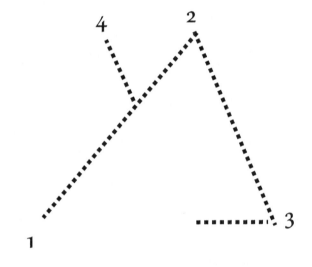

Draw line starting at 1

Draw line starting at 2

Draw line starting at 3

Draw line starting at 1

Draw line starting at 2

Draw line starting at 3

Draw line starting at 4

Practice

MEM sofit

מ

Hand-writing

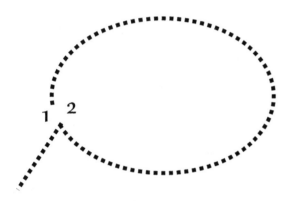

Printing

Draw line starting at 1
(round clockwise)

Draw line starting at 2

Draw line starting at 1
(Right, down, left, up)

Mem is written like this when it is at the end of a word

Practice

NUN
נ

Hand-writing

1

Printing

1

Draw line starting at 1

Draw line starting at 1 (Down, left)

Practice

NUN sofit

ן

Hand-writing	Printing
1	1 2

Draw line starting at 1

Draw line starting at 1 (down)

Draw line starting at 2 (left)

Nun is written like this when it is at the end of a word

Practice

SAMEKH

Hand-writing

Printing

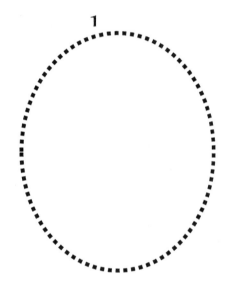

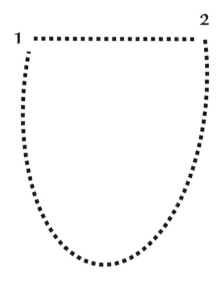

Draw line starting at 1

Draw line starting at 1 (right)

Draw line starting at 2 (clockwise)

Practice

AYIN

ע

Hand-writing	Printing

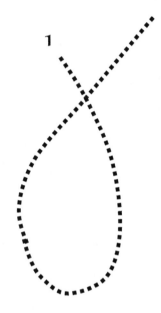

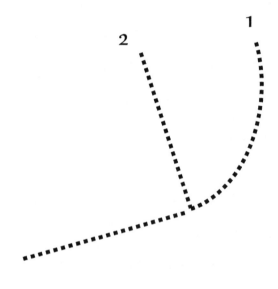

Draw line starting at 1

Draw line starting at 1

Draw line starting at 2

Practice

PEH

Hand-writing	Printing

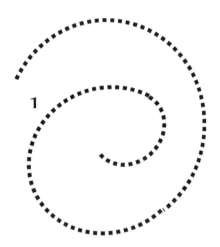

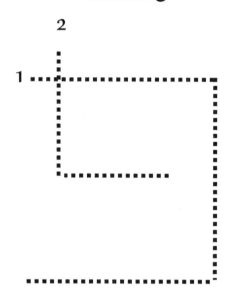

Draw line starting at 1

**Draw line starting at 1
(Right, down, left)**

**Draw line starting at 2
(Down, right)**

40

Practice

PEH sofit

Hand-writing	Printing

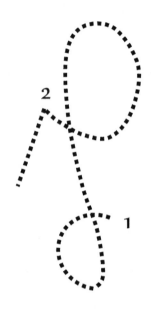
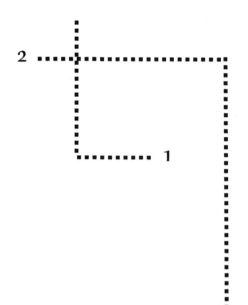

Draw line starting at 1

Draw line starting at 2

Draw line starting at 1
(left, up)

Draw line starting at 2
(right, down)

Peh is written like this when it is at the end of a word

Practice

....

....

....

....

....

....

....

....

....

....

....

....

....

....

....

....

....

TZADI

Hand-writing

Draw line starting at 1

Printing

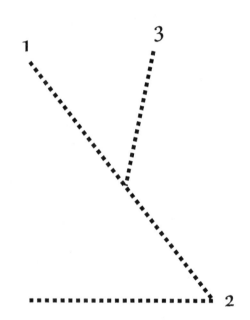

Draw line starting at 1

Draw line starting at 2

Draw line starting at 3

Practice

TZADI sofit

Hand-writing

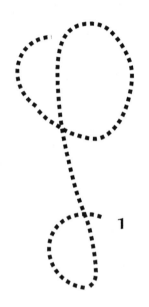

Draw line starting at 1

Printing

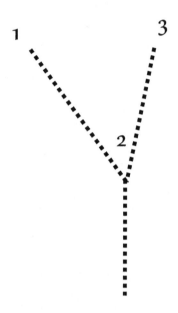

Draw line starting at 1

Draw line starting at 2

Draw line starting at 3

Tzadi is written like this when it is at the end of a word

Practice

QOF

Hand-writing	Printing
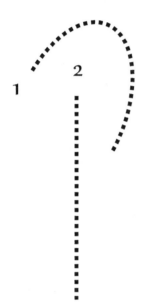	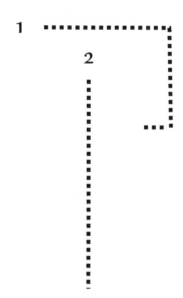

Draw line starting at 1

Draw line starting at 2

**Draw line starting at 1
(Right, down, left)**

Draw line starting at 2

Practice

REISH

ר

Hand-writing

Printing

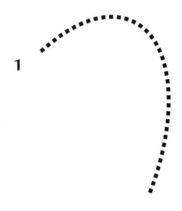

1

Draw line starting at 1

**Draw line starting at 1
(Right, down)**

Practice

SHIN

Hand-writing

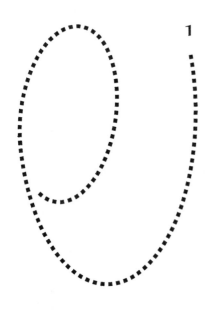

Printing

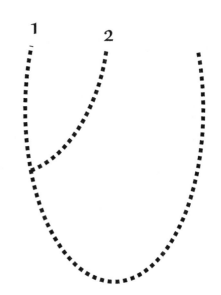

Draw line starting at 1

Draw line starting at 1

Draw line starting at 2

Practice

TAV

Hand-writing	**Printing**

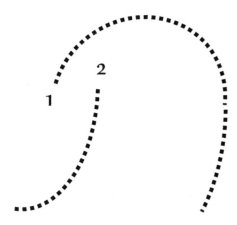

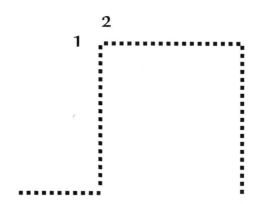

Draw line starting at 1

Draw line starting at 2

Draw line starting at 1
(Right and down)

Draw line starting at 2
(Down and left)

Practice

. . . .

. . . .

. . . .

. . . .

. . . .

. . . .

. . . .

. . . .

. . . .

. . . .

. . . .

. . . .

. . . .

. . . .

. . . .

. . . .

. . . .

WHAT DID YOU THINK?

First, thank you for purchasing this book and reading it through to the end!

We know you could have picked any number of books to read, but you picked this book and for that we are extremely grateful. We hope you enjoyed your reading experience.

If so, would you mind taking a minute to leave a review on Amazon? We read every review and they help new readers to discover our books.

Besides, if you think this book could be of interest to family or friends, please feel free to share it with them.

On the contrary, if you did not like the book, please don't hesitate to email us at: judaismrhythm@gmail.com and share your ideas for improvement. We will gladly receive your constructive feedback and keep your comments in mind for our next books.

PS: Don't forget to download your free bonus (see below).

YOU LIKED THE BOOK AND WANT TO KNOW MORE ABOUT THE

JEWISH TRADITIONS?

⇨ **DOWNLOAD THIS FREE PDF TO GUIDE YOU THROUGH THE**

SHABBATH RITUALS

ABOUT JUDAIMS RHYTHM

Judaism Rhythm

Judaism Rhythm is passionate about the Jewish Culture.

Its mission is to provide simple and helpful information about Judaism: its origins,

history, culture, traditions, rituals, and values.

Such information is for knowledge seekers, both adults and children, curious about this

topic and regardless of their religious backgrounds and/or involvement.

Printed in Great Britain
by Amazon

HOW TO BUILD AN
ONLINE
BUSINESS

Australia's Top Digital Disruptors Reveal Their Secrets for Launching and Growing an Online Business

BERNADETTE SCHWERDT

WILEY

First published in 2018 by John Wiley & Sons Australia, Ltd
42 McDougall St, Milton Qld 4064
Office also in Melbourne

Typeset in 12/15pt Liberation Serif

 A catalogue record for this
book is available from the
National Library of Australia

Cover design by Wiley

Cover image © filo/iStockphoto

Internal figures: figure 7.1: © Mtsaride/Shutterstock;
© tehcheesiong/Shutterstock

Printed in Singapore by C.O.S. Printers Pte Ltd

10 9 8 7 6 5 4 3 2 1

Disclaimer

To my wonderful family who make it all possible and worthwhile

Phil, Darcy, Cameron and Maddi

And to the best parents a girl could hope for

Rosemary and David Schwerdt

CONTENTS

ABOUT THE
AUTHOR

Bernadette Schwerdt is a writer, keynote speaker and entrepreneur. She is the founder of the Australian School of Copywriting, the head copywriting tutor at the Australian Writers' Centre, and a former senior account director with Wunderman Cato Johnson Advertising, where she created campaigns for clients such as Apple, American Express and BHP.

She has a business degree in Marketing from the University of South Australia, is the author of the best-selling book *Secrets of Online Entrepreneurs*, the producer of a video series of the same name for Fairfax Media and a popular TEDx speaker on a topic close to her heart: 'How to bumble your way to success'.

She is on the board of Writers Victoria, a mentor with the Layne Beachley 'Aim for the Stars' foundation, and a judge for the Anthill Cool Company Awards and the Online Retailers Industry Awards (ORIAs). She has been featured in *BRW, Money* magazine, *HuffPost* and on Sky News.

She took three years out of the corporate world to study acting at the Victorian College of the Arts, has since worked extensively as an actor in film and television and is a leading public speaking coach for senior executives.

You could say she's had what is now known as a 'portfolio' career. Her mother still doesn't know exactly what she does.

ACKNOWLEDGEMENTS

I would like to thank all those who made this book possible.

To the fantastic team at Wiley Publishing: Lucy Raymond, Chris Shorten, Peter Walmsley, Ingrid Bond and Sandra Balonyi.

To all the amazing online entrepreneurs and expert contributors who participated in the book. Thank you for your time, honesty and generosity of spirit.

To my wonderful family, friends and business colleagues:

Patrick and Sandy Schwerdt, Edmund and Sheryn Schwerdt, Stephen and Rosalind Schwerdt, Monique Eddy, Heather Fraser, Judyth Wiley, Jenny Thurlow, Karen Claren, Theresa Miller, Karen Eck, Ami-Leigh O'Donnell, Meri Harli, Paul Greenberg, Toby Tremayne, Glenn Flood, Andrew Romeo, Samuel Tan, Alex Sapurmas, Sylvia Young, Jane Carbone, Michelle West, and Gina Battista.

PREFACE
What's your
'pinch of salt'?

I have a confession to make.

I don't like cooking. But ironically, I really like watching cooking shows.

The show I love most of all is *MasterChef* and the reason I love it is not because of what they cook; it's about *how* they cook and how that cooking process reveals their true entrepreneurial personality. I'll give you an example.

There's a segment on the show where all the contestants are given a recipe. This recipe is often prepared by a famous chef—such as Heston Blumenthal—a chef renowned for creating fiendishly difficult recipes. The contestants' job is to re-create this recipe to the letter. If a contestant gets it wrong, they run the risk of going home. If you watch the show, you'll know that going home is to be avoided at all costs.

So, the contestants start cooking. Halfway in, the recipe calls for a pinch of salt. One contestant—let's call her Sue—puts in the pinch of salt, stirs it, stares into space, tastes it and declares to no-one in particular, 'I think it needs more salt!'

At this point, people like me at home start throwing popcorn at the screen, yelling, 'Are you crazy?! It's a recipe! It's been salted! Don't mess with the recipe!'

You can see Sue wrestling with her decision. 'Will I put more salt in ...? Won't I ...? Will I ...? Won't I ...?' and then ...

Boom! In goes the salt! And all hell breaks loose.

The judges descend and declare Sue to be 'crazy' for messing with the recipe.

The fellow contestants hover like ghouls and call Sue 'crazy' for taking such a stupid risk. People at home, like me, yell, 'Are you crazy? You are *so* leaving the *MasterChef* kitchen. Your journey is *over.*' Sue panics. She second guesses her decision. 'Did I make the wrong call? Has that extra pinch of salt cost me my place in the competition?'

And then it gets to the judging. This is when it gets interesting. It goes one of two ways.

The judges taste Sue's dish, screw up their noses and say, 'That tastes *terrible.* It's too salty. What were you thinking?' Sue starts to cry.

Or they taste it, smile and say, 'That tastes *amazing.* What were you thinking?' Sue starts to cry.

And more often than not, the contestant—people like Sue—who took the 'crazy' risk goes on to win the competition!

So why does *that* contestant win when those who follow the rules and stick to the recipe don't?

Having watched every season since it started, I've seen the pattern. People like Sue win because they're the innovators, the mavericks, the risk-takers, the ones who say, 'I know what I *should* be doing; I know what the judges are telling me to do and I know what the audience is telling me to do. But I'm going to do it my way, because I believe in *me.*'

And they're exactly the sort of people I wanted to interview for the book you're reading right now. Not people from the cooking community of course, but people from the *online business* community—people who have taken risks, gone out on a limb, given up their comfortable day jobs, done something others considered 'crazy', and succeeded.

With that in mind, I wanted to explore two key aspects.

First, are entrepreneurs born or made? Is there an entrepreneurial 'gene' that automatically hardwires them for success? Are they born with an abundance of traits that naturally predispose them to the rollercoaster ride that is entrepreneurship? Or can training, commitment and exposure to advanced entrepreneurial strategies be enough to create success? Or is there a third option where entrepreneurial ability is a combination of heredity and environment?

What's clear is that while some entrepreneurs are born risk-takers, mercurial in nature and driven to buck the trend, these qualities are not in and of themselves pure indicators of success. Entrepreneurs come in all shapes and sizes, launch their startups for a wide variety of reasons and bring a range of skills and abilities to the table. I wanted to discover not so much what *natural* traits are needed for entrepreneurial success, but to uncover the mindsets and behaviours that successful entrepreneurs exhibit that lead to success. After all, one can argue that traits can't be learnt but mindsets and behaviours can.

Second, I wanted to explore the practical side of building a successful online business: the nuts and bolts that enable that crazy idea to be launched to a global market. After all, having the idea is one thing; building it from scratch is another. Here's what I wanted to find out:

- How did they come up with the idea and get it off the ground?
- What challenges did they face getting started and how did they overcome those challenges?
- How did they know what idea to run with and how did they test whether their idea had merit?
- What is their point of difference and how did they come up with that?
- What trends do they follow and how do they stay ahead of their competitors?

- What was the minimum viable product (MVP) that got them started?
- What online tools and templates did they use to launch their online business?
- What are their marketing strategies for growth when they've got no more money to burn?
- What social media strategies do they use to gain new market share?
- What content do they create to build influence and generate sales?
- How do they compete with businesses 10 times their size?
- What role does advanced technology such as artificial intelligence, virtual reality and other disruptive tools play in their business?
- How do they get found on Google when they can't afford to pay for AdWords?
- How do they get media coverage when they can't afford a publicist?
- How do they influence and persuade investors and staff to come on board when all they have to show is a crazy idea?

… and much more.

Who's this book for?

This book will be of great value to you if you:

- *run a small business* … because you need to know how to fend off competitors that weren't there yesterday and are here today: competitors founded by tech-savvy geekpreneurs who spot a sleepy industry and even sleepier CEOs and think, 'We can take them on'. If you're not thinking at least a year ahead, you're a target. Don't get caught sleeping at the wheel. Stay up to date.
- *employ millennials* … because if you have millennials handling your marketing, managing your social media or

building your website, they're probably telling you what to do and how much it's going to cost and you can't do a thing to challenge them except agree, pay the Facebook advertising bill and then scratch your head wondering, 'What do they really do?'

- *are a millennial* ... because you have a great idea and the tools to bring it to fruition, but you just can't get traction. You know what needs to be done, but struggle to build a team or manage it once you do. Maybe you've been ripped off one too many times by a 'partner' and you're wondering what you did wrong and what you could have done better.

- *are in middle management* ... because if you've only ever had one career, you're aged 50 or over and you get retrenched, you, my friend, are in trouble. I don't mean to scare you, but you'll need to retrain 'tout suite' so why wait for the axe to fall? Retrain now, get savvy with the new tech tools of business and take control of your future while you have the luxury of employment.

- *are a stay-at-home parent* ... because you stayed at home to raise your little ones and now you want to get back 'out there' (wherever 'out there' is). But you've lost your confidence and instead of 'feeling the fear and doing it anyway', you just feel the fear. You haven't lost your brain. It's just gone a bit mushy. You've got ideas galore; you just need the confidence to bring them to life.

Why you should read this book

For the past few years, I've been privileged to be a judge for the Online Retail Industry Awards (ORIAs), the peak body for internet business in Australia. I was privy to the award applications submitted by Australia's best and brightest online businesses. As a result, I got to see 'under the hood', so to speak of how leading entrepreneurs built their multimillion-dollar businesses. I had access to the inside story on how and why they started their businesses, the challenges they faced, the launch strategies they applied, the website platforms they used, the marketing software they chose and the systems they followed for success. I've also been a judge for Anthill Australia's Cool Company Awards and seen how dozens of other mavericks got started. I've conducted dozens of industry panels featuring the heads of Australia's most innovative startups, such as Uber, Vinomofo, Milan Direct, Pozible and Deals Direct and had the opportunity to ask them questions many would like answers to but didn't have the platform from which to do so.

Prior to that, I spent 12 months creating a five-part video series for Fairfax Media's *The Age* and *The Sydney Morning Herald* newspapers and got to interview disruptive digital leaders, including Matt Barrie from Freelancer, John Winning from Appliances Online, Tony Nash of Booktopia, Jodie Fox from Shoes of Prey and dozens of others. Those interviews formed the basis of my first book, the best-selling *Secrets of Online Entrepreneurs* and now, three years on, I'm back with this book.

I've taken all that knowledge, conducted fresh in-depth interviews with a host of new online entrepreneurs and gone back to some of those I interviewed before to find out what they've been up to and what they're doing differently. All up, I've interviewed more than 100 of Australia's top digital entrepreneurs and had additional creative input from the world's most innovative thinkers on specialist topics such as PR, content creation, search engine optimisation, business storytelling, data analytics, marketing automation and user testing.

I've taken all those insights, overlaid that research with my 25 years in advertising and digital marketing and synthetised it to create this five-part-strategy playbook—the ultimate guide, if you like—for creating a successful online business. If you're looking for shortcuts to building an online business and want to stand on the shoulders and leverage the learnings of those who have gone before you, this book is it.

I hope you enjoy it.

INTRODUCTION
The state of play

I was born in 1966. Life seemed simple then. There was no mobile, no email, not even videos. 'Social' was called 'going outside' and the internet was the Funk & Wagnalls encyclopaedia.

Work was simpler too. In the advertising agency where I cut my teeth, a 'hard decision' was choosing between placing a full-page advertisement in *Cleo* or *Cosmopolitan*. Tough decision. Kept me up at night.

Fast forward 25 years and here we are, smack bang in the middle of a technical revolution and boy, does that 'hard' decision to choose between *Cleo* or *Cosmopolitan* seem easy. Now, when scheduling media, the discussion is had between data scientists and it sounds something like, 'We'll just do an A/B test using the multivariate vector points as mutable factors for sub-segment n-2 utilising the regression coefficients.' I know. It doesn't make sense to me either, but that's how complex the media-buying discussion has become.

It's not just work that's complicated. Simple things, such as children's toys, have become unbelievably complex.

For example, my son turned 11 last week. We bought him a drone helicopter. It cost $50. Five years ago, it would have cost $700. Eight years ago, it didn't exist. The gyro that makes it work cost NASA engineers $100 million to invent and you need to be a computer programmer to use it. When I was 11, we got Pong and we thought that was the height of technical sophistication.

Things move much faster now too. A TV commercial that took a team of creative professionals three months to make can now be produced by a 13-year-old with an iPad in under 30 minutes. A website for a new business can be built within an hour for just a few dollars.

In short, things are changing, fast. For the better? Depends on where you stand. One thing is clear. Digital disruption is not just 'Web 2.0 on steroids'. It is a fundamental restructuring of the way business operates and indeed, the very way we live. All businesses—from child-care to aged care, from car repair to stocks and shares—will be affected. Who will be the winners? Who will be the losers? The answer is in your hands and the solutions are in this book.

The democratisation of knowledge

When I was a kid, you were seen and not heard. Parents were the king and queen and what they said went. Our sources of knowledge and wisdom were our families, the church, the school and the library. Information was in the hands of the few and it was doled out according to their views, perspective and experience, so even if we wanted to stretch our wings and build a business, we needed help from others to make it happen.

Now, we have Google, and the democratisation of knowledge it enables has transformed our society so quickly, widely and deeply (I'll stop with the adverbs) that many people, especially those over 50, don't know how to keep up with it. The impact Google has on our lives cannot be understated. Now, for example, everyone has access to the factors of production (more on those later) and where we live, what we know, who we know and how much money we've got, are no longer barriers to building a business. Now, anyone with an idea and access to the internet can get started, which means everyone has the potential to become an entrepreneur.

So, what the heck is an entrepreneur anyway?

The technical definition of an entrepreneur is a person who undertakes some task, takes a risk, initiates an action or makes things happen. There's no one-size-fits-all or cookie cutter definition for a person who becomes a successful entrepreneur. Some are natural-born salespeople with the gift of the gab and a higher-than-usual tolerance for risk, ambiguity and uncertainty. Others are introverted idealists who find comfort in the cool calculations of an Excel spreadsheet. Irrespective of their innate differences, many entrepreneurs exhibit similar behaviours that contribute to their success. Here's what I have observed. For the most part, they:

- are humble—they know they don't have all the answers and ask better questions than most
- are obsessed with their business and pursue one business idea at a time
- have clarity on what they want their business to achieve, be it to make a million or be home by 3 pm to pick up the kids
- get started quickly without worrying about the end game or what their exit strategies might be
- start small and gain momentum by openly sharing their idea and collaborating with others who complement their skill set
- do basic tasks—such as following up with prospects, keeping an eye on cash flow and building the sales funnel—meticulously and consistently
- don't accept defeat or loss gracefully, if at all, and accept that at times they may annoy a great many people with their actions
- regularly test and measure the results of their marketing efforts and tweak those marketing levers to create incremental improvements
- reinvest profits back into the business to make it a better, faster, leaner operation

- get involved in every aspect of their operation and do everything themselves until they can afford to hire others
- work harder and put in longer hours than anyone else they employ.

If this sounds like a life you'd like to lead, the entrepreneurial world is for you. If not, you'd best get back on the 7.19 am train for the city commute, take instructions from a boss you neither like nor respect, complete tasks that mean little to you and add nothing to the world, and let faceless men and women in corner offices dictate your future.

The choice is yours.

If you're standing still, you're going backwards

I have a friend called Sophie. She's a talented business coach and great at what she does. She paid a colleague to build a Wix website for $500. It looks terrific. She loaded up her content, got her headshots done, promoted her first public workshop and got approximately zero enrolments.

'What am I doing wrong?' she wailed. 'I built my site, I got the testimonials. I have an offer on the home page. I've got my AdWords happening. I hooked it up to Mailchimp. Where are all the customers?'

Five years ago, those marketing efforts would have been enough. Even three years ago, they would have been sufficient. Now? Not so much. So, what's different? What's changed? A lot.

As Sophie so painfully discovered, what worked before may not work now.

Back in the early 2000s, it was easy to build a database, and even easier to get on page one of Google. There were few competitors. Facebook was free, and consumers were enamoured and easily led. Early tech adopters such as Catch of the Day, Kogan, Deals Direct,

Freelancer and Milan Direct came and conquered. Those early days of the wild wild west set them up and gave them the edge. I interviewed many of those founders for my first book, *Secrets of Online Entrepreneurs*, and they say quite honestly, 'If I had to start my business now, I don't know if I could achieve the same level of success. It's much harder now.'

Many who didn't catch the tech wave saw their businesses go under; many found they couldn't compete, but many also found that they didn't *want* to compete. The introduction of the GST in July 2000 saw many old-school business owners just give up the ghost — it was all too much. Now, retailers of many years standing are doing the same, not because of new government regulations but because of the threat of online competitors and the sheer effort it takes to keep up. They're giving up because they don't like the way people shop now, where a customer tries on a dress or a shoe, sources a cheaper quote online (while they're in the shop), thrusts their mobile phone in the retailer's face, and says, 'Match that price or else.'

You only need to wander up high streets across Australia and see the plethora of 'For lease' signs to know that retail is under threat. And Amazon is just warming up.

The way we do business has changed dramatically and you may not believe me when I say this, but for those with the right skill set and attitude to technology, it's for the better. Yes, only the good survive in business nowadays, but it's never been easier, cheaper or faster to work out how to *be* good and to harness the tools of technology that can *make* you good.

The change factors that I will elaborate on in the book — the tools that underpin all successful modern online businesses — are for the taking. They enable ordinary people to build businesses that let them do what they want, when they want and for how long they want, and to get paid what they want. They give people like you and me the tools to create businesses that matter to us and help us achieve our personal goals, be it to own a water-front property or buy a pony for the kids. These tools help make it easier for people to connect with collaborators, customers, suppliers, partners and investors more easily than ever before.

These change factors are marvellous and terrible all at the same time, and they're changing the way we live. What are these change factors? Read on to find out.

There's no I in TEAM—but there is ME

If you've been around long enough, you'll know most things come full circle.

When big, pure-play operators such as Amazon, Kogan, Catch of the Day, Deals Direct and the like got started, we could get what we wanted with all the boxes ticked: right product, good price, great range, fast delivery … perfect!

But then customers—being fickle and pernickety, and fussy, and self-focused—wanted more. They said, 'I really like what you're giving me, but I want it done slightly differently for me, you see, because I'm special and my needs are paramount and in this post-modern age where my needs trump everything, I've decided that …

- I want to talk to someone in customer service about *my* purchase because I'm not sure if I'm buying the right thing and I need to know *now*.
- I want *my* product to be a bit different from what you've got on offer; I want it done *my* way so that it suits *my* values, *my* diet, *my* lifestyle and *my* budget.
- I want to spend less time scrolling through a website and more time reviewing customised offers that reflect *my* taste, *my* needs and *my* past purchases.

This focus on the individual gave rise to all manner of niche products that had to be 'just right', as evidenced by the rise of the mass personalisation of goods: almond-milk-decaf-not-hot-but-warm-cappuccino; personalised handbags with gold-encrusted monogrammed initials; books featuring storylines with our children (and their best friends) as the main characters; values-based buying that reflects our need to buy ethically, sustainably and locally, and 3D-printed running shoes built specifically to accommodate our pronated left foot and dislocated metatarsal. Welcome to the era of mass personalisation.

When done well, mass personalisation offers a better experience for customers, increases loyalty and leads to higher value orders. It curbs decision fatigue and cuts down on the effort a customer has to spend finding what they are looking for.

Why mass personalisation is a good thing

This rise of 'mass personalisation' is good news. Why? Because it means small-scale business owners can create bespoke, niche products that serve a tiny sector of a global market and still find enough customers to make a healthy profit; and because we have the tools of digital disruption at our fingertips (such as cloud services, mobile technology, big data analytics and social media—more on these later) we can build the business quickly and cost-effectively. In short, it's never been faster, cheaper or easier to give those self-centred, narcissistic, pernickety people exactly what they want. I'm not judging those people. I'm one of them. We all are to some degree. We've all become so *demanding* and it's the businesses that respond to that demand by offering extreme customer service that succeed.

WHAT EXACTLY IS DIGITAL DISRUPTION?

Technically speaking, digital disruption is when emerging digital technologies and business models create change within an industry. They impact the value of existing products and services offered in the industry and cause the need for re-evaluation.

Is mass personalisation bad? Heck no, it's great! It's great for the little players who can't compete on price, range, service and delivery, all at the same time. It's brilliant for them because now they can find a way to compete that enables them to focus on the *tiny bit* they do brilliantly; the *tiny bit* that only they can do; the *tiny bit* that separates them from the pack; the *tiny bit* that enables them to be found on Google. That *tiny bit* could be the 'pinch of salt' that creates that all-important point of difference.

So, when a customer wants a cobalt-blue, mohair, jewel-encrusted dog jacket monogrammed with 'Fido' on the collar, and they want it delivered overnight, gift-wrapped in gold-flecked tissue-paper with a personalised note to Fido (written on Schmacko-scented parchment paper), they can find the exact supplier online to do it at the right price.

That's why we love the gig economy (more on that later) and why the gig economy has flourished: it enables people to be brilliant at their little bit (making cobalt-blue, mohair, jewel-encrusted dog jackets) and through the tools of digital disruption enables them to offer their specialised service to a global market.

If you like the thought of being able to offer your *tiny bit* to the world, the bit that you can be brilliant at, then the tools and templates in this book will help you to do it. So, what will you sell? What will your *tiny bit* be? If you're stuck for business ideas, take a look at some of the hot online niches in the next section. They are predicted to be fast growing sectors in the future.

20 hot online niches to consider

Being a successful entrepreneur begins with asking one important question: What will you sell? I'll keep reminding you of this throughout the book because, first, it's the most important question to ask, and second, it's really easy to get bogged down in the minutiae of building a business and to forget that people pay you to solve a very specific problem.

This decision needs to be made carefully as you'll live and breathe it for the foreseeable future. To increase your chance of success, it's worth looking at what trends are occurring and ride those waves to see where they take you. You may find the business changes direction as you get started, but you've got to get started with something so you may as well choose a category that's predicted to grow. Take a look at what fads are occurring because fads become trends, trends become niches and niches become mainstream. If you pick the right fad at the right time and get in early, you can set yourself up for success.

> **QUICK TIP**
> If you really want to keep your finger on the pulse of what the next trend is, just Google 'Amazon is about to buy ...' and wait for the predictive drop-down menu to reveal 'the next big thing'.

For example, remember when the 'organic section' was a few misshapen carrots in a wicker basket tucked away in the corner of the green-grocer? Now organic means Amazon paying $US13.7 billion for US-based grocery store Whole Foods Market. In other words, niche groups that were considered 'fringe' or 'outliers' two decades ago are now viable markets of interest. If you're keen to build an online business that has huge potential for growth you would do well to look at the niches that are emerging and see if any match with a product or service you're passionate about. It's not essential that your business idea be focused on a passion, but it will make those hard times easier to get through. To whet your creative appetite, here's a list of 20 online niche hot spots for you to consider. Take a look at these to see if any appeal to you as potential business ideas:

1. organic and vegan products
2. cruelty-free products
3. house-made produce

4. sustainable farmed products

5. baby equipment

6. pet care

7. vintage fashion

8. plus size clothing for men and women

9. petite size clothing (that doesn't have a Barbie logo on it)

10. the hipster brigade: beards, barbershops, baristas, blogging

11. the maker movement: micro-producers of everything—furniture, beer, bread, cheese...

12. yoga for men

13. mindfulness for corporates

14. composting and recycling

15. ethical investing

16. fair trade

17. repairing and sharing (from clothes and computers to toasters and toys)

18. subscription models (from software to shavers to socks)

19. marketplaces (for anything) that connect buyers and sellers

20. products that target the specific needs of older women, cashed-up boomers and millennials.

These niches are all trending up to become mainstream markets. Get in early and own your 'corner' of the market before they get saturated.

To see the future, we must look to the past

These emerging hotspots may seem new and trendy but they're not. We need only speak to our frugal parents—those born in the 1930s and 1940s—to see that nothing has really changed. Take a minute to ask them about these fads/trends/niches and you'll quickly discover that everything old is new again. My dad had 11 brothers and sisters. They lived on a farm and within their means. The way they sourced and used products and services would now be called 'self-sustaining' and 'hipster', but their financial circumstances at the time dictated that nothing be wasted or taken for granted.

For example, they:

- fished for yabbies in the local dam (fad: sustainable farming)
- grew wild strawberries in the garden (fad: organic low-miles food)
- made jam out of what was left over (fad: preserving)
- raised hens for their eggs (fad: farm-laid, free range)
- fed the food scraps to the chooks
  (fad: recycling and composting)
- made their own beer and stored it in the garage for later consumption (fad: micro brewing)
- walked 3 kilometres to school and back each day
  (fad: 24/7 gyms)
- used household ingredients such as yoghurt and cucumber to create beauty products (fad: organic facial)
- added some sugar to the facial mix (fad: microdermabrasion).

My dad's family lived that way because they had to. Now, living simply/sustainably/fashionably like this is no longer a necessity, it's a lifestyle choice, and technology has made it easier, cheaper and faster to buy those products and services that enable that lifestyle.

People haven't changed. What has changed is *how* and *why* we buy these products. Now, we've worked our way to the top of Maslow's Hierarchy of Needs and we buy these products because they reflect our values and how we want to be seen by those closest to us.

So enough with the talking. Let's get going by introducing you to the entrepreneurs I interviewed for this book.

Who's in the book?

Some entrepreneurs featured here are high profile and will be well known to you. Some will be lesser known, but with equally successful businesses.

Some have been in business for decades; others are just getting started. Don't be dazzled by the glamour of the big names and big success stories. Yes, those experienced hands have much to share. But it's the ones getting started—who are in the thick of it, living and breathing it every waking hour—from whom you can learn just as much.

Table I is a snapshot of some of the Aussie online entrepreneurs you'll discover in this book:

Table I: the entrepreneurs or their chosen representatives

Tony Nash	Booktopia	www.booktopia.com.au
Andre Eikmeier	Vinomofo	www.vinomofo.com
David Rohrsheim	Uber	www.uber.com/en-AU
Jane Lu	Showpo	www.showpo.com
Matt Barrie	Freelancer	www.freelancer.com
Adrian Fittolani	Envato	www.envato.com
Melanie Perkins	Canva	www.canva.com
Jules Lund	TRIBE	www.tribegroup.co
Kate Morris	Adore Beauty	www.adorebeauty.com.au
Darren Rowse	Problogger	www.problogger.com
	Digital Photography School	www.digital-photography-school.com
Daniel and Justine Flynn	Thankyou Group	www.thankyou.co
John Winning	Appliances Online	www.appliancesonline.com.au

Shaun O'Brien	Selby Acoustics	www.selby.com.au
Paul Greenberg	DealsDirect	www.dealsdirect.com.au
	NORA	www.nora.org.au
Sandy Abram	Wholesome Hub	www.wholesomehub.net.au
Simon Griffiths	Who Gives A Crap	www.whogivesacrap.org
Mark Bevan	Joust	www.joust.com.au
Morgan Coleman	Vets on Call	www.vetsoncall.pet
Nik Merkovic and Alex Tomic	HiSmile	www.hismileteeth.com
Lucy Glade-Wright	Hunting for George	www.huntingforgeorge.com
Lucy Mathieson	Bake Play Smile	www.bakeplaysmile.com
Anna Whitehouse	Mother Pukka	www.pukka.co.uk
Alex Ouyens	Ouwens Casserly Real Estate	www.ocre.com.au
Sarah Leo	Openbook Howden	www.openbookhowden.com.au

I've also sought contributions from consultants at the top of their game whom other entrepreneurs turn to for wisdom, advice and expertise. To seek their advice would cost you a year's salary. It's all here in the book.

I've sourced the best in the business. Experts in PR, web development, user experience, site optimisation, social media, influencer marketing, digital marketing, content creation, professional speaking and more (see table II, overleaf).

Table II: the specialist expert contributors

Karen Eck	eckfactor PR	www.eckfactor.com
Jocelyne Simpson	IDoMyOwnPR	www.idomyownpr.com
Toby Tremayne	Magic Industries	www.magicindustries.net
Adam Franklin	Bluewire Media	www.bluewiremedia.com.au
Jim Stewart	StewArt Media	www.stewartmedia.com.au
Meri Harli	Fat Cake Media	www.fatcake.com
Phil Leahy	Retail Global	www.retailglobal.com.au
Lyndal Harris	Podcast VA	www.podcastva.com
Kevin Bloch	CiSCO	www.cisco.com

The five steps in this book

I've created a 5-step process for you to follow when building your online business (see figure I). This roadmap will provide signposts for what to look for, what roads to take, what shortcuts to follow, and what dead ends to avoid.

Figure I: the five steps of the book

Each step contains chapters that will cover different aspects of the journey. The book is best read from start to finish but you can also dip in and out at any point along the way. Everyone will be at different stages of building their business, so take what's right for you and leave what's not.

If you're looking for the ultimate strategy playbook for launching, building and growing an online business, this roadmap will help you get there faster.

If you want things in your life to change, you have to change things in your life. That starts with changing the way you think and what you believe is possible. So what set of beliefs do you need to build an online business? What mindset is needed to be a successful entrepreneur? Welcome to Step 1: How to develop an entrepreneurial mindset.

Mindset

How to develop an entrepreneurial mindset

If someone said to you, 'Here's how I made a million dollars and I'm willing to share my secrets with you', you'd listen to them, wouldn't you? It'd be insane not to. We all know that success leaves clues, so it makes sense to follow those who have gone before and learn from what they've done.

Having interviewed dozens of successful online entrepreneurs, I've discovered that there are certain things they all have in common. Developing an 'entrepreneurial mindset' is one of them—a way of thinking that is slightly different from the way most people think. I've condensed those differences into five qualities. These entrepreneurs:

1. *trust their crazy ideas*—they back their judgement, listen to their instincts and persist in the face of relentless criticism

2. *get started*—they start small, pivot quickly and are hands on (especially at the beginning)

3. *have depth of vision*—they look at what the trends are and look further ahead than most (which is why their ideas are sometimes considered 'crazy')

4. *know what business they're in*—they know what sector they operate in and who their competitors are

5. *know what problem their business solves*—they know exactly why a customer will buy their product and the revenue model that underpins that transaction.

The entrepreneurial mindset is not something most people are born with, but it can be learnt. That's what Step 1 is all about.

Chapter 1

Mindset #1: Trust your crazy ideas

Do you remember Apple's iconic TV campaign from the 1990s featuring scientists, artists and mavericks, with the famous grammatically questionable tagline 'Think Different'?

Here's to the crazy ones. The misfits. The rebels. The troublemakers. The round pegs in the square holes. The ones who see things differently. They're not fond of rules ... You can quote them, disagree with them, glorify or vilify them. About the only thing you can't do is ignore them.

Entrepreneurs think differently too, which is why entrepreneurship often attracts the crazy ones, the ones prone to breaking the rules, the ones who don't say, 'Why?' but 'Why not?' This 'craziness' is often borne out of a passion—a passion to right a wrong, make a difference, solve a problem, make a million.

This begs the question, 'What's the difference between someone being seen as crazy and someone being seen as visionary?' The answer? The crazy ones just take longer to give up. Jeff Bezos' Amazon started in 1994 but didn't turn a profit until 2001. Alibaba's Jack Ma and Google's Sergey Brin and Larry Page also struggled to make money in the early days. Yet all persisted and stuck to their vision in the face of immense criticism and public pressure.

People said Trump was crazy when he declared in the 1990s he would one day become President of the United States.

People said Musk was crazy when he said that Mars travel would become a commercial reality.

Trump's and Musk's crazy ideas took nearly two decades to manifest, and here we are, watching the consequences of those ideas play out in our news feed each day. When an entrepreneur's audacious idea fails, they're considered crazy. When their idea succeeds, they're considered visionary. Musk is both crazy and visionary. As for Trump? History will be the judge on that one.

From zero to hero

Take a look at some of the crazy ideas that are succeeding right here in Australia and you'll realise that anything is possible. And the factors of digital disruption are compressing the time frames, which means fortunes that would have taken a lifetime to amass are now being made within years, as evidenced by former corporate executive-turned fashion entrepreneur Jane Lu, founder of Showpo. What started off with a laptop and two shelves of clothing is now an online juggernaut. Jane's business got started in her parents' garage, became a pop-up store, then a retail store and is now a pure-play online retailer that's dominating the fast fashion market.

Showpo

What started off in 2010 as a pop-up store is now an online global fashion empire, shipping to 80 countries. Through being disruptive in the retail space and capitalising on the use of social media, Showpo now boasts a cult social following of more than 2.9 million. On track to turn over $100 million by 2020, Jane Lu's days of being a cubicle warrior at Ernst & Young (EY) are well and truly over.

Just as Jane Lu harnessed the power of social to create a business from nothing, the founders of digital marketplace Envato created a digital product out of thin air and leveraged the 'creativity of the crowd' to make that creativity accessible to a global market.

Envato

Envato is a group of digital marketplaces that sells creative assets for web designers—assets such as themes, graphics, video, audio, photography and 3D models. Its co-founders Collis and Cyan Ta'eed worked out of a Bondi garage, putting everything on the line to build the startup. Most people at the time called their idea 'bizarre'. Not anymore. Envato has more than eight million community members, and five million digital items for sale. The couple were listed in the top 10 of the 2016 *BRW* Young Rich List.

Not all startups start in garages, but an uncommon number do. Amazon, Apple, Disney, Google and HP are just a few that did.

WHAT IS PURE-PLAY?

Pure-play operators don't have retail storefronts. They can only be found online.

Sometimes a crazy idea is borne out of necessity, as Sandy Abram found when she realised that people wanted to shop according to their values.

Wholesome Hub

Melbourne entrepreneur Sandy Abram started Wholesome Hub, an organic food and grocery marketplace, due to a medical condition that compelled her to investigate the healing power of organics and to treat food as medicine.

Her 'pinch of salt' is that people can search for products on her website based on the values that are important to them. She now stocks 1000 products and has more than 3000 customers. She's only been in business for a few years but she's rapidly snaffling market share from the bigger players by making it easier for people to find the products they need.

So, what's going on? What's enabling these crazy ideas, and many others like them, to succeed so quickly?

Why *are* crazy ideas succeeding?

What's driving this phenomenon is *information*. As Ray Kurzweil, Google's director of engineering, observed, 'Once any domain, discipline, technology or industry becomes information-enabled and powered by information flows, its price/performance begins doubling approximately annually.'[1]

WHAT IS MOORE'S LAW?

A book about the technology revolution would not be complete without a mention of Moore's Law. Gordon Moore, co-founder of Intel, famously predicted in 1965 that the overall processing power for computers would double every two years. He believed this would happen because he could see that the number of transistors you could fit onto an integrated circuit (per square inch) was doubling every year since their invention and would continue to do so. In other words, the computers would get smaller and faster.

And the doubling pattern as described in Moore's Law doesn't stop. We design faster computers, which in turn enables us to build faster computers, and so on. It's like a hallway of mirrors. We are living in unprecedented times. Never in human history have we seen so many disparate but connected technologies moving at such a pace. There are many technological factors underpinning these changes. Let's look at the main four, which are loosely termed 'the factors of digital disruption'.

Four factors that enable digital disruption

There are many factors enabling businesses such as Envato and Showpo—and smaller startups such as Wholesome Hub—to get started and grow so quickly, but we'll focus on the big four here.

Independently, these four factors (or technologies) are all game changers, but when combined, they become exponentially disruptive.

The four factors that have enabled these startups to go from zero to hero in such a short space of time are:

1. cloud
2. big data
3. social
4. mobile.

I'll go into greater detail throughout the book, but here's a quick-start guide to each one.

1. Cloud

Remember when a simple website cost $5000 to build? Now it costs just $500 or even $5. The cloud went some way to making that price reduction possible. Cloud-based companies such as Amazon Web Services (AWS) now enable anyone to cost-effectively host a website, stream video and pump out massive amounts of content to the world. This 'factor of production', once only accessible to large corporates, those with money or those with sophisticated coding skills, means anyone with an internet connection can set up an online business. For example, Melbourne-based blogger Darren Rowse has five million readers each week; the esteemed *The New York Times* has around the same, meaning a one-man-band can potentially have as broad a reach and be as powerful as a media conglomerate.

The cloud also untethered us from the desktop, allowing us the freedom to work from wherever, whenever and to collaborate instantly with people around the globe.

WHERE IS THE CLOUD ANYWAY?

By the way, when we say we've stored something in 'the cloud', it's not really in the cloud, or even in the sky. It's on a physical computer, somewhere. The cloud refers to many computers housed in massive warehouses all over the world.

AWS in particular has removed the major problem of infrastructure management and planning and allowed startups to grow quickly and easily.

WHO USES AWS?

• Qantas	• Unilever	• McDonald's
• Netflix	• Kellogg's	• Sony
• GE	• G4S	• Spotify

2. Big data

Big data is the ability to take vast volumes of data (or even small volumes of data) and quickly analyse it to gain greater insights. Kevin Bloch is the Chief Technology Officer at CiSCO, a company that makes the technology that securely connects nearly everything that can be digitally connected. In other words, it is a significant player in the Internet of Things (IoT). His example of big data shows why this development will impact the work of vast numbers of white-collar workers, potentially eliminating some positions altogether.

A radiologist of 20 years standing would see around 20 million images, and all of their prior training would be focused on helping them read those images so that they can better help the patient. Now, with machine learning, our computers can 'ingest' 20 trillion images in less than an hour. Machine learning and artificial intelligence (AI) will also leverage all of the world's intelligence on radiology and 'teach' that machine what all of the radiologists in the world have learned. This means machines can now look at images and provide a much higher statistically correct diagnosis than a single radiologist can. Therefore, the question is, 'What is the role of the radiologist in the future?'. AI will have a big impact on that industry and indeed all professions that rely on processing data as their main form of currency will also experience high levels of job loss. I have no doubt that we will still need radiologists in the future, but I think that part of the job — in terms of looking at images — will have to change.

WHAT IS THE INTERNET OF THINGS?

The Internet of Things (IoT) is a scenario in which physical objects (cars, fridges, roads, even animals) are embedded with a unique identifier (or sensor) and the data that those objects collects is able to be instantly transferred over a network without needing person-to-person interaction. This data is then used to make decisions.

For example, sensors in the road can determine traffic patterns so that traffic light sequences can be amended to keep traffic flowing smoothly. Sensors in rubbish bins tell the council how much rubbish needs to be collected and therefore what capacity the rubbish trucks need to have (before they leave the depot). Sensors in fridges have 'spoiler alerts' letting you know when the milk is off.

Security experts are concerned that having connected devices in the house — like a 'smart' fridge or air conditioner — leave you open to a cyber-attack. For example, your fridge may have direct access to your network and could be used to spread malware to other devices in your home.

A tip for the paranoid: Before you buy any connected device for the home, check out the 'software update' policy in the warranty. If you're going to buy smart devices, be smart about it.

Big data can also predict with accuracy what people plan to buy. For example, an online book retailer could feasibly know from its data that a customer is pregnant before she has told her family, simply by looking at the books she is researching. Knowledge is power. Big data is going to be a big deal.

3. Social

Social advertising is relatively cheap to buy and can reach vast audiences instantly. It's disrupting every industry, and in particular the media sector. For example, the advertising industry used to make

10 per cent on whatever media they booked. Now, that media spend is diverted to Facebook and Google AdWords, and the mainstream media guys miss out. Plenty of other people are monetising social though, and they're also bypassing the traditional media channels to do it. It's the network effect that makes social so powerful.

WHAT IS THE NETWORK EFFECT?

The network effect describes a situation when a good or service becomes more valuable as more people use that good or service. In other words, the more people use the product or service, the more valuable it becomes. eBay was one of the first online auction markets. It had the most sellers and the widest range of products. As a result, it attracted more buyers. As a result of that, it attracted more sellers. The more sellers it had, the more buyers it attracted, and so on. This is the network effect in action. The more valuable something (like a website) becomes, the more people use it. This cycle feeds on itself until one platform arises to dominate all others. The telephone was an early example of the network effect in that the value of a phone increases if everyone has a phone. More recently, Facebook, TripAdvisor and Skype have benefited from the network effect.

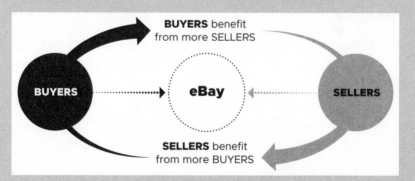

PS: This is not to be confused with 'data network effects'. This is when a product (generally powered by machine learning) gets smarter as it is fed more data. In other words, the more data a community contributes, the smarter the product gets.

One of those people monetising social media is Jules Lund, the TV and radio personality. He created a social media marketplace called TRIBE, a site that turns everyday bloggers, photographers and creatives into paid social influencers. He says:

Our mission is to unlock the world's creativity through everyday content creators. In the past brands turned to celebrities for endorsements. That's not sustainable for a small brand. Our marketplace matches brands with social influencers. A photo shoot involving models, props, extras, locations, that might have taken a week to get completed, and would have cost thousands, can now be fulfilled almost instantly.

While Jules helps micro bloggers make money, the celebrity endorsement still has its place. *Vogue*'s Anna Wintour hosted an exclusive Instagram video studio at the New York Met Ball, where A-list celebrities such as Madonna and Blake Lively posed for photos and clips on the app. That one event generated 283 million likes and comments across 42 million accounts in just four weeks.

Social's ability to reach millions instantly is largely why many startups have been able to fast track their success so cost-effectively.

4. Mobile

You don't need me to tell you what an impact mobile technology is having. Everyone has a device and we're using it to search, compare and shop with ever-increasing frequency. Australia-wide, the current percentage of mobile transactions is 42 per cent, but for the savvy entrepreneurs who are optimising for mobile, the figures go much higher, with some pushing 65 per cent.

Google is encouraging this explosion in mobile shopping by prioritising sites that have been optimised for mobile in its search rankings. Digital marketing expert Adam Franklin from Bluewire Media says:

Google will penalise your site if it's not optimised for mobile so if your site is not yet working well on a mobile, it's time to take action. If you're just starting out, design your site for mobile first and work backwards from there as mobile is well and truly the default device for search.

My son's version of digital disruption is having his mobile phone taken from him.

***

Look closely at the business models of the following startups and you'll see that these same four factors (cloud, big data, social and mobile) underpin their success. Adoption of these technologies enables them to scale without friction, which means they can grow exponentially without incremental increases in costs.

- Skype
- Lyft
- Uber
- Airtasker
- Airbnb
- Yelp
- WhatsApp
- GoToMeeting
- Slack
- Expedia
- Tumblr
- Expensify

If you're keen to create a disruptive online business, you'll want to look more closely at these four tools of disruption and identify how you can leverage them in your own business. They are the master keys of disruption. How they are wielded and in what propensity will determine how disruptive your business will be. But first, you need to get started.

Chapter 2
Mindset #2: Take action

Let's recap. You've got a passion to start an online business. You've got a crazy idea that might work. You've got access to the tools of disruption...but there's a key element missing. It's called taking action. Some entrepreneurs have great ideas but they take too long to get started and by the time they do, the market has moved on or a competitor has taken the lead.

In order to succeed, you have to start.

This sounds obvious, I know, but it's easy to forget that having an idea, talking about it and attending meetups and hackathons are all well and good, but ideas are a dime a dozen. What separates successful entrepreneurs from the others is that they *do* something with their idea. They create something that gives momentum to their idea. The best way to bring an idea to life is to create something for others to look at. That 'something' is often referred to as a minimum viable product (MVP). The MVP could be a pop-up shop at a shopping centre or a market stall, a one-page website to show prospects or a paper mock-up of your invention. It has to be something that others can see. Without that it's just an idea—and everyone has an idea. I'll cover MVPs in more detail in Step 2.

Why entrepreneurs start their businesses

How and why entrepreneurs get started is as varied as the businesses they create. Some start out on their journey because they personally experienced a problem that needed solving, saw a gap in the market that needed filling or had a bad sales experience they felt they could improve upon. Others start because they want to make a lot of money, while others start off selling one thing and that leads them to selling something else.

Uber got started because its founder couldn't find a cab.

Uber

Uber founders Travis Kalanick and Garrett Camp were stranded on a snowy evening in Paris and couldn't get a cab. They mused, 'Wouldn't it be great if one of the cars driving past could give us a ride and we would pay them for the privilege?'

That musing led to the creation of one of the world's most disruptive startups.

For one Western Australian entrepreneur, the idea for an online business grew out of frustration.

Canva

Melanie Perkins is the CEO and co-founder of Canva, a free online graphic design platform. The idea for the company began in 2007 after feeling frustrated with how long it took to design a simple marketing brochure.

'I was in university, giving other students lessons on how to use design software, and soon found myself writing long instructions to do the simplest things. It seemed insane to me that it took 22 clicks to export a high-quality document,' Perkins said.

After coming up with an idea for a user-friendly online tool to help students design their own yearbooks, Melanie and Canva co-founder Cliff Obrecht took out a loan and brought in a tech team to build Fusion Books.

Fusion Books is now the largest school yearbook publisher in Australia and has expanded into France and New Zealand. Melanie and Cliff believed their technology had applications beyond the yearbook market, and they knew they had to pursue their vision so they set up Canva. In January 2018, the company was valued at US$1 billion and today has more than 10 million users in over 190 countries.

Vets on Call started because Morgan Coleman was horrified at the experience he had with his vet.

I took my pet to see the vet and could see how stressful the experience was for him. The foreign environment, the noise, the bright lights, the car trip just to get to the vet. Everything about it was stressful. I thought, 'there's got to be a better way'. What if the vet could come to the house? And that's how Vets on Call got started.

Kate Morris from Adore Beauty started because she couldn't buy what she needed.

I grew up in Tasmania and I've been a beauty junkie from as far back as I can remember. I used to read all the magazines and drool over the products in them but could never actually buy most of them in Launceston. Of course, there was no online shopping then. When I moved to Melbourne I worked part-time on the cosmetic counters [of retail stores] and online shopping started to come in around 1997 and I came to realise two things: as a beauty junkie living in Launceston it would have solved all my problems to be able to access products online; and most people hated the intimidating experience of dealing with the girls behind the counter.

Online marketplace Freelancer got started because founder Matt Barrie needed the service.

> I used a small website to get something done and it just blew me away that I could actually get someone on the other side of the world to do a job for me that I couldn't get done locally. Long story cut short I basically bought the company and then used it as a platform to acquire the competitors.

As you can see, these entrepreneurs all got started because they found a problem they were keen to solve.

Others got started almost by accident.

Businesses that start as one thing and become another

Often a business starts by offering something and as a result of being in the market, discovers the customer wants something different. Being open to change is the hallmark of entrepreneurial success.

For example, if Shaun O'Brien, founder of Selby Acoustics, hadn't started his first business, there's no way he would have launched his second. Like many in the early 2000s, Shaun was attracted to the high margins that could be made selling TVs and other big-box electronic items online direct to the customer. But what he didn't bank on was the plethora of hassles and hurdles that came with eliminating the middleman.

> I didn't realise until I got into it that firstly, it's really expensive to repair electronics like TV and audio systems. They are enormously intricate, require stocking of lots of different parts and require quite high levels of skill to fix. Add to that the high costs of shipping bulky goods to and from the customer across Australia and the fact that servicing the customer can be very time consuming, and I discovered very early on that all that glitters is definitely not gold when it comes to selling electronics online.

But fortunately, what he also discovered was that the accessories that people needed to make their televisions work—the cables, the wall mounts, the nuts and bolts, the brackets—were much easier to sell than the televisions.

I could see pretty quickly that the accessories were smaller so they were easier and cheaper to ship, had fewer moving parts so they had fewer technical problems and therefore required little or no servicing and I realised, after lots of sleepless nights, that maybe I should be selling accessories instead of electronics.

So, that's how Selby Acoustics got started. Like the phoenix rising, his second business grew from the creation of his first.

When failure leads to success

Andre Eikmeier loved wine. He loved it so much that he and his brother-in-law created Quoff, an online wine community, to share their love of it with other like-minded wine lovers—things like which wine they drank, why they liked it, what food it went with, how much it cost, was it good value, what was better value, and so on. Their aim was to unite a tribe with a shared love of wine 'without all the bowties and bullshit'. However, after four hard years slogging it out they had to come to terms with the painful realisation that in Andre's own words, 'Nobody wanted to pay for what we were offering. Wineries didn't actually want their customers talking about their wines in a public forum, and they certainly weren't willing to pay to be able to reach those customers.'

The business had failed. Or had it? Although they hadn't sold many memberships, what they did have was an engaged community with lots of members. As the primary breadwinner, with two children in private schools to support and four years invested in the business, Andre—along with his brother-in-law Justin Dry—had to make a decision. Should they just walk away from what they had built or give it one more shot? What that 'shot' was they weren't too sure, but they knew they had a passionate community of wine lovers.

'We said to ourselves, instead of just recommending wine, why don't we sell it too!' Andre says.

'Justin suggested "what about a wine deals site"' Andre says. Though initially reticent, their decision was vindicated when, within just a week of launching their first product, they were inundated with sales. Andre says, with a wry smile:

> Our initial success was largely due to the Quoff community we had built up over those first four years. They were our first customers. It was as if they were saying, 'You've been telling us what to buy for four years—it's about time you sold us something!' To be honest, we felt pretty stupid that we hadn't cottoned onto that more quickly.

A little site called eBay

For some people, a burning passion to help others is the foundation of their 'why' and the reason they do what they do. For Paul Greenberg, his burning passion was to give his family a fresh start in Australia, away from some of the challenges in Southern Africa. Unable to transfer the wealth he had at the time due to government currency restrictions and unfavourable exchange rates, he had to get creative.

> We were only allowed to take the equivalent of $30000 with us to Australia—which is not a lot when you're starting from scratch—and a few personal effects. Fortunately, I was allowed to take my vintage guitars with me, which was a decision that changed my life. When I got to Australia—and I have to say times were a little tough—a friend told me about a little site called eBay so after getting online and seeing the potential, I put my guitars up for sale and couldn't believe how much people paid for them! It got me thinking: what else could I sell on eBay?

That small decision to sell a few guitars led him to co-create Australia's first online department store, Deals Direct, which subsequently gave rise to the 'fixed price' function that is now a staple on eBay and other auction sites. Deals Direct went public in 2014 and Paul retired to become the executive chairman of industry group NORA (National Online Retailers Association).

From little things, big things grow

Some business owners start with a crystal-clear intention: to make money. And lots of it.

When Dean Ramler and his mate and co-founder Ruslan Kogan hatched their plan in 2007 to launch their online furniture site Milan Direct they didn't just go home to think about it, they bought a plane ticket to China to start sourcing factories. With Ruslan's experience in e-commerce and Dean's family history in furniture manufacturing, they knew they could do it as well as anyone.

In 2015, after only eight years in business, Milan Direct was purchased by online homewares site Temple & Webster for $20 million. Not a bad rate of return.

Whatever you sell and why you sell it, the most important thing you can do is get started. The market will tell you what to do next.

So, what will you sell? What niche will you explore? What market has a problem that needs solving? To find a gap in the market that needs servicing, and to create a product to meet that need, you need an entrepreneurial quality called 'depth of vision'.

In short, you need to be able to look ahead.

Chapter 3

Mindset #3: Look ahead

Business owners are busy people, but sometimes they get so bogged down in the running of their business, they fail to look up and see where the market is headed. By the time they do, the market has moved on and so have their customers. Successful entrepreneurs keep an eye on the current trends but also look ahead to see what's coming. Tracking industry trends helps you stay relevant to your existing customers, but it also helps you identify opportunities that others are yet to see.

QUICK TIP

To find a point of difference you have to look ahead.

To find out what those trends are and what your market will need, you must look ahead—a long way ahead. In fact, you may have to look so far ahead that people may actually think your idea is ... crazy.

Uncovering crazy ideas that are yet to be discovered needs depth of vision: the ability to look deep into the future and see what no-one else is seeing.

This is why an idea first perceived as crazy (most likely a fad that's trending in a very small pocket of an outlier fringe group) seems crazy—because no-one has ever done it before.

And yet, when that idea does become reality, the entrepreneur is considered visionary. The question is: can you stick with your idea long enough for the market to realise they have a problem that needs solving? We all know people with revolutionary ideas who've started a business but were too early to market and/or couldn't financially (or mentally) stay the distance.

WHAT DO YOU SEE? THE ACORN OR THE HOUSE?

Visionary entrepreneurs don't look at things the same way as others. For example, when most people look at an acorn, they just see an acorn. But when an entrepreneur with depth of vision looks at the acorn, they see what's made possible by the acorn: the oak tree; the wood from the oak tree; the house that's built from the wood; the suburbs of houses that are built from the wood. Entrepreneurs don't just see what's *there*; they see what's *possible*.

Having depth of vision isn't hard. It just means getting close to your customer and being obsessed with serving their every need before they even know what that need is. It's called being 'customer centric'.

Extreme customer centricity

People often think technology itself is the real threat to the status quo. It's not. Being non-customer centric is the biggest threat to any business. Putting the customer at the front and centre of all business decisions sounds obvious, but it's not always easy. United States-based advertising executive Alberto Brea described it well when he shared his views on why legacy industries failed so spectacularly.

Amazon did not kill the retail industry. They did it to themselves with bad customer service.

Netflix did not kill Blockbuster. They did to themselves with ridiculous late fees.

Uber did not kill the taxi business. They did it to themselves with [a] limited number of taxis and fare control.

Apple did not kill the music industry. They did it to themselves by forcing people to buy full-length albums.

Airbnb did not kill the hotel industry. They did it to themselves with limited availability and pricing options.

Technology by itself is not the real disruptor.

Being non-customer centric is the biggest threat to any business.

Putting customers front and centre is not a new concept. We've always sent out surveys; asked for feedback; professed to 'listen' to what they want. But do customers even *know* what they want? Surveys and the like are reactive in nature, and most people don't know what they need until they see it. In their book *The Third Industrial Revolution in Global Business*, management consultants Gary Hamel and CK Prahalad famously wrote, 'consumers are notoriously lacking in foresight and are unable to imagine products that do not yet exist.'

To find out what a customer really needs, we have to look ahead and predict what those needs are; we need to look at the niches, the fads and the trends that are brewing because those outlier markets, although small in number, reveal what the future needs of our current customers will be.

When Jane Lu from Showpo built her website back in 2010, she looked into the distance and predicted that people would find shopping on their mobile more convenient than their desktop. That observation seems obvious now, but it wasn't then. She took mobile seriously, long before others did, and that 'early adopter' behaviour contributed to her fast growth.

Booktopia's founder Tony Nash has a simple strategy for staying ahead. He goes overseas.

I have always looked offshore in terms of seeing what's happening next. Some say, 'You've been so incredibly visionary', but a lot of the time I've simply gone to the US

or the UK and looked at what's going on over there with the internet, with e-commerce and then came back to Australia and basically implemented it.

Domino's goes digital

Don Meij looked further than most when he decided he would turn Domino's from a pizza chain into a technology powerhouse. While his innovation team was busy being first to market with tech-enabled services such as online ordering, SMS notifications and delivery drones, his competitors were twiddling their thumbs and losing market share by the minute. Meij's depth of vision enabled him to make the decision early on that Domino's would not be a pizza company that dabbles in technology, but a technology company that happens to make pizza, and that, as they say, made all the difference.

That decision to identify as a tech company was borne out of Meij's personal decision to be a visionary leader; a leader who would have the courage to look deep into the future and see what they needed to do as a company to stay ahead of the curve—to be willing to be considered crazy.

How not having depth of vision failed Kodak

If I had a dollar for every time Kodak was mentioned as the poster child for how not to manage digital disruption, I wouldn't be writing this book. I'd be in the Bahamas sipping on a Mojito...having a handsome pool boy hand-feed me hot chips...But I'm not, so I will mention it.

I'll use Kodak (just this once) to demonstrate a key tech trend that underpins the principle of digital disruption.

The main reason Kodak collapsed was because their leadership team failed to look ahead, to see the perfect storm that was brewing and to take steps to avoid it. What they failed to see was that photography, their core business, was based on a scarcity model. In other words, people were careful about the photos they took. They had to decide which photos were worthy of keeping and which weren't. They were judicious.

When digital photography came along, that conservative approach went out the window. Now you could take shots of anything: that ant crawling on the table; that puddle on the pavement; that mole on the back of your hand. Photos became disposable because the marginal cost of taking an extra photo didn't just diminish (as it would with a linear improvement in the technology), it shrunk to zero. Whether you took three pictures or 300 pictures the cost was the same: zero marginal cost. The result? No-one needed cameras anymore. Sales of cameras plummeted.

It got worse for Kodak. Not only did we not need to buy their cameras or film, we stopped needing photographic paper too. When we were careful with our shots, we diligently took the film to the Kodak shop (remember those?) and got them printed out. We'd eagerly await their return and then dutifully file them in our photo albums (remember those?). When was the last time you put some films in for processing or even printed them out on your printer? You don't need to of course—you can store them on your phone for free. Zero marginal cost.

Kodak was hit by unprecedented technological change coming at it from multiple directions. Cameras, film, processing, distribution, retailing, marketing, packaging, storage. The works!

This is the very essence of a paradigm shift. Shifts like this are creating thousands of similar disruptions across the global economy. To stay ahead, you have to see what's coming down the line.

Here's a cautionary tale of an Australian leader who didn't look ahead.

How the head of Godfreys lost his job

In 2016, the CEO of Godfreys was sacked by the board because, in their words, he 'failed to spot a market shift'. In my words, he lacked depth of vision. The market shift he failed to spot was the migration of users from floor vacuum cleaners to stick vacuum cleaners. That inability to spot the shift cost Godfreys a large chunk of market share and it cost the CEO his job.

You may be asking, 'What's the CEO of Godfreys got to do with me? He ran a public company answerable to a board. I run my own business. No-one can sack me!' You're right. You may not be answerable to a board, but you are answerable to your customers and they are the ones who can sack you. They won't tell you that they're sacking you; they'll just leave and find another supplier who is looking ahead.

How not looking ahead cost taxi drivers their livelihoods

A taxi driver I spoke to bought three licences from the Victorian government in 2012, borrowing against his house to the tune of nearly $800 000. At the time those licences seemed like a sure bet.

But in August 2016, a mere four years later, the Andrews Government announced an overhaul of the commercial passenger vehicle industry, buying back licences at a fraction of their worth. The taxi driver now had a debt of $670 000 hanging around his head, 'like a noose', he said.

However, other taxi drivers I've talked to saw the writing on the wall and sold their licences before the value was wiped out. They had the depth of vision to see what was happening and got out before everyone else.

Even sectors as innocuous as associations need to look ahead. For example, an association that has millennials or Generation Y as members or future members should be looking ahead and taking steps to rethink their membership models. Unlike their Generation X and Baby Boomer cohorts, these digital natives are increasingly turning to the freelance economy for work—for some because the flexible nature of that work suits their lifestyle; for others because there is no full-time work to be had. The result? Association membership is on the slide and without forward thinking and a restructuring of their membership model, associations will find themselves unviable and at risk.

Who needs depth of vision?

Does every entrepreneur need to have depth of vision or is it just for those who seek to disrupt a legacy industry? For example, does a café owner need depth of vision? A car wash company? A financial planner? You bet. Everyone does. The decision to *not* stay ahead of the curve shows up in the smallest of ways.

- It's a hipster café that doesn't offer soy milk, or PayPass or wall sockets to charge laptops.
- It's a high-end car wash company that doesn't offer a brushless eco-wash, a café with barista-made coffee or a kids' play corner.
- It's a financial planner who doesn't know what Stockpot, Society One or Joust are.

Depth of vision is not just about being ahead of the competitors, it's about being ahead of the customer. Customers look to us for leadership, to tell them what's happening next, what to care about. If we stop adding value to their lives, we lose their trust, and in this era, if we lose their trust, we lose everything.

Those who don't look ahead remain behind

How far ahead do you need to look? One year, five years or 15 years?

Elon Musk looks decades ahead. The Chinese government looks a hundred years ahead. Japanese conglomerate Softbank has a 300-year plan. It's a tricky concept to get right. We need to look far enough ahead to see what the customer needs before they know they need it, but not so far that we offer them gimmicks that have no impact on the bottom line.

Here's how Tony Nash of Booktopia assesses the value of new tech tools such as virtual reality goggles.

> In terms of virtual reality and being able to put on a headset and pretend that you're walking through a mega bookstore that's three miles long and browsing around in there for two hours—is that really going to add value? Will that really help generate the sales based on the investment you're making? At this stage, that's hard to justify. I think what we'd probably end up doing is find somebody who's built that kind of product and then we just load our images and our data into that system so then people can have that kind of shopping experience. [In terms of where we invest our time and money,] I'd be looking more at international expansion and spend a lot more in investing in that delivery piece and holding more stock.

For other industries, advanced technologies create a point of difference that is meaningful.

Virtual reality (VR) and the real-estate industry

Alex Ouwens runs Ouwens Casserly, a boutique real-estate firm in Adelaide. He got started earlier than most on the digital innovation journey and invested in 3D videography. His YouTube video shows him introducing his firm as 'the first real estate firm to use virtual reality'.

Alex says, 'We're preparing for a time when everyone has a VR headset. We believe it will go some way towards replacing on-premise inspections. It's not there yet but it will happen'.

Here's how his virtual reality (VR) product works. If you list your house for sale with his agency, they will create a short video of a walk-through. When you put the VR goggles on, you get to see the property in a new perspective. Everything feels real and you can see the house in its correct proportions. It's great for researching floor plans, getting a feel for the house or just collecting ideas with minimal effort.

More importantly, the content is portable and if you have a set of VR goggles you can download the content from the App Store and watch it without ever visiting the house.

Think about the impact this has on real estate and related industries.

Open inspections as we know them will become obsolete and the thought of strangers in our house, browsing through our undies drawer and nicking spare change from the fruit bowl, will become a thing of the past (not that I'd do any of those things, of course).

The impact of that shift? We won't need a real-estate agent standing guard at the doorway anymore and instead of 30 'units' walking through—most of them nosy neighbours—there'll be three and it will be by appointment.

If there is an 'open for inspection', potential buyers won't need to give their name and details because the facial recognition scanner will identify them as they walk in the gate. You won't need to worry if they can afford the house because those facial data points will call up their financial risk profile to reveal their credit history. If they do qualify, they'll be able to buy the house on the spot by transferring the deposit that they just borrowed from a peer-to-peer lending network. Or they'll just pay it with Bitcoin and the government won't have a clue where the money is going to or where it came from.

CAN YOU BUY A PROPERTY WITH BITCOIN?

In 2017, British entrepreneurs Michelle Mone and Doug Barrowman created Dubai's 250-million-pound luxury development, Aston Plaza and Residences. They claim that it will be the 'first major development' to be priced in the virtual currency Bitcoin.

Nigel Dalton, REA Group's chief inventor says, 'By 2020, most Australian homes will have VR headsets, and we're confident the leading real estate agents will embrace VR to create a brand-new experience for a whole new generation of property seekers.'[1]

Will this dystopian scenario happen now? Should every real estate agent run out and invest in VR technology? No, but bit by bit, like the frog in boiling water, these tech developments are putting the heat on every industry—some more than others.

While VR and other technologies may not add immediate value to all industries, they absolutely will to the real estate industry, and those who ignore it do so at their peril. Knowing what trends to pay attention to and invest in and what not to is the hallmark of a visionary entrepreneur.

What's your 'pinch of salt'?

We've established that the future belongs to those who can take an existing 'bit' of a service and give it a twist and do it better than anyone else. So, what's that tiny bit going to be for you? What's going to be your point of difference? What's going to be your pinch of salt?

This trend to find a 'bit' of a business model, twist it and find a way of doing that bit differently is a huge asset to the smaller underdogs in the online world because it enables them to compete. They don't need to be the biggest, the cheapest or the fastest anymore. And that's good because those three points of difference were what enabled the bigger players to dominate.

Points of difference that were once too expensive, too technically difficult or too niche to be viable to offer (such as hyper-personalisation, home delivery, ethical investing) are all now possible.

For the first time in history current technology enables you to hone in on one aspect of a business model, twist it and thereby compete in almost any sector with any product.

Here are a few examples to help you identify the various ways in which businesses have taken a *bit* of an existing business model and twisted it to create a valuable point of difference.

Make it quick: Menulog

Menulog is a popular online ordering app. You order food online. You get your meal delivered. What's so different about that?

What's different is *how* the order is taken. Instead of ordering directly with the restaurant, you order via the Menulog app, and then you get your meal delivered. What's different is the extra digital layer—the interface—provided by Menulog. That little interface makes a big difference to all the stakeholders. The customer gets instant access to hundreds of restaurants, gets those meals home delivered and only has to enter their address and credit card details once.

That interface is a game-changer for the restaurant owner too. It enables restaurants to get an online presence at a very low cost and be seen by thousands of new customers.

Menulog and other platforms like it have not been great for all restaurants. For example, if you owned the only Malaysian restaurant in your area that offered home delivery, Menulog's arrival unleashed a raft of new competitors for you to battle it out with. The main point, however, is the customer used the app and liked it, which means that nothing else really matters. The customer is king. Menulog is a great example of how to harness the four factors of disruption—cloud, mobile, data and social technologies—to create an interface that scales without friction at virtually zero marginal cost.

PS: Menulog was sold to UK-based Just Eats in May 2015 for $855 million. That 'little' interface generated a very big return.

Make it fun: Vinomofo

Vinomofo created their point of difference by offering great wine, at great prices, without the 'BS'. That point of difference, coupled with their unique brand personality, informs every aspect of their business, from the website design and imagery, to the copy they use on their website, to the people they employ. Here's how their unique customer 'voice' shows up in their website copy:

- 'You should be boozing like a baller on a dirtbag budget, drinking $30 wine for 15 bucks...'
- 'There's no lock-in contract and no bullshit. You just pick a club that works for your budget, personalise it to suit your tastes and decide how often you need your wine delivered.'

You wouldn't see Dan Murphy's creating copy like that. That small but important focus on a 'mofo' brand personality gives Vinomofo an edge in a cutthroat market. They haven't reinvented the market for home delivery of wine. They just picked one aspect of the business—extreme customer service and a 'mofo' attitude—and made that their point of difference.

Make it cheap: fiverr.com

Fiverr.com didn't create a new product or service. Upwork, Freelancer and 99Designs had all gone before, but fiverr identified one little aspect of those competitive sites—pricing—and gave it a twist. Their pinch of salt was that you can get anything you like from the site and it will cost just $5. Whatever it is you need—a logo, a piece of code, a song sung, a cartoon drawn—they will do it for $5.

This narrow focus was a gift that kept on giving as it provided them with meaningful points of difference that the customer would:

- appreciate—what's not to like about getting a $5 logo design?
- easily understand—'You mean everything is $5?' Yep.
- enjoy sharing with colleagues and friends—'Hey, check this out! Everything's $5!'

The creative supplier liked it too. It gave them a chance to rise above the clutter they experience on other marketplaces and helped them generate new leads. Importantly, the media would find it interesting and novel to write about too as it's a fun and slightly zany concept. This one-price-point concept is not new. The $2 Shop pioneered it and Japanese retailer Daiso has certainly taken it to the wire with their $2.80 price point for every product.

Like many one-price-point concepts, fiverr.com's offering evolved and now offers higher priced services to those who seek them, but the $5 price point creates cut-through, awareness and that all-important customer trial.

Make a difference: Thankyou

Thankyou didn't make a better, tastier, cheaper bottle of water. They just did one thing differently: they offered customers the chance to *feel good* about choosing their product instead of the competitors'. That's all. They did this by adding a unique code to each bottle so people could go online and see what humanitarian project their purchase had contributed to. Customers reasoned, 'If I have to buy a bottle of water, I may as well buy one that helps someone else.'

Make it easy: Wholesome Hub

It's not what Wholesome Hub stocks that makes them different. Their unique 'values-based' search function enables you to quickly find products that are not easily found. Each product has been tagged according to a range of different 'values', which enables shoppers to buy according to their conscience or dietary needs. For example, are you searching for cruelty-free products? Made by Fairtrade? Kosher? Gluten-nut-dairy-egg-free? Shopping for hard-to-find products has never been easier with the Wholesome Hub search functionality. Is this a world-shattering or life-changing point of difference? No. But the 'values-based' search function is helpful and meaningful to customers who have specific needs and want to find those products quickly and easily.

Make it a subscription: Dollar Shave Club

'Shave time and money' is the cute tagline for razor-blade disruptor, Dollar Shave Club. The Dollar Shave Club is a subscription-based service that delivers a disposable razor to your house each month. You pay a fraction of the retail price, you get them delivered to your door and it continues month by month until you opt out.

They launched the service with a funny, irreverent 90-second videoclip that went viral. You can check it out at www.bernadetteschwerdt.com.au/book. Three months after posting the clip on YouTube, it racked up 4.75 million views and in the first 48 hours after the video debuted 12000 people signed up for the service. The video went on to get more than 20 million views and rocketed Dollar Shave Club to more than $240 million in revenue.

Their point of difference? They focused on one product (razor blades), one audience (men who shave and want to save money and time) and one 'twist' (we'll deliver it to your door). The subscription delivery mechanism is the disruptive point of difference.

PS: In July 2016, *The New York Times* reported that Unilever allegedly paid $1 billion for Dollar Shave Club after just five years in business. A perfect example of how a little startup can compete with the big players and beat them at their own game, simply by creating a meaningful point of difference.

Make it fairly: Everlane

Ever wondered how the discount chains sell $5 T-shirts and still make a profit? I do. I think someone's missing out on a pay cheque somewhere along the line. In most cases it's the factory worker. This has led to the creation of the fair-trade movement, which works hard to get factory workers a fair deal.

Some serious fashion identities are getting on board. Punk rocker and fashion royalty Vivienne Westwood's clothes labels tell people where the product was made, in what village and by whom. Others are using the clothes price tag to list a detailed breakdown of who in the value chain got paid what.

Everlane.com, an ethically-driven, US-based fashion label, has taken it one step further. They have videos on their website and extensive summaries showcasing the factories they work with. They are transparent in who they use and each factory is given a compliance audit to evaluate factors such as fair wages, reasonable hours and environment. Has Everlane.com reinvented fashion or created a new product? No. They've just made it easier for people to choose who and where they buy their clothes from.

Make it fun: Openbook Howden

Companies such as printers are increasingly turning to advanced tech tools such as augmented reality (AR) as a new source of revenue. For example, Sarah Leo, General Manager of Brand, Strategy and People at leading South Australian printer Openbook Howden uses AR to create a point of difference for her clients.

They printed a book for entrepreneur Scott Boocock (the 'peg with a hook' guy from the *Shark Tank* reality show). He wanted to showcase his unique approach to business so they collaborated to create a book featuring AR. The author inserted various images throughout the book that were AR activated, which turns it from being a standard book into an engaging and involving experience. World shattering? Life changing? No, but it does create interest, a bit of fun for the reader and that all-important point of difference. It's a smart business move on their part as it demonstrates to their clients that they have depth of vision and are keeping ahead of the trends. To see exactly how this application of AR works, check out my site www.bernadetteschwerdt.com.au/book.

WHAT IS AUGMENTED REALITY (AR)?

AR blends digital content with reality. Unlike VR, where you wear a headset that blocks out the real world, AR places a digital layer between you and reality. For example, an engineer could wear an AR 'visor' (similar to a sun visor) that calls up a specific page of a manual, a graph, a web page or map whilst they're working. This content appears in front of them as if on a transparent screen. They can reference the content and continue working, so they don't have to 'down tools'. The game Pokémon Go was an example of AR.

***

Let's recap. You've got your crazy idea, the tools of disruption at your disposal and you've looked ahead to find a niche, trend or fad in your sector that has the potential to grow. You've put your depth of vision goggles on, seen what the market will need in five years' time and picked a sliver of that market to focus on. But what industry will you be operating in and who will you be competing with? That may seem obvious at the outset but once you delve deeper, it may not be as simple as it seems and if you get the answers to those two questions wrong, it could cost you a lot of money, time and effort.

Chapter 4

Mindset #4: Know what business you're in

In the early 1990s I worked as an account director for a Sydney-based, multinational advertising agency. One of our clients at the time was Australia Post. At our first 'get to know you' meeting, we asked them the standard question we dutifully asked all new clients: 'What business are you in?'

'We're in the letters business,' they said confidently.

We accepted that answer as valid and moved on. After all, they were Australia Post so it seemed pretty obvious.

Twenty-five years down the track and seeing the decline of their letters business, it's pretty clear we all got the answer to that question wrong. So what business *were* they in? With the benefit of hindsight, the answer should have been *'We're in the 'transmission of information and products' business.'*

Is this just word play? Semantics? After all, what's the difference between 'the letters business' and the 'transmission of information and products' business?' As it turns out, a lot. The difference shows up when you ask the next question, 'Who are you competing with?'

Who are you really competing with?

After Australia Post answered, 'We're in the letters business', their answer to our second question (who are you competing with) was,

'No-one. We have no competitors. As a semi-government authority we are the only ones who can deliver letters.'

So what do you do when you have no competitors? You get complacent; you overlook opportunities; you ignore the need for innovation. I believe the seeds of Australia Post's first financial loss, posted in 2015, were sown in the early 1990s due to this erroneous belief that they had no competitors.

It could have been so different for them.

If they had answered, *'We're in the "transmission of information and products" business'*, then the competitive landscape would have looked very different (and very crowded) and their marketing would have taken a more aggressive approach.

For example, at that point in time, telemarketing was huge; fax marketing just as big. Couriers such as Federal Express and DHL were entering the Australian market and email was bubbling up too. The internet was simmering on the horizon, and the arrival of internet service providers such as OzEmail were hot topics of discussion.

As you can see, there were lots of competitors in the 'transmission of information and products' business. If you change the answer to the question, 'What business are you in?', you instantly change the competitor landscape too.

The consequences of getting the answer to this question wrong have been enormous. Australia Post has had to play catch-up ever since. In the interim, they lost a massive opportunity to own the space that other tech companies now occupy. Other players, such as OzEmail, took early market advantage and owned the territory that Australia Post could have owned and, by rights, should have owned.

On the upside, Australia Post is working their way back and they have their digital fingers in a range of pies.

WHO WANTS TO BE A MILLIONAIRE?

Malcolm Turnbull purchased his stake in OzEmail in 1994 for $500 000 and reportedly sold it for $57 million in 1999.

What business is Australia Post in now? In the words of former CEO Ahmed Fahour, 'We are a technology company.' That's a long way from being in the letters business.

What business are you *really* in?

As you can see, asking the question, 'What business are you (really) in?' is not as straightforward as it seems.

The reality now is that your business is an amalgamation of many business processes and at any one time, depending on what process the business is working on, you will need to 'act as if' you are in that business in order to understand the demands of it.

John Winning, founder of Appliances Online, said it well:

We are a logistics company that happens to sell appliances. We are a technology business that happens to sell appliances. We are a marketing and advertising agency that happens to sell appliances. Each area of the business needs to be the best at what it can be.

When you know what business you're in, you do things differently.

Andre Eikmeier, co-founder of online wine curator and retailer Vinomofo, reflects on how he would have done things differently.

When we started, we thought we were in the 'wine' business so we hired wine experts. But the trouble was, we weren't getting any sales and the website wasn't working as efficiently as it should have. It's really important to understand right from the get-go that as an online business we are as much an internet company as we are a wine company. What we would

have done differently is invite a developer or tech guy to be one of the founders. Ideally, for an online business, what you want is a hacker who can code and a hustler who can market as part of your founding team. Otherwise, you're in the hands of dev [web development] agencies, which are expensive and not particularly productive, or you're in the hands of a young guy who's building the site after his day job but doesn't have real experience, and it just doesn't work. We had a lot of problems early on working with part time dev contractors.

We're all in the technology business

As demonstrated by the Australia Post example, the consequences of getting the answer to this question wrong can be serious. It can bring a company down. The message is clear: irrespective of what you sell, online or offline, if you have a website, even a simple blog or a one-page website, you're in the *technology* business and you need to think and act like a technology business.

Knowing how important it is to get the right answer to 'What business are you in?' I was curious to see how each entrepreneur would answer when I asked them that question. As expected, they were way ahead of the game.

We are a tech business that connects influencers and brands.

Jules Lund, founder of TRIBE

We are a logistics company that sells books.

Tony Nash, co-founder of Booktopia

We are a logistics business that sells appliances.

John Winning, founder of Appliances Online

Once you've established the business you're in, you need to work out exactly what your business does. Smart companies are using a process called 'functional mapping' to identify the core activities that make up their business.

What does your business really do?

The best way to work out what you do and what your business does is to strip it right back to basics.

WHAT IS A FUNCTIONAL MAP?

A functional map is useful for quickly identifying all of the processes involved in bringing a product or service to market. Once the list is compiled, identify who is in charge of each process. This gives accountability and ownership and helps identify the roles each team member plays.

When Andre Eikmeier and Justin Dry bought back their company, Vinomofo, from Catch of the Day in 2013, they took the opportunity to rebuild it with the future in mind. Andre reflects on how they did it.

When we restructured we needed to get back to basics and work out exactly what we do. We conducted a functional mapping process to identify every step in our business.

When we looked at the components of the business, it worked like this. We:

- buy wine in boxes
- photograph those boxes of wine
- write the copy for the boxes of wine
- put that copy on the website
- write emails and other content pieces to advertise the wine
- ring people up to see what wine they want
- send the wine out.

The functional mapping process helped us simplify what we did, to see exactly what we do. When we looked at it like that,

it helped us work out what skill sets we needed, what teams we needed and who needs to do what. It helped us take the complexity out of it and work out what business we needed to be at every stage of the process.

What we learned was very valuable. We saw where our pain points were, where we had gaps and we realised of course, that's why there's problems in that area, because there's no ownership of that task. It has been an incredibly valuable process. The business has grown so much we now do it on a regular basis now.

Functional mapping allows leaders to explore where accountability lies, especially in areas where cross-functional co-operation is needed.

Identifying what business you're in is important as it dictates how you run a business: from the people you employ, to the competitors you face, to the promotions you run. Here are a few examples that demonstrate how it's not always as clearcut as it seems.

Westfield shopping centres: What business are they *really* in?

Westfield shopping centres are not just shopping centres. On any given day, you will find a range of arcane activities taking place in the forecourt: fashion parades, hackathons, cooking competitions, dog parades—sometimes it's all of them at the same time. So what business are they in? Retail? No. Entertainment. The promotions manager for the centre needs to know this as it will dictate the type and scale of promotions they run.

A hardware store is just a hardware store. Or is it? What business is Bunnings in?

Bunnings hardware stores: What business are they *really* in?

One of the big secrets behind Bunnings' success is their ability to convert the female renovator into a skilled tradesperson. Their two-hour workshops have been instrumental in helping women get the inside running on how to fix stuff. And once they've got the knowledge, the women can take a stroll down the aisle and buy what they need.

They're as much in the education business as they are in the hardware business.

Like a lot of writers, I love stationery, which is why I love hanging out at Officeworks. (I know, I should get a life!) But what business are Officeworks really in?

Officeworks: What business are they *really* in?

If you look at who shops in Officeworks, you'll find it's mainly small business owners. And what does Officeworks help them do? Build their business. After all, without a computer, a printer, paper and a desk, how can you start, let alone build, a business? Officeworks doesn't just sell office goods, it sells the dream of owning your own business. In some respects, it's an incubator for startups.

How can this valuable question, 'what business am I in?' demonstrably help small businesses? I have a client in the landscaping business. He sells plant packages online and he asked me what sort of blogs he should be writing for his website.

If he's in the 'landscaping' business, the obvious answer is blogs about gardens and plants. But that's not overly inspiring for people (like me) who may need plants but aren't interested in reading blogs about plants. But if he's in the business of 'creating beautiful lifestyles' then his blog content can cover a much wider array of topics and be infinitely more interesting. For example, under the broader definition, here's a few topics his blogs could cover:

- How to make your dead lawn 'kid friendly'
- 5 ways to fit a luxury pool into a small backyard
- 3 mistakes townhouse owners make when choosing indoor plants.

These blogs are far more interesting, will attract a wider array of people and target people's need to create beautiful lifestyles—and that's the business he is really in. A small difference, but important.

What about libraries? Yes, they're in the book-lending business, but they're much more than that. I think they're in the 'inspiration' business.

LIBRARIES ARE THE NEW BLACK

Want to learn how to code? Use an iPad? Edit a video?

Your local library is the place to go. If you haven't been in one for a while, go. They are mini-incubators and offer a feast of courses, talks, events and resources that will give you the tools to get tech-savvy. Great for the kids, the seniors and everyone in between. Best of all, most services are free or very low cost.

Knowing what business you're in helps you accurately focus all aspects of your activities—from hiring people, to the blogs you write, to the website you build and the suppliers you engage.

All great businesses know who their customers are and what needs they have. This is called 'knowing what problem you solve'. As with all important questions, the answer is not always obvious.

Chapter 5

Mindset #5: Know what problem you're solving

When you have Paul Greenberg, the godfather of the Australian online retail industry, sitting in front of you—a man who created Australia's first online department store; a man who disrupted the retail landscape and has met the likes of Jeff Bezos, Jack Ma and Elon Musk—what question do you ask him?

For me, that question was: 'Paul, what's the Next Big Thing?'

Paul looked at me and he said two words: 'Wrong question.'

So, what's the right question? He answered,

> **To discover the next big thing—the IPO that goes off, the next Unicorn in waiting—the question isn't 'What's the next big thing?' The question has to be:**
>
> *What problem is yet to be solved?*

Are all the good ideas gone?

I often get asked, 'Have all the good ideas been taken? Have the big disruptors such as Facebook, Uber, Airbnb and Alibaba sucked the oxygen out of the ideas atmosphere, leaving no room for new ones to grow?' The answer is, unequivocally, *no*.

All the good ideas have *not* been taken. In fact, the market is ripe for big, bold, audacious ideas precisely *because* of the big disruptors. Their very existence creates opportunities for new ideas to thrive.

The trick is to identify the disruptor in your industry, look at the problem it creates and create a business that helps solve *that* problem.

Note: Don't seek to be the next Facebook or the next Snapchat either. You just need to solve the problems they create. Their girth creates a market plenty big enough for everyone.

Disruptors solve big problems but they also create new ones — problems that others can solve.

So, don't try to beat these disruptors at their own game, or even contemplate doing so; just focus on a problem they create and solve that. The bigger the disruptor, the bigger and broader the opportunity that awaits you.

Finding a problem to solve

So how do you find out what problem needs solving? You may want to look at the current disruptor within your own industry, and see what problems it's creating, to work out what problems need to be mopped up.

That's as good a basis as any for coming up with a disruptive business idea. So, who's the big disruptor in your industry and what problems have they created that you could solve?

Who's the 'whale' in your industry?

It's helpful to think of the distruptors in your industry as whales in the ocean. Whales 'own' the ocean in which they swim. They intimidate all with their over-sized presence. They also control the ecosystem around them and help a raft of other creatures such as plankton and krill to survive. Just by existing, whales enable other creatures to live.

Facebook, Airbnb, Uber and other disruptors are just like the whale. They move through the ocean taking everything in their wake, and while doing so, inadvertently spawn ecosystems of their own, without even knowing what or who those suckers are.

Take Facebook. As one of the first social media platforms to create a major disruption, it spawned an ecosystem of industries.

Look at all the industries that Facebook has breathed life into simply by existing:

- Social media *content creators* exist because of Facebook.
- Social media *defamation lawyers* exist because of Facebook.
- Social media *data analysts* exist because of Facebook.
- Social media *competition creators* exist because of Facebook.
- Social media *community managers* exist because of Facebook.

Without Facebook, those industries, and the thousands of businesses within those industries, wouldn't exist.

There's a disruptor—a whale—in your industry. Find out what it is, see what problems it is creating and build your business idea around that.

But first, here's what *not* to do when deciding on your business idea.

Why business ideas fail

A lot of business owners start a business simply because *they* think it's a good idea or *they* have a passion in that area and therefore think that a business can be built around it. That's inspiring and all, but starting a business because *you* think it's a good idea is what I call 'the push mentality', which goes something like, *I've got a great idea and I'm going to 'push' it out to the world, whether the world needs it or not.* That's a recipe for failure.

What if we were to reverse the thinking and see what the market needs first: discover what problem is yet to be solved and then create the product or service that meets that need?

Wouldn't it be great if ...?

After 25 years in business, I have finally stumbled on a powerful question that instantly reveals an unmet need, and along with it, a never-ending supply of unique business ideas.

This question taps into a 'pull mentality' that allows you to pull from the collective unconscious of unmet needs an idea that no-one has ever thought of.

With this one simple question, you can access a never-ending supply of unique, profitable and sustainable business ideas. Here is the question that reveals those unmet needs. Drum roll please ...

Wouldn't it be great if ...?

That's it! I know it seems ridiculously simple, but it works. Here's how existing entrepreneurs have used this simple but powerful phrase to come up with world-class disruptive ideas. Take the quiz, 'What am I?' and guess what product I'm describing:

- *Question:* Wouldn't it be great if ...
  ... we could take a photo, see it for 10 seconds and delete it?
  What am I?: Snapchat
- *Question:* Wouldn't it be great if ...
  ... there was an app that told us where all the whiting is swimming today?
  What am I?: Fishfinder
- *Question:* Wouldn't it be great if ...
  ... there was a website that helped me compare insurance policies so I could get the best deal?
  What am I?: iSelect.com
- *Question:* Wouldn't it be great if ...
  ... I could raise money directly for someone close to me?
  What am I?: GoFundMe.com

- *Question:* Wouldn't it be great if ...
  ... I could find local, trusted, cost-effective tradies to help me with odd jobs around the house?
  What am I?: Airtasker.com

This question doesn't just help uncover new business ideas. It helps existing businesses uncover new marketing ideas and resolve long-standing problems. It assumes nothing and that is part of its power. Here's a real-world example of how I used this very simple question to help a client unlock some creative marketing strategies.

ABC University

I ran a brainstorming workshop for a leading Australian university. They specialise in creating English-language training products for the South-East Asian market. For privacy reasons I'll call them ABC University and the training product 'English For Beginners'. The situation was dire: sales were down, morale was low and their channel partners were starting to push competitive products. They asked me to conduct an innovation session to establish what was going wrong, and to crowdsource with the group some suggestions for what could be done better.

There were 30 people from seven different South-East Asian countries at the workshop. I put them into small groups and asked them to consider this question:

If the university could give you a magic wand that would enable your every marketing wish to be granted, what could we do to help you? When you present your answers, we'd like you to start each sentence with the phrase ... 'Wouldn't it be great if ABC University could ...?'

At the end of the brainstorming, a representative from each group stood up and presented a list of all the things they would like ABC University to do differently that would help them better market the education product in their home country.

(continued)

ABC University (*cont'd*)

The results were revealing.

In just 15 minutes they came up with a range of initiatives that the marketing team had never considered. For example, a woman from China got up and said, 'Wouldn't it be great if we could ... change the name of the course?'

The university marketing team gasped! 'Change the name of the course!' they spluttered. 'What's wrong with the name of the course? Surely we can't be so off track that even the most basic element of marketing, the course name, is wrong?' they muttered.

'Why do you want to change the name of the course?' I asked.

She said, 'In my country the brand name of the course 'English for Beginners' means 'boring'. So, in effect, when we're asking people to sign up to this course we're saying, 'Please sign up to 36 hours of this really boring English-language tuition course.' This has not been helpful to our marketing efforts.'

This small insight dramatically changed the way the university marketed the course.

Ask your clients to complete the phrase and see what they'd like you to do differently. It could be very illuminating.

How disruptors create 'feeder' industries

Here's an example of how industry disruptors create problems, and how businesses within those industries use the creative question — 'Wouldn't it be great if ...' — to create a product to solve it.

For example, if you apply the question, 'Wouldn't it be great if ...?' to these ideas, you can reverse engineer how some of them came into being.

Here are some examples of how this brainstorming question reveals unmet needs.

- *Industry disruptor:* Airbnb
  Question that reveals unmet need: Wouldn't it be great if ...?
  Solution: ... I had a digital lock to put on my Airbnb property that enables me to send tenants a personalised code so that I can remotely track who comes in and when.
  Problem it solves: I can't be at the property to let new tenants in every time they change over. There are too many keys to the property in circulation and I don't feel my property is secure.
  Result: Save money, reduce risk
  Provider: Smart locks by RemoteLock

- *Industry disruptor:* Uber
  Question that reveals unmet need: Wouldn't it be great if ...?
  Solution: ... I could hire a female-only ride-share service to pick up my children when I can't get there.
  Problem it solves: I prefer to have female drivers who are mothers or understand the particular needs of mothers to be the ones who pick up my children.
  Result: Peace of mind, reduce risk
  Provider: Shebah.com.au

- *Industry disruptor:* Wotif.com.au
  Question that reveals unmet need: Wouldn't it be great if ...?
  Solution: ... I could find all the current hotel deal sites on one page so I can easily see and compare them on one screen, rather than flip between multiple sites.
  Problem it solves: I can't tell what the best deal is without creating a spreadsheet to do it and I don't have time to cut and paste all the deals.
  Result: Save time, save money, convenient
  Provider: Trivago.com

WHAT IS CROWDFUNDING?

Crowdfunding is used by individuals or groups to raise money to fund a project, any project. It could be a movie, a startup venture, a charity or even a funeral. It works on the premise that a large group of people will give an amount of their choosing in return for a 'reward' — be it a ticket to the movie's opening night, an early version of the product that you have funded, or it could be just a feeling of goodwill that you've helped others.

- *Industry disruptor:* Crowdfunding
  Question that reveals unmet need: Wouldn't it be great if ...?
  Solution: ... we could donate money directly to the people who need it most rather than giving it to an organisation and having it eaten up in admin and wages.
  Problem it solves: I don't like giving money to big charities because I don't think it gets to the people who need it.
  Result: Trust, personalisation
  Provider: GoFundMe.com.au

- *Industry disruptor:* Drones
  Question that reveals unmet need: Wouldn't it be great if ...?
  Solution: ... we could use drones to fly into the vineyards and take high-quality images of the grapes so we can accurately tell if they're ready for picking or damaged by frost.
  Problem it solves: It's time consuming and expensive to look at each vineyard and see up close whether the crop is ready for picking.
  Result: Fast, safe, cheaper
  Provider: riseabove.com.au (agricultural drones)

To create a successful startup, you need to understand what problem you solve. The question, 'Wouldn't it be great if ...?' is a great way of helping you uncover a new opportunity that has yet to be serviced.

Let's recap

You've got your:

- crazy idea
- access to cheap technology (and tools of disruption)
- depth of vision
- problem that needs solving
- business idea that solves that problem
- point of difference that's meaningful to the customer…

…now what? You need to breathe life into your idea and get your business off the ground. After all, we all know ideas are a dime a dozen but it's the execution that matters—and that's where most novice entrepreneurs fall down. They simply don't have the know-how, confidence or expertise to manifest their idea and make it real.

Takeaways:

- What's your crazy idea? Don't discount an idea because others say 'it's crazy'. It could be the next Snapchat!
- What's your 'pinch of salt' that creates a point of difference? You don't need to reinvent the wheel; you just need to offer something that sets you apart from the competitors.
- Who are you really competing with? Make sure you get this one right or you will find that you have competitors that you didn't anticipate or prepare for.
- To detect unmet needs in your sector, ask the question: 'Wouldn't it be good if…" and see what new ideas this uncovers.

- What business are you *really* in? Take time to answer this question carefully—it may not be as obvious as you think and it will dictate every aspect of what you do.
- Who's the disruptor in your industry? Are they creating a new problem for you to solve?

Coming up...

So how do you bring an idea to life? How do you get it started and give it the best possible chance of success? You need to take action! That starts with creating something that others can see and get excited about.

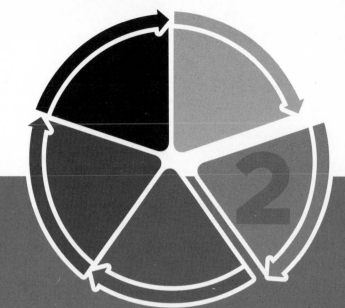

Minimum viable product (MVP)

How to create an MVP to launch your startup

Most people think Uber arrived in Australia fully formed and ready to rock. That's not the case. Take the quiz to see if you know how Uber really got started in Australia. Did they:

A. launch a crowdfunding campaign?

B. get a profile piece featured in *Taxi Weekly?*

C. create a flier and stick it under taxi drivers' windscreens?

The answer? C. Yes, the billion-dollar startup's minimum viable product (MVP) was a single-sided, A4 flier. From little things, big things grow.

David Rohrsheim, General Manager of Uber Australia and New Zealand, shared with me the inside story behind Uber's start in Australia.

> **At the start, Uber was just me and two colleagues. We drove down to the parking lot at Sydney Airport, where all the limo drivers would wait between jobs. We put a flier under their windscreen wipers. The flier was an 'expression of interest' asking them to get in touch if they were interested in trying a new way to work. We'd hoped that some drivers would see it as an opportunity to grow their business and we'd get a pool of drivers to test out our new app.**

It worked. They got enough drivers to create an MVP and they rolled it out in a small test launch that led to the Uber juggernaut we've come to know and love. Even the most disruptive of the disruptive get started with the most basic of MVPs.

Having an MVP is key to testing the validity of your business idea. But how do you come up with an idea in the first place? And how do you know which idea is the best idea? Having a system for assessing the validity of an idea is helpful for sorting out the chaff from the grain so let's use some strategies to test how robust your business idea really is.

Chapter 6

How to come up with a great business idea

Ideas alone won't make you rich but the correct execution of an idea just might. So where do great business ideas come from? And where and who can you turn to for inspiration? Funnily enough, sometimes the person with the best idea may not be the best person to bring that product to market. In fact, it's often the very people who come up with the idea who *shouldn't* bring the idea to market.

Deals Direct co-founder Paul Greenberg expands on this paradox.

Often, it's a person who has worked in one job all their life who comes up with a brilliant invention. They may work on a production line and see the same problem occurring on the conveyor belt day after day. They think to themselves, 'You know, if only someone would invent a bolt that stopped the conveyor belt doing that, then it would make this whole machine work better'. Often an idea for a new product will come from a person who has a detailed knowledge about a particular occupation. But of course, as is often the way, the people who have the idea often don't have the ability to bring it to market, which is why so many great ideas fail to manifest. A successful enterprise often requires both the inventor and a marketer and it's rare that someone can be both. Not impossible, but rare.

Often, the person with the idea has a personal stake in the product and has been touched deeply by the need to get that product made. Don Di Giandomenico is one such person.

Marveloo: A transportable, wheelchair-accessible restroom

Don works as a team leader in horticulture and maintenance for a large Melbourne council. He has been an employee all his working life. His daughter has cerebral palsy and uses a wheelchair. As a result, Don has an insight into the services his daughter can't access. One of those services is an accessible restroom/toilet when she attends community events such as music festivals or outdoor festivals. These events have port-a-loos, but most are not accessible to people in wheelchairs. As a result, Don's daughter misses out on attending events that are a rite of passage for others.

Don and his family, wife Angela and daughter Jessica, got to thinking and asked that key question we established earlier ('Wouldn't it be great if...?'). They came up with a wish-list that looked like this:

- 'Wouldn't it be great if... we could build a restroom that made it easy for people in wheelchairs to access when they attended outdoor events?'
- 'Wouldn't it be great if... we could build a mobile restroom that could be relocated from event to event as needed?'
- 'Wouldn't it be great if... we could make the mobile restroom available for rent at cost-effective rates so lots of people could use it?'

Based on this premise, and in consultation with his daughter, Don jotted down on the back of an envelope what this invention might look like, what features it would have, how big it would be and how it could be transported.

From there he took the jottings to his manager and director for approval to proceed with the concept. The concept was approved and endorsed by council to proceed. The sketches were taken to a designer who toyed around with what would be required to make it all work. A formalised structural plan was developed in preparation for construction. The plan was redeveloped in 3D so the total concept was apparent as a model.

The council put together a small team and proceeded to build it. With something to show, they could now take it around to various stakeholders and get their buy-in and feedback.

Those early jottings on the back of an envelope became the prototype for the Marveloo, a mobile restroom that enables users of wheelchairs to access public toilets.

Great ideas often come from those closest to the problem.

You need an expert

Along with the hacker and the hustler—whom Andre Eikmeier of Vinomofo identified as integral team members of a tech-based business—you'll want to add a third person to the team—the Expert. Together they form a team, as illustrated in figure 6.1 (overleaf). Don's case study demonstrates that great business ideas often come from someone 'on the ground', people who know what needs are yet to be met, have a personal insight into that world and can guide the innovation process.

Experts such as Don are everywhere. They're often older, experienced people who have retired, been 'let go' or have not kept up with technology.

HARNESSING OUR SENIORS AND RETIRED WORKERS

We discard our older workers, as if their use-by date has expired at 65. What a waste. Tech savviness and university degrees are important, but we mustn't confuse education with experience. Our older cohort have much to offer and the younger startups would do well to harness the retirees' knowledge and passion for mentoring, partner with them to find new ideas or put them on their board of advisors.

Figure 6.1: together these three experts can help you manifest a great business idea

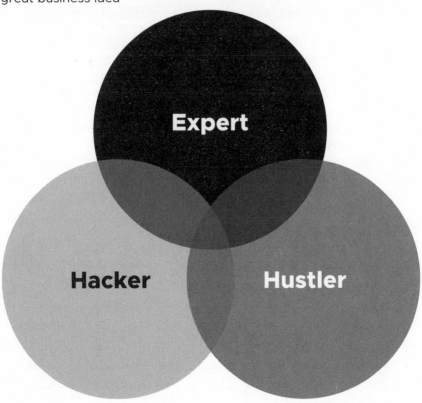

Experts can be young too. Maybe they're your children or grandchildren? After all, who knows more about what a toy, game or app needs than the children who use it?

Experts are your customers. They are often closer to your products than you are because they use them every day. They know what's missing or what features need to be added. Experts are all around us: people on public transport, at work or in the coffee queue. Listen closely to what's being said by those around you and you'll hear about ideas for products that are ripe for invention.

Choose your business idea carefully

As an entrepreneur, you are going to live and breathe your idea for many years to come. It will dominate your thoughts and cost you tens, maybe hundreds, of thousands of dollars so don't rush in with the first idea you come up with. In the old days, when the internet was in its infancy, fortunes were made with just a good idea and a website. That's not the case now. People are savvier and there are thousands of businesses competing with you.

So how do you find a new business idea? Or if you've already got one, how do you prove it has merit before you commit to it? There are some nifty tools to help you work that out. Here are 20 of them.

20 ways to research, test or find a great idea

Here are a few ways to test whether your idea has merit.

1. Use similarweb.com to find out how much traffic the top-ranking competitive sites are getting. If it's not much, maybe the demand for the product is not there.
2. Check out what's trending on Google Trends:
   - You can type in any keyword and it will show you whether the search volumes are increasing or decreasing for that particular word.
   - You can also compare words to see if one word is more powerful than another.
3. Check out what's trending on Twitter.
4. Search on Amazon to see how many books are being published on that topic. This will tell you whether those books are doing well and whether there's a demand for that topic.

5. To find out what topics are 'hot', you can type any topic into www.buzzsumo.com and it will show you the most-shared content using that keyword.

    - You can also type in your own website's URL or a competitor's and find out what content is being shared.

    - After a while you will see certain types of content get shared a lot and you can pick your niche. You'll begin to see the trends of what's popular and what's not.

6. Check out what people are talking about: listen to conversations with your friends or just read the news; listen out for 'Wouldn't it be great if ... ?'

7. Run an AdWords campaign to see if people click on your link. Use a few variations of the offer to test which version gets the best click-through rate.

8. Visit a local newsagency to see which magazines have been published and ask the newsagent which magazines sell well.

9. Share your idea with everyone you know and see what reaction you get. Their response will tell you volumes.

10. Take in those responses and let that feedback inform your idea. Does your idea confuse them? If so, what bits don't they understand? Let their confusion and questions help you refine your idea.

11. Write a survey, share it with your friends and get them to pass it on to as many people as possible. Use www.survey-monkey.com to send free surveys to your market.

12. Research the Australian Bureau of Statistics reports to find growing niches.

13. Find out where your customers are online by asking them, 'What social media are you using?'

14. Check engagement levels on your blogs to see what headlines people are responding to.

15. Check out what's selling on eBay and for how much.

16. Attend hackathons and get feedback on your idea from the technical community.

17. Run the idea as a short course at a community college to test if there is a demand for this type of information.

18. Commit publicly to attending a pitch festival so you are forced to share your idea with someone other than your cat.

19. Click on www.hubpages.com, look up your topic and see which articles are really popular.

20. Visit Facebook fan pages to see how many people are in your target market catchment.

Collaboration: Building your team

Some entrepreneurs are big-picture people. They are brilliant at galvanising the troops and creating excitement around their idea, but they struggle with the technical side and can't get their website up and running. Other entrepreneurs are tech-savvy, tinkering types: they love toying around with software and tools but prefer to stay behind the scenes and minimise their contact with people. Both sets of skills are needed if you're to build and spruik your product to the world.

Does it matter which type you are? From my research, there is no one-size-fits-all recipe for success but every startup team needs a blend of both types of people.

So do you have all the skills you need to succeed? Possibly not. That's why you need to collaborate with people who are not like you—people who can compensate for your weaknesses and people who can complement your skill set.

Your past does not equal your future

Don't let lack of skills or experience in online entrepreneurship stop you from getting started. Take a look at the occupations these people had before they started their online endeavours. Few had any technical know-how but that didn't stop them from getting started:

- Jane Lu worked in corporate finance for KPMG and EY before starting her online business, Showpo.
- Jules Lund was in TV and radio before launching TRIBE.
- Andre Eikmeier was an actor, a telemarketer and a range of other things before he started his business, Vinomofo.
- Paul Greenberg was a psychologist before launching Deals Direct.
- Sandy Abram was a nurse and then a marketing manager before setting up Wholesome Hub.
- Daniel Flynn studied property at university before creating Thankyou.

Their strength is their ability to get people excited about an idea. If you watch their videos or hear them speak, you can see that they are naturally predisposed to the role of being the 'front person'.

People with technical or coding know-how have a decided edge in starting an online business as they inherently understand how websites work.

- Envato co-founders Collis and Cyan Ta'eed are web and graphic designers.
- Tony Nash was a professional SEO consultant prior to starting Booktopia.

Both groups need each other's skill sets. If you've done any professional-development work you'll know that everyone has different predispositions and tendencies. It's about knowing yourself and finding others who can fill in the skill gaps.

Leadership skills

Interestingly, many people I interviewed for this book have no formal background in human resources or people management, yet most named leadership as the make or break factor in their success.

Andre Eikmeier of Vinomofo credited a leadership coach with taking his team to the next level.

We hired a leadership coach and she helped us have the conversations we needed to have to build our team and create higher degrees of trust. She helped us reveal who we are as people, as men and women, with families and busy lives outside of work: people with great talents no-one else knew about. I credit those sessions with helping us redefine our core purpose, which is to be authentic and honest.

Being a successful entrepreneur entails understanding your strengths and weaknesses. Knowing what gaps exist in your entrepreneurial makeup enables you to find those talents in others and to work with them so the project can succeed.

> ## QUICK TIP
> There's an old saying: You can have results or excuses, but not both.

Don't let limiting beliefs about what you're capable of define your future. Anyone can succeed in online business. You just have to get started. It's time to quit talking and start doing. It's time to show the world what your idea looks like. It's time to build your minimum viable product (MVP).

Chapter 7

What is a minimum viable product (MVP)?

The MVP concept was made popular by Eric Ries in 2011 in his book, *The Lean Startup*. His methodology suggests that the question is not, 'Can this product be built?', but is in fact two questions: 'Should this product be built?' and 'Can we build a sustainable business around this set of products and services?'

Figure 7.1 (overleaf) portrays perfectly what an MVP is. On the left is a plain doughnut, ready to eat. It represents the essence of an MVP: make something with the minimum functionality that enables it to be tested and then improve on it later. The elaborate doughnut on the right is the final product — the version that comes after you've launched the plain doughnut. To kickstart your business idea, start with the simplest version (a plain doughnut) and go from there.

Figure 7.1: the doughnut on the left is the basic version—the MVP. The doughnut on the right is the next iteration of that MVP. Get the simple doughnut to market first.

minimum viable product

product

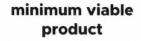

Why do you need an MVP?

When asked why businesses need an MVP, Bluewire Media's digital marketing expert Adam Franklin says:

> **Where some entrepreneurs go wrong is they try to manufacture the fancy doughnut first. They spend too long developing it—getting the shape, the texture, the sprinkles, the icing just right—so by the time they launch it, a competitor has come along and scooped up the market. Getting the most basic product to market as quickly as possible is key to success.**

An MVP forces you to get something to market quickly; to get feedback from your customers; to pivot, change, amend, adapt and then release it back to the market.

Who is the MVP for?

What slows down the MVP process is deciding what target market to focus on. Adam Franklin says:

> **The MVP is not for every possible target audience. That would take too long to make and would weigh down the MVP with**

too much functionality. It's best to select one target market [also known as a 'user persona'], get really clear on what their needs are and build the MVP for them.

What should an MVP look like?

Ideally, the MVP is a 'thing' that other people can look at, touch or experience. This takes it from being a nebulous thought or concept to making it real. The important thing is to *make* it and get it out there. There are dozens of ways to create MVPs. It just depends on what you're selling. Your MVP could be:

- a stall at the local flea market selling your product.
  Example: Catch of the Day started as a stall at a suburban Melbourne market

- a one-page flier showing your customers what you've got planned to launch.
  Example: Uber started in Australia with a one-page 'expression of interest' flier handed out to taxi drivers

- a two-hour workshop teaching people the 'secrets' of your topic.
  Example: My copywriting school got started as a 10-hour short course

- a simple app that lets you test your product on real customers.
  Example: Jules Lund started TRIBE using www.invisionapp. com, a platform that turns screenshots into a working app

- a podcast featuring interviews with experts on your topic of choice with a 'comments' section that allows listeners to provide feedback.
  Example: Sarah Koenig and host Ira Glass produced the ground-breaking podcast, *This American Life,* which laid the foundation for a range of other blockbuster podcasts.

- a short introductory video explaining how your product solves a problem.
  Example: Dropbox's famous MVP was a three-minute video offering people extra storage space if they shared the link with friends. Upon release, Dropbox's sign-up list grew from 5000 to 75 000 overnight. Watch the video on my site: www.bernadetteschwerdt.com.au/book.

- a landing page website that promotes your eBook and collects the details of those who'd like to receive it.
  Example: Tim Ferriss tested the name of his book *The 4-Hour Work Week* with an AdWords campaign and collected traffic from the landing page to sell the book

- a 250-word blog asking people to submit their comments about your topic or idea.
  Example: Blogger Darren Rowse asks his readers to submit ideas in the comments box on what products he should review and what topics they'd like to learn about

- a three-question survey that collects input from your ideal target market.
  Example: Vets on Call founder Morgan Coleman used a Facebook survey to test whether vets would use his service

- a miniature model or pared-down version of the final product so that people can see what you're trying to achieve.
  Example: Don Di Giandomenico's Marveloo mobile restroom prototype helped others understand what he was trying to achieve

- a crowdfunding video to see what level of interest your product gets.
  Example: Who Gives A Crap launched their toilet-paper business with a three-minute crowdfunding video that raised $50 000 in 50 hours

- a five-page whitepaper outlining your thoughts and concerns about your key topic.
  Example: Membership guru Belinda Moore's whitepaper 'Membership is Dead' generated over a million dollars in consultancy and speaking fees.

If you build it, they will come ... maybe

There's only one real way to build a business, and that's one customer at a time. In other words, you only need one customer to validate your proof of concept. Creating an MVP increases your chances of finding that first customer.

Buffer and the landing page that launched it

Buffer is a popular app that allows you to automate your social media posts and send them at a time and frequency of your choosing.

Buffer's founder, Joel Gascoigne, wanted to test the market first to see if anyone would even want to use it. His MVP consisted of a landing page that described what Buffer did, and a summary of its plans and pricing. If people clicked on that landing page, they'd be taken to a page that said, 'Hello! You caught us before we're ready — leave your email address and we'll let you know when we're ready.' He tweeted out the page and enough people left their email addresses for him to take the next step, which was to test if people would pay for the service. Experienced entrepreneurs know that even if people want something, it doesn't mean they'll pay for it. Gascoigne updated his landing page to include a detailed Plans & Pricing page featuring three options:

1. free
2. $5 per month
3. $20 per month.

(continued)

Buffer and the landing page that launched it (*cont'd*)

He continued tweeting to let people know about the page. The clicks on the paid plans indicated his pricing models were working. After reaching a critical mass of registrations, Gascoigne built a simple app containing limited features, launched it and secured enough paid users to generate revenue to keep it going. It now has millions of users.

Fun facts:

- Buffer was launched in 2010.
- Four days after launch it had its first user.
- A few weeks after that it had 100 users.
- Within nine months it had 100 000 users.
- By September 2013, it had 1 million users.
- By February 2014, it had 1.3 million users.

The moral of the story? If you build it, they will come (but find out whether they'll pay for it first!).

How to pick a user persona

It's important to understand that an MVP doesn't need to be all things to all users. If you're trying to completely cover all your personas in your MVP, you've missed the point of using MVPs in the first place. The purpose of an MVP is to get your product to market quickly and efficiently so that you can learn and iterate from those who use it. If you focus on targeting too many users at the start, you'll never launch anything.

WHAT EXACTLY IS A USER PERSONA?

A user persona (also known as the 'target market', 'avatar' or 'customer profile') is simply a description of the type of person you'd like to reach. It helps to have a clear picture of your user persona before launching as it determines many things: the features you include in the MVP, the tone of your copy and where you advertise. For example, Sandy Abram from Wholesome Hub has a clear picture of her user persona. She calls this persona 'Jennifer'. Giving the persona a name helps Sandy remember that all her customers are real people and not just faceless automatons. Here's how Sandy describes 'Jennifer':

'She's a busy mum of two children, juggling a lot of balls in the air. She likes to eat healthily and prepare food for her family that's both nourishing and tasty. She cares about the environment and wants to buy as ethically as she can without sacrificing taste in the process.'

This process is easier to complete when you've been in business a while and you have an idea of who your customers are. But what if you are just starting out and don't have any customers to use as a reference? How do you decide what user persona to start with? It's simple. You make it up. When you get some customers, you can refine it further.

What did Uber do?

There are three factors to consider when choosing a target market (or user persona) to go after: Your market must be:

- big enough to be viable
- able to afford your product or service
- willing to pay for it.

When Uber launched, they had a range of user personas to choose from including young women travelling alone, senior citizens and rural residents. But they chose just one specific user persona, the city commuter, because this met the criteria listed above. They tested the app using that one target group and, over time, added features to attract other target markets. Those target markets included large groups (uberXL), ride sharing (split fare feature) and price-sensitive commuters (uberPOOL).

Uber followed the MVP process: start small, build it, release it and then get feedback from customers on what to do next. This is what's known as creating a 'feedback loop'.

What does 'minimum' really mean?

Once you've chosen your user persona, you need to identify what features to include in your MVP. In other words, how do you make sure you're not wandering off the path and creating an MVP for another user persona altogether? The key question to ask is: 'Do the users *need* this feature to solve their problem, or do they *want* this feature to solve the problem?' The answer to this will tell you how much functionality to launch with. When it comes to creating your MVP, it's best to include what customers *need* rather than what they may want.

> **WANTS VS NEEDS**
>
> Q: What is the difference between a want and a need?
>
> A: A want is a feature that would be a 'nice to have' but is not essential. A need is a feature the product or service can't exist without.

For example, Uber's MVP needed some basic functionality to make it work: the driver needed to know the exact location for pick up; and have the ability to debit the passenger's credit card; the passenger needed to know the make of the car and the driver's name. Could Uber have added more functionality to the MVP? Sure. In an ideal world, the passenger may have wanted to change their pick-up location address; to see a photo or ID of the driver before getting in the car; to know if the car had air-conditioning/heating or not, and so on.

But were these features essential to the launch of the first MVP? No. They would have been useful features, but not *essential* to the core function of the Uber app, therefore they could be omitted and included at a later stage. This streamlined approach enabled Uber to move quickly, launch the app to market and get feedback.

Which 'wants' should you include?

Making decisions as to what gets included in the MVP, and what gets left out, should be made in light of what the competitors are doing. For example, to create a unique point of difference from the taxi companies, Uber included in its early MVP features such as real-time ride tracking and automatic credit card payments. Is real-time tracking a core function of the service? No. Could it have been included in a later iteration? Yes, but Uber needed to stamp its authority on the market quickly and provide a valuable point of difference that would convince customers to choose it over taxis.

Are MVPs just for startups?

Have you ever wondered how the big players use MVPs to launch products? With enormous resources at their disposal, do they still use the tried and proven principles of test, measure, learn? I spoke with Adrian Fittolani, General Manager of Content at Envato, to find out how they use MVPs to research new ideas and products.

Bernadette: What business idea did you want to test?

Adrian: We thought there was a strong need for a photography service, so, for example, if you needed a photo shoot done somewhere you could have a photographer come out and take professional photos and provide you with the finished results. We made an early shippable value product (ESV*), we mocked up a little website, we had direct relationships with some local photographers who could test it out for us and we started to see whether or not local businesses in Melbourne would be prepared to engage a photographer in that way.

(*Adrian calls their MVP an ESV.)

Bernadette: **What happened?**

Adrian: We found over a very short period that there wasn't really a need, or there wasn't really a desire, to engage with that service—not in Melbourne at least. The website was a classic MVP. It had the appearance of a business but behind the scenes it was really stuck together and very experimental.

Bernadette: **How did you know it was the product that was wrong? Could the marketing of it have been to blame?**

Adrian: We tried different marketing techniques and different campaigns. Some worked, some didn't. Through the process we had convinced ourselves that it wasn't just the marketing—it wasn't the reach, it wasn't the things that we were trying—it just wasn't getting traction. It was six months of experimenting in trying to reach customers and engage them as well.

Bernadette: **What marketing channel campaigns did you use to trial it?**

Adrian: We had access to quite a number of customers through our existing businesses so we were marketing to people who might engage with it. We had access to email marketing campaigns and banner advertising; we used tracking tools and quite a few other things.

Bernadette: **What did you learn from that experience and how do you take those ideas and apply them to other parts of the business?**

Adrian: That experiment shared its lessons with another product called Unstock. Maybe users would be interested in having access to a higher quality stock image, even if they were priced at a higher rate. In turn, that Unstock experiment provided even more knowledge and we put that into our PhotoDune product. Everything is about iterating, trialling and testing.

As you can see, even established startups use the MVP methodology to constantly assess if a new product or innovation is worthy of further investment.

How to test pricing points before you launch: Bounce and crowd testing

Ever wondered how long it takes to get from Parramatta to Manly in peak hour? Quick answer: A long time. But if you wanted your phone to notify you of the exact time you need to leave to get there on time, you'd use Bounce.

Bounce is a mobile app, similar to Google Maps in that it calculates travel times but it also syncs the destination with your calendar and notifies you when you have to leave. Bounce used an open source crowdfunding site called Kickstarter to launch their MVP. Not only did crowdfunding help them generate pre-sales to fund the development of the product, it enabled them to conduct A/B tests to work out how much people were willing to pay for it.

The results?

Price point	Percentage of people who would purchase it	Learning?
$5	1.4	If you charge more, more people will buy it
$10	1.7	

That simple test proved more people would buy it if it was more expensive. What a great lesson to learn so early on in the launch phase.

MVPs are essential 'tools of the trade' when launching a new online concept. They help you establish whether your product has a market, whether people will pay for it, how much they are willing to pay for it and what functionality you need to offer.

WHAT IS A/B TESTING?

John thinks the 'buy' button should be red. Sacha thinks it should be blue. Dani thinks it should be orange. Who's right? Don't rely on the loudest voice in the room to make an important marketing decision. Test it. A/B testing (also known as split testing or bucket testing) works by serving up two versions of the same landing page with just (ideally) one variation to test which page performs better.

Chapter 8
Anatomy of a startup

I've studied the MVPs of many startups and there are as many different pathways to success as there are entrepreneurs. There is no one-size-fits-all roadmap to success, but it's reassuring to know that there are signposts you can follow that can guide the way.

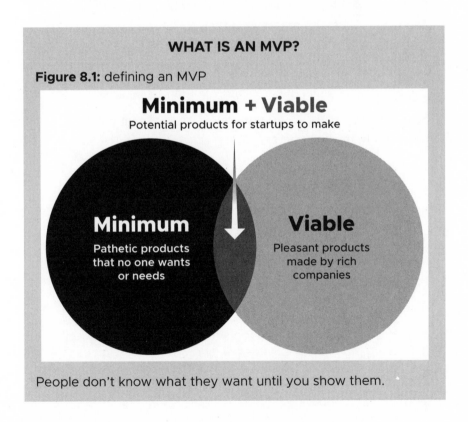

WHAT IS AN MVP?

Figure 8.1: defining an MVP

Minimum + Viable
Potential products for startups to make

Minimum
Pathetic products
that no one wants
or needs

Viable
Pleasant products
made by rich
companies

People don't know what they want until you show them.

Based on the MVPs I've researched, I've created a general MVP blueprint you can use to help you get your MVP up and running. It may not fit your business model exactly, but it will help you get some momentum and overcome 'paralysis by analysis'.

13 steps to launching your MVP

If you've never created an MVP before, it's hard to know where to start. Here are 13 basic steps many entrepreneurs follow to help them get their MVPs up and running. If you're not quite sure how to launch your MVP, this blueprint may help.

Step 1: They use the product or service, discover there's something wrong with it and feel certain it can be improved; or they have a burning desire to make a bucketload of cash and have no attachment to what they sell. Either way, they have a business idea they'd like to bring to life.

Step 2: They see what others are doing in the sector or elsewhere and ask, 'What's this like…?' and 'Wouldn't it be great if…?'

Step 3: They tap into a growing niche market that displays the potential to be much bigger.

Step 4: They create a basic 'no frills' MVP.

Step 5: They ask for feedback to validate whether their idea has merit.

Step 6: They find collaborators who bring complementary talents or assets to the business.

Step 7: They start small and roll out using a small test market that targets one user persona.

Step 8: They use cheap tech tools to grow the business and deliver efficient customer service.

Step 9: They gradually add extra functionality and launch it again to get feedback.

Step 10: They back themselves and trust their instinct.

Step 11: They get involved and are hands-on at the outset.

Step 12: They create a point of difference that's meaningful and relevant to the user.

Step 13 (optional): They connect their business idea to a higher, more important purpose than money alone.

How Vets on Call used the 13-step process to create their MVP

If you've ever struggled to locate your sick cat and put it in a box, and then transport it across town to the vet without it getting out of the box and scratching you to smithereens, then you'll know what a great idea it is to have a vet who comes to your house. This is Vets on Call founder Morgan Coleman's 13-step MVP story.

Step 1: They use the product or service, discover there's something wrong with it and feel certain it could be improved.

Morgan described his vet experience as 'just so awful for my pet that I walked away thinking that there had to be a better way. I thought about the pain points I felt as a consumer and they were: the lack of convenience; the stress it causes for the pet but also for the owners; and also, the lack of affordability.'

Step 2: They see what others are doing and ask, 'What's this like…?' and 'Wouldn't it be great if…?'

Morgan asked, 'Wouldn't it be great if… the vet could come to my house?' Based on that core premise he asked the question, 'What's this like?' and realised that the idea is similar to Uber in that the service allows pet owners to book a vet to come to their home. (Uber's core asset is an algorithm that links vacant drivers and cars with people who need a driver and a car, thereby helping the drivers utilise their unused time.) Similarly, Vets on Call creates value for both the pet owner and the vet by utilising the vet's down time.

(continued)

How Vets on Call used the 13-step process to create their MVP (*cont'd*)

Step 3: They tap into a growing niche market that displays the potential to be much bigger.

With incomes and insurance levels on the rise, people are more willing to spend money so their pets can live longer. 'People are also investing in pets the way they once invested in children so pets are receiving a lot more attention and special treatment than they once did.'

Step 4: They create a basic 'no frills' MVP.

Morgan conducted a three-minute survey via SurveyMonkey on Facebook to see if the idea was of interest to the vets.

Step 5: They ask for feedback to validate whether their idea has merit.

'I surveyed a lot of vets and pet owners to see if there was a need. Once I validated my idea that there was a need for it I started meeting with pet owners in dog parks and places and asked them to trial my service,' Morgan says. 'Once I'd done this our MVP was really me being the middle man between vets and the owners, trying to set up vet trial appointments for pet owners and getting feedback from them afterwards.'

Step 6: They find collaborators who bring other talents or assets to the business.

Morgan teamed up with vet Henry Wong and tech partners Nathan Sinnott and Rael Kuperholz, who each took an equity stake in the company.

Step 7: They start small and roll out using a small test market with one user persona.

Vets on Call will initially launch in Morgan's home town of metropolitan Melbourne before expanding further, and will be focused on city-based residents.

Step 8: They use cheap tech tools to grow the business and deliver efficient customer service.

Morgan uses Optus Loop, a low-cost call-management system so pet owners and vets can ring one number to reach him across all devices.

Step 9: They add extra functionality and launch it again to get feedback.

Morgan created a basic version of the app, which enabled users to book a vet online. He is now building in extra capabilities such as the ability for the vet to order services such as pharmaceuticals and x-rays. On the pet-owner's side, their pet's history and product purchases are all available via the mobile app, which makes it very convenient to keep track of their pet's needs.

Step 10: They back themselves and trust their instinct.

Morgan is funding the startup himself and sold his house to pull together the $60 000 needed to start the business. 'I really believe in what we are doing and the value we are bringing to the market,' says Morgan, who has since taken on seed funding to get to the next level.

Step 11: They get involved and are hands-on at the outset.

Morgan says, 'As a startup entrepreneur you will be doing literally everything and you need to know the most intimate details about your business, without exception.'

(continued)

How Vets on Call used the 13-step process to create their MVP (*cont'd*)

Step 12: They create a point of difference that is meaningful and relevant to the user.

'Vets on Call will be priced from $80 for a general consultation, which is the going rate for a vet at a clinic, but the big point of difference is the vet will go to your home,' says Morgan.

Step 13: They connect their business idea to a higher, more important purpose than money alone.

'Growing up in Bendigo I was the only indigenous kid in my school. I grew up with a single mum who is not indigenous so that brought its own challenges,' he says. 'For me it is really important to be the change you wish to see. I want to create change not just for myself and my family but for indigenous Australia,' he says. 'That's the reason I'm starting an internet business—it's scalable to the point where hopefully it will inspire other indigenous entrepreneurs around the country.'

If you need to create an MVP to launch your online idea, try using these 13 steps to help you get started.

When you build your MVP you'll almost certainly be filled with self doubt and uncertainty as to whether your idea will succeed or not. Being comfortable with being uncomfortable is part and parcel of being a startup entrepreneur and it's a feeling you'd better get used to.

Chapter 9

How to bumble your way to success

Launching a startup may make you feel like you're making it up as you go and lurching from one chaotic situation to another. Expect that. I asked entrepreneurs of many years standing a very specific question: 'How did your business get started?' While some had meticulous business plans in place, many openly acknowledged they had nothing of the sort and had no idea what they were doing. In other words, they bumbled their way to success. Management consultants call this process 'managing uncertainty', 'negotiating complexity' or 'dealing with ambiguity'. I call it bumbling. Lots of entrepreneurs bumble their way to success. They put one foot in front of the other and hope that it all turns out. Don't judge yourself too harshly if you feel like you're bumbling. It's part of the process of getting started.

EVERYBODY BUMBLES

I did a TEDx talk called 'How to bumble your way to success'. After the talk, a man came up to me and said he was a bumbler. I asked him what he did for a job.

'I'm a surgeon.'

I didn't get his card.

Visit www.bernadetteschwerdt.com.au/book to watch the speech.

What *not* to ask when you're getting started

When I created the video series 'Secrets of Online Entrepreneurs' (which was the MVP for the book of the same name), I have to be honest and admit that I didn't know what I was doing. I was bumbling. I had a clear goal (to make the video series), but I was a bit hung up on the 'how' I was going to do it. All I knew was that I wanted to interview leading entrepreneurs about how they'd built their online businesses.

I was working with a business coach at the time, and every time we spoke I bombarded him with a bunch of questions about how I could get the video series off the ground. Here's how our coaching conversation went:

Bernadette: **I have some questions for you, coach. There's a few of them. Here goes:**

- How am I going to afford a five-part video series that requires a three-person camera crew, interstate travel and full production facilities?

- How am I going to get the entrepreneurs to come onto the show for free and share their hard-won secrets with me?

- How am I going to distribute the show so people can watch it?

- How am I going to find the time to do all this while I run my core business?

Coach: Stop!

Bernadette: **Why?**

Coach: You're asking the wrong questions.

Bernadette: **What do you mean?**

Coach: When you ask too many 'how' questions like, 'How am I going to afford it?; How am I going to get the entrepreneurs to come on the show?; How am I going to distribute the show?' and the like, the only possible answer to those questions at this early stage is 'I don't know'.

Bernadette: I know I don't know and that's why I'm asking you how to do it.

Coach: Here's the thing: If you get too many 'I don't knows' at this early stage of the project, you run into what I call the 'wall of no' and it just gets too hard. You get despondent, you lose energy, you get distracted with other shinier objects that take your focus away and before long, you lose interest in the idea and you go back to living your sad little life ...

[He didn't say that last bit, but he might have thought it.]

... and then, a year or so later, you're reading the newspaper and you see an entrepreneur take the podium to win a trophy, and you see that they've taken _your_ idea and made it work, and you say, 'Hey! That was my idea! I came up with that a year ago! How come _they're_ winning all the awards! That was _my_ idea.' The difference is, _they_ asked better questions at the early stage of the journey. They didn't focus on 'how' questions and that's why they were able to have success with the idea, and you weren't.

Bernadette: Okay smarty pants, so what do I ask?

[I didn't say that first bit, but I might have thought it.]

Coach: It's very simple. You do what journalists do and ask the five basic questions that get to the heart of any matter. The five Ws or what I call 'the 5 Widows'. They are:

What?

When?

Where?

Who?

Why?

Bernadette: Please explain.

Coach: You take your earlier 'how' questions and convert them into 'W' questions instead. This turns them into tasks that can be actioned. For example, instead of asking all those 'how' questions, we would now start each question with a 'W', like this:

- '**Who** has already created a show like this and **what** can you learn from them?'

- '**Who** could be interested in coming on the show and **what** would they get out of it?'

- '**When** would you start filming?'

- '**What** questions would you ask?'

- '**Where** could you shoot the first episode?'

- '**Who** could be interested in sponsoring the show?'

- '**Why** do you want to do it and what do you hope to achieve?'

…and so on.

He had a good point. It became very clear that taking the 'how' questions and converting them into 'W' questions 'cracks open' the project and turns unanswerable questions into achievable tasks. It was quite a revelation. If you're trying to get an idea off the ground and you keep going in circles, it may be because you're asking 'how' questions. Turn them into 'W' questions and see the difference it makes.

Creating trust: The only currency that matters

When you launch your MVP to the world, few may know about it, or about you. When they do get to see it or try it out, trust is going to be an issue. Without a track record, or a Google presence, you may struggle to convert visitors into paying customers, especially if they have to give you their credit card number.

Trust is the currency of the internet, so you need to spend time thinking about how you can trust-hack your way to create an MVP people will take seriously.

> ## WHAT'S A HACK?
>
> A hack is a shortcut.

Here are 15 tried and tested ways to help people trust you, your product and your website. You should work towards acquiring these for your startup. It will take time, but you do need to take the first step. Start small and build from there. Here's what helps build trust:

1. media stories and photographs about you or your product
2. high-quality product photos and well-written product descriptions
3. logos of associations or membership organisations you belong to
4. number of followers on social media
5. testimonials — written and video
6. clearly stated warranties and refund policies
7. generous money-back guarantees
8. fast responses to email or phone queries
9. well-written, accurate website copy
10. blogs on your website and guest blogs for other sites
11. videos of you in action — on stage, being interviewed, at industry events
12. mentions about you and your business on Google
13. Google Customer Reviews (which has replaced Google Trusted Store)
14. credit card logos and SSL (Secure Sockets Layer) certificates on your payments page
15. awards (being a finalist can be as helpful as being a winner.)

Why winning awards pay dividends

Even if you're not at a stage where you feel you can apply for awards, it's immensely useful to look at the award applications anyway and notice what the judges look for. For a start, take a look at the questions they ask you to answer. That will tell you what you should be focusing on in your business. If you have to focus on these when you apply for awards, why not focus on them at the start?

Are awards worth the effort? Yes, the award application takes a long time to complete but once you've done one, you can 'rinse and repeat' and use the same content for another award.

How one award generated $800 000 in sales

Awards are not about ego. They're about conversion. CEO of Booktopia Tony Nash reveals why.

'As an online retailer we need to do everything we can to reduce the perceived risk of buying from us. So, when we won the Telstra Business Award we put the logo of the award on the top, right-hand side of our site. But we wanted to test it to see if the logo made any difference. It made a big difference. We conducted split testing where one version of the home page (with the award logo) gets served up and then another version of the page (without the logo) gets served up. It's called A/B testing and it's super easy to do—all you need is a bit of code and you can test and measure a variety of elements.

'After two weeks the results were clear. The page with the logo generated an extra 2 per cent in sales compared to the page without the logo. This may not sound like a lot, but at the time, our turnover was $40 million, which translated to more than $800,000 in sales in one year! Not a bad return for putting a logo on your home page.'

It's amazing how powerful one award logo can be.

So, who's going to do all this work?

Startups are not cheap. They'll cost you not just emotionally but financially too. And without investors or funding, you'll need to pay for it yourself. You can get suppliers to contribute and pay them in 'sweat equity' — but be careful. Jane Lu had this to say about equity partners:

Partnerships are like getting married without the courting and relationship part. You might get lucky, but often if you haven't had the opportunity to work closely with them before (and it's different being colleagues to business partners), it's really hard to know what it's going to be like.

So, if you go it alone, you're going to need things done cheaply. That's where the gig economy comes in.

WHAT IS THE GIG ECONOMY?

The 'gig economy' refers to the growing number of workers, particularly millennials, abandoning traditional nine-to-five employment in favour of working independently on a task-by-task basis for various employers. By 2020, it is forecast that contingent workers will exceed 40 per cent of the US workforce.

The gig economy will help you gain access to skilled people who can help you complete expensive tasks like coding, copywriting and web design cost-effectively.

If you're going to hire freelance contractors using digital marketplaces like Upwork, Freelancer or 99Designs, you will need to accept that finding competent, reliable and trustworthy suppliers may take longer than you think so factor that potential time delay into your plans.

The MVP equals the end of your dream

Creating an MVP is the alchemical art of bringing together the people, tools and technology that breathe oxygen into your concept and make it real. That process requires action, effort and faith. It also requires you to give up your dream because once your idea takes root in the real world, the fantasy of what it *could* be, or *should* be, is over. The reality is sitting there in front of you, as an MVP, and it may not look as good or as exciting as it did in your imagination. It also means you have to go out there and sell it to the world. It takes courage, guts and conviction. It's not for the faint-hearted or the easily discouraged. You have to believe in it with all your heart. And be constantly thinking about how you can make it better. You'll encounter criticism, skepticism and complaints along the way. How you manage that feedback will determine how successful you will be. Just remember this: they don't build statues of those who criticised but of those who did something, or at least tried to achieve something. Which one will you be?

Let's recap

You've selected the best business idea to run with, tested it and feel comfortable it's the right choice.

You've built your MVP, tested it on real people and got some real feedback.

You've accepted the process of starting may involve some bumbling and stumbling and you know that's all part and parcel of the journey.

Next stop. Building your website. All aboard!

Takeaways...

- Use an MVP to test whether your idea has merit.
- Get it to market quickly; learn what's working and then reiterate.
- The person with the idea may not be the best person to bring it to market.
- Collaborate with those who can offer something you don't have.
- You'll need to build trust in your MVP. There are dozens of ways to achieve this but pick one or two and commit to them.
- Read award guidelines even if you don't plan on applying. You'll learn a lot just by discovering what the judges look for.
- The gig economy is great for finding low-cost talent.

Coming up...

We're at the point where big decisions need to be made — what will you sell, for how much, to who and how will it get delivered — the nuts and bolts of building an online business. The answers to these questions will determine the type of website you'll need and what resources you'll need to build it.

And yes, we will get a little bit technical. This is exactly where most people abandon their online dream. Don't let that be you! Don't let the technical turn you off. You can do this.

Hey wait! Come back! It'll be fun. I promise.

Momentum

How to harness the technical tools to build your online business

You've looked ahead to see what the trends in your market are and you've come up with a business idea. It may be a massively disruptive idea that seems crazy to others and could earn you a billion, or it could be a simple idea that earns you some extra income to pay for a family holiday.

You know what problem you solve, what business you're in, who you're competing with and who your target market is. You know you need to create something for the market to look at (an MVP) that will enable you to test your idea and get valuable customer feedback.

But now you need to ramp things up, build that MVP, your website or app, gather a team of like-minded collaborators to work with and get into the nitty-gritty of making it all work.

This chapter is all about moving forward. It's about giving you the momentum to take your business to the next level using the tools and technologies that the best and brightest entrepreneurs use.

But before we go too far, we need to address some basic questions that you may have at this stage—questions that may be hindering you from moving forward. For most people, those questions are:

- How will I build my website or app?
- How will I find the right people to help me build it?
- How will I scale it all and make it grow big on a budget?
- How will I make enough money from my online business to keep it going?
- How will I find the time for this 'side hustle' while I work my first job and look after my family?

Notice what all those questions start with? That's right: 'How'. And as we established in chapter 9, 'how' questions are the least helpful, especially in the early stages of getting your business started.

We've also established that great online entrepreneurs don't always know what to do next, but they do know what questions to ask that will help them gain momentum. So what questions should you be asking at this stage of the game? What questions will help you move forward?

Here's seven critical questions you must ask before taking any further steps or investing any further dollars.

Chapter 10

7 questions to ask before you build your online business

The big disruptors know something most don't. They know that if the goal is to create a seriously disruptive business, that impacts millions of people, that can scale quickly without a commensurate increase in costs, then they must choose carefully what they sell, how they sell it, to whom they sell it and the business model that underpins each transaction.

Here are seven questions that all the big disruptors ask to help them make those important decisions. Founding Executive Director of Singularity University Salim Ismail covers these in greater detail in his ground-breaking book, *Exponential Organisations* but here's the quick-start guide to the questions you should be asking before you take any further action.

1. What will you sell?

Before you decide what you're going to sell and how you're going to sell it, it's worth hearing what Tony Nash of Booktopia has to say about choosing business models. He runs a business that turns over $100 million, so he knows what he's talking about.

> People often come to me with an idea and I hear them out. And then I ask, 'So when are people going to hand over the money?' And they'll say, 'Oh, when they subscribe, or the site will generate advertising.' But it's all very vague. It

won't cut it. I'm trying to be fair and honest with them, but in the beginning, it's all about cash flow rather than financial statements. Where's the money coming from? What have I got to pay out? Make sure you've got more money than you need to pay out. When you're starting out you must focus on the cash. Money must be coming into the company.

Indecision surrounding the right or best business model to pursue is often the number-one reason why people fail to get started; they simply can't make up their minds about what they want to sell and how they're going to generate revenue from it.

When it comes to working out what you will sell, you generally have four options to choose from:

1. You can sell products/services that are purely information-based.

   Examples: LinkedIn, Facebook, Instagram and GitHub are all information-based businesses. As a result, they have been able to scale quickly, without friction, and benefit from the network effect—that is, the bigger they get, the bigger they get. Closer to home, TRIBE and Joust follow this model. Information is their currency.

2. You can sell products/services that are physical, but the underlying services sold are information-based and revenue-generating.

   Examples: Apple's iPhones are tangible products, but they facilitate information-based businesses such as the buying of online music, the downloading of apps, and so on; Fitbits are tangible products, but they generate data that companies will buy.

3. You can sell products/services that are physical in nature, but they use information-based technology to deliver or produce them.

   Example: Amazon sell books, but their information-based infrastructure (website, algorithms, size, commission system, automation) enables the business to scale.

4. You can sell products/services that are physical in nature.

   Examples: Gloria Jean's, Cotton On and Tiffany's all sell physical products—tangible products you can eat, wear or touch.

WHAT DOES SCALING MEAN?

Scaling means to grow revenue with minimal or no increase in operating costs such as admin, sales, and so on. For example, in Year 1, a company delivers $10 million in revenue with $1 million in operating costs. In Year 2, the company delivers $12 million in revenue with $1 million in operating costs. The company scaled because it grew revenue by $2 million without increasing its operating costs.

Disruptive businesses often choose to sell information-based products as this enables them to monetise software at low marginal costs over time. They also re-calibrate their services to make them more able to scale. For example, Airbnb went from using PayPal to their own custom-built payments collection system because they couldn't effectively scale the PayPal system to meet their needs. This radically changed the way they were able to accept payments and deal with refunds and this in turn enabled them to scale their service and operate in multiple countries.

Best practice strategy

The most disruptive disruptors embrace the first model: an information-based business that inhabits the 'sharing' economy.

These disruptors generate multiple sources of revenue ranging from advertising fees to subscription models to premium versions of their free products. They may also be marketplaces or platforms that connect suppliers/producers/makers with buyers, and then take a clip of each transaction for their efforts. Marketplaces are massively disruptive models and they are changing the face of business, threatening legacy industries like never before and creating enormous opportunities for startups that demonstrate depth of vision. (More on marketplaces in chapter 12.)

Note: I've also included in chapter 14 a detailed example of how you can build an information-based business using free or low-cost tech tools. This demonstrates that the principles I outline here are not just 'pie in the sky' stuff but strategies that work and can be applied in real life.

2. What staff will you hire and on what basis?

When Instagram was acquired by Facebook in April 2012 for $US1 billion in cash and stock, it had only 13 employees and a handful of investors.

When Google acquired Waze in 2013 for $US1.1 billion, the company had no infrastructure, no hardware and fewer than 100 employees. It did, however, have 50 million users.

So much success; so few staff. It begs the question: On what basis do you engage/hire your staff? One of the hallmarks of successful startups (such as Instagram and Waze) is that they have a small, full-time core team providing stability and leadership, and they complement this with a range of on-demand contractors who can be upscaled or downsized as the business needs.

WHAT IS WAZE?

Waze is the world's largest community-based traffic and navigation app. Waze's active community of users share real-time traffic and road information.

Using on-demand contractors enables startups to engage highly specialised, flexible, cost-effective talent to complete micro-tasks.

This work is often conducted outside the organisation and is regularly done by suppliers in other countries. Many of Envato's staff work are based overseas and work at a time that suits them and their personal needs. Envato welcome this and believe it creates a well-balanced, more dynamic team. They focus on team results rather than team attendance. Many startups access the gig economy, which makes the hiring of top staff at lower costs possible.

This principle of 'on demand' staff also extends to the assets a company engages. Disruptive entrepreneurs use on-demand assets to remain agile and minimise overheads. For example:

- they use co-working spaces instead of leasing office space
- they use cloud-based solutions such as AWS for data storage instead of buying expensive hard-drive storage units
- they use Trello, Yammer, Slack and other cloud-based software products for fast, accurate and flexible communication between stakeholders
- they use Uber for company vehicles, (or if they're seriously on the move, they'll use Netjet, the 'Uber of jets'.)

Best practice strategy

Accessing staff and assets on demand enables you to get the skills you need without the overheads and risk attached to hiring full-time employees and buying expensive fixed assets.

3. What social tools will you use to engage your community?

How extensively do you use social technologies to engage with your users, customers, partners and fans? Does your community heavily influence your product development, product innovation and market testing, or is social simply a passive tool that you engage on an ad hoc basis to help with sales, listening and market research? Most successful disruptors rely heavily on a range of social technologies to fast-track decision making and get immediate results.

Matt Barrie's Freelancer knows a thing or two about harnessing the power of social technologies to get a massive result. They activated a global competition on social to get its community to promote the Freelancer name and logo. The competition spread to multiple countries. Matt says:

> The amazing thing with the internet now with two billion people online is you've got this 'one to many' relationship. You can, for example, put up a contest and a prize and you can now crowdsource a result from billions of people online.

> We used our contest platform, which is usually used to get something like a logo designed. So, for example, you put up $100 in prize money and you might get a thousand logos submitted and you can say, 'I don't like these — change the colour or change the font', etc.

> But we thought, 'How far can we push this paradigm?' So, we said, 'Let's put $25 000 into the platform and just see what happens.' And the prize was distributed based on people downloading our logo, printing it out and just promoting it in their local area.

So what was the result of the contest?

> We gave all the freelancers four weeks to come up with something and it was pretty mind blowing. One team in Bangladesh got 3000 people involved and they printed 3000 shirts, 3000 bandanas and 3000 flags with our logo. They marched 3000 villagers into a stadium, unveiled a 2400-square foot sign of Freelancer and then, using laptops, taught 3000 villagers how to use my website. That was pretty amazing.

Harnessing the power of your social community helps customers feel engaged. It's also good for business. Here's how online fashion retailer Princess Polly did it.

The Patchelorette Influencer Competition: 'Seven Instagram stars. Seven jackets. One Winner.'

Fashion site Princess Polly created The Patchelorette Influencer Competition to activate their social community, get engagement and increase sales of their denim patches.

They chose seven Instagrammers to be the designers, all with big followings, such as Cartia Mallan, Sally Mustang and Emily Gurr. Using the patches from Princess Polly's latest collection, these 'Insta-famous' girls had to design covetable denim jackets.

Princess Polly's community would vote for their favourite creation to win the jacket and a $500 voucher, and the winning designer would be crowned The Patchelorette.

They conducted live eliminations, much like the 'rose ceremonies' on *The Bachelor* TV show, and broadcasted them live via Snapchat to thousands of viewers. This assisted in building constant anticipation and excitement among the audience.

Princess Polly drove sales of the patches by offering a discount code to each customer who voted, which provided a further incentive to get involved and resulted in new email sign-ups and increased website sales. A win–win!

An engaged community can be very useful. They can even convince supermarkets to stock your product. Here's how social enterprise Thankyou activated their social community to get the big supermarket chains to stock Thankyou's bottled water.

Co-founder Justine Flynn explains how it worked.

> **We asked our social community to post a video or send a message to the large supermarkets asking them to stock the Thankyou range. On the first day of launching, the supermarket's Facebook pages were flooded with people saying, 'Please stock the Thankyou range'. The supermarkets relented, the product got stocked and the rest is history.**

Justine and Daniel also launched a business book using their social community.

> **We launched our *Chapter One* book campaign, where we said, 'Pay what you want' and told them that the profit of *Chapter One* will be funding the future of Thankyou and starting new initiatives. We had people pay as little as five cents for the book and some people paid up to $5000.**

Best practice strategy

The most disruptive businesses have social technologies at the heart of everything they do and rely heavily on their community for product development, product innovation, market testing and sales.

4. What gamification tools will you use to increase customer usage?

Disruptive entrepreneurs embrace gamification and deliberately gamify their product to increase user uptake. You need only watch a six-year-old play on their iPad to see the power of gamification in action. You'll notice they want to keep playing to 'get to the next level', 'win a badge', 'open the next door' or 'unlock the vault'. Here's some common gamification strategies that increase user engagement.

Quizz *Gemknch*

> ## WHAT IS GAMIFICATION?
>
> According to the Oxford Dictionary, gamification is the application of typical elements of game playing (e.g. point scoring, competition with others, rules of play) to other areas of activity, typically as an online marketing technique to encourage engagement with a product or service.

Progress bars

Online education provider Khan Academy uses the filling of the 'progress bar' to incentivise children to finish a maths module: '3 more questions to complete the module'; 'You're nearly done!'; '2 more steps to go 'til completion'.

Netflix uses a similar progress bar to show you how much of a show you have already watched.

Leaderboards

Minecraft, an online game that lets users build virtual worlds, has gamification down to a fine art. One 'game within the game' allows players to compete against each other to be the best 'builder' of a random object. Once the 'build' is finished (you get three minutes to build it), the players vote and the online leaderboard displays the winner's name. I watched my son play it and took ridiculous pride in seeing his name top the leaderboard for building the best 'pineapple' out of Minecraft blocks. These are the small moments a mother treasures.

Quizzes and polls

Asking people to take a quiz or complete a poll are other ways to gamify an online offering and thereby engage an audience. Business coaching companies often use provocative questions such as 'How entrepreneurial are you?' to inspire you to take their online quiz. After filling in the quiz you receive a report back outlining where your strengths are and what you need to work on.

Holiday
?

Unsurprisingly, the coaching company can help you manage your weaknesses simply by enrolling in their course.

Travelshoot is a global marketplace that connects travellers with local photographers in over 100 cities. When you visit their site, a 'chocolate wheel' pops up that lets you give it a 'digital spin'. You can win prizes ranging from a $100 voucher, to a 5-per-cent discount code or nothing at all. The user experience is fast, colourful and dynamic. You'd visit the site again just to have another turn.

Games and polls are ideal devices for collecting data. The more data you provide, the more 'helpful' they can be to you. Companies use that data to fine-tune their marketing and then send you tailored messages based on the data you've given them.

Online alcohol delivery service Tipple use gamification for market research purposes. For example, in order to work out if your suburb is in their delivery zone, you need to hand over your postcode. Then they reveal whether you are in their delivery territory or not. The process feels like you're playing a game when it's really a clever data-collection technique.

Best practice strategy

The most disruptive businesses fully embrace the principles of gamification to incentivise and engage users.

5. What level of failure will you accept from your staff?

Disruptive entrepreneurs don't just tolerate failure, they expect it. They also reward it. Believe it or not, companies such as Grey Advertising, Proctor & Gamble and Google hand out Heroic Failure Awards to those who have failed spectacularly. It's not without purpose. Their belief is that great innovation comes from trying new things, measuring, testing and then pivoting if changes need to be made. They're not fearful of failure; they just want to do it faster so they can move on to the next iteration. They also take care to set goals around the innovation process so that valuable learnings are captured.

Successful disruptors sometimes provide their staff with '20 per cent time', a concept that enables staff to take one day a week to ruminate, play and develop personal or passion projects on the company dime, in the hope it uncovers innovation 'gold'. Google was one of the early pioneers of the concept. Much has been made of their decision to terminate the concept, but it allegedly led to the creation of products such as Gmail, AdSense and Google Talk.

Best practice strategy

The most disruptive businesses have enormous tolerance for failure but set goals and processes around how that failure is monitored and measured.

6. What goals and metrics are used to track staff performance?

Disruptive entrepreneurs may reward failure, but they systemise and measure staff performance and results too using detailed goal-tracking mechanisms such as:

- Objectives and Key Results (OKRs)
- Net Promoter Score (NPS)
- Key Performance Indicators (KPIs).

NPS and KPIs are well documented and used widely by leading companies. What's not so well known is the concept of OKRs. Google is famous for using OKRs as their executive measurement tool of choice as it offers a simple way to create structure for teams and individuals.

What are OKRs and how do they work?

OKRs work on the principle that the objective must be ambitious and feel a tad uncomfortable, and that key results must be quantifiable and lead to objective grading.

Here's an example of the activities and metrics that a fintech entrepreneur may nominate as part of her OKR plan:

- Increase profile by applying for the Woman of the Year award by the end of the year.
- Re-establish blogger leadership by speaking at three key industry events.
- Identify and reach out to the top-10 Australian-based finance bloggers to be a guest contributor.
- Create a five-part video series for YouTube addressing key challenges for home-loan borrowers.

Best practice strategy

The most disruptive businesses use detailed goal-tracking mechanisms such as OKRs to measure and track innovation and progress.

7. What data will you rely on to make business decisions?

Using data to personalise an offering is the hallmark of great disruptors. Netflix uses your previous viewing habits to offer recommendations on what you should watch next. Amazon offers the same service: 'If you liked that, you'll love this'.

On a more prosaic level, Domino's used data sourced from their own social-media channels to produce self-deprecating TV commercials that openly acknowledged the negative feedback their customers had given them. They even showed screenshots of the real Facebook comments in the TV commercial. It was a gutsy move that could have backfired, but that's the risk all great disruptors take if they choose to share data with their customers.

Kate Morris's Adore Beauty uses data to help customers select a shade of foundation that matches their skin tone.

> **We use Findation, a widget that helps shoppers find their perfect foundation shade when shopping online. Customers enter any foundation they have previously used and the Findation widget will recommend the closest shade match so they can be 100 per cent certain that the foundation they purchase will be right for them.**

Findation uses data from more than 6 534 000 foundation users worldwide and a sophisticated proprietary algorithm to match shades between brands.

Serious online players use data to measure everything. And why wouldn't they? The tools are there. As Jane Lu from Showpo says, 'Most of what we do with marketing can be measured now, so it's not as hit and miss as it used to be. We can see what post is working, what headline had cut-through. We can see what email worked and what image got a better response. It's so much easier to measure now.'

Leading entrepreneurs use data to measure increases or decreases in:

- orders
- revenue
- refunds
- website traffic
- customer database statistics
- average order value
- active emails
- items sold each minute
- percentage of orders shipped the same day

- percentage of cart abandonment
- new email addresses gained per day
- Google review ratings
- followers on all social media platforms each day
- average customer support response time
- average time until second purchase
- brand recall

… and much more.

I asked Tony Nash what he measures and he said 'sales'.

Best practice strategy

The most disruptive businesses rely heavily on data to make business decisions and to personalise their marketing.

***

Asking these seven critical questions at the start of your entrepreneurial journey will help you choose the right business ideas and revenue models to match your personal goals.

Chapter 11
Open Access, Open Sesame!

There is one game-changing technology I have yet to mention and it's a principle that has enabled disruption to occur at lightning pace. It's called Open Access Technology (OAT). This principle has reduced the barriers to starting an online business so it's worth understanding what it is so you can harness the power it offers you.

What is OAT?

Put simply, Open Access Technology facilitates inventions, skills, data and technologies to be designed, developed and deployed at a rapid rate and to create disruption on a vast scale.

WHAT IS OPEN ACCESS?

Open Access means making information (documents, software, and so on) available on the internet for any user to read, download or copy for any legal purpose. A hallmark of Open Access is that the material is free for others to use.

Here are four examples of how OAT has made starting an online business more accessible to everyone.

Democratised access

Google has democratised knowledge, which means anyone, anywhere can access information anytime, in any format they choose, in almost any language. This creates a level playing field. In the past, people held onto the reins of knowledge and only made it available if they were rich, obliging or pious. In other words, it was at their discretion. Not anymore.

Now, a nine-year-old child can access free knowledge as quickly as (or probably more quickly than) a 50-year-old CEO. What impact does this upending of knowledge-holding have on the market? In short, massive. OAT has made entrepreneurship open to anyone, including children, who are ironically better placed to harness the tools of disruption than almost anyone over 50. Here's an example.

The nine-year-old coding whiz

'Wouldn't it be great if... if we could use an app to teach pre-schoolers the names of animals?' That could have been the launch question that got Anvitha Vijay started on her entrepreneurial journey. Anvitha is a grade four student from Mount View Primary School in Melbourne, and she created an educational app (Smartkins) as a way to help her little sister identify animals. Anvitha has well and truly harnessed open access technology to build her app. She learnt coding on YouTube, used design app Sketch to nail the interface, Photoshop to tidy up the interface and Xcode to code the app. For her efforts, she was awarded a coveted scholarship to Apple's annual Worldwide Developer Conference.

The democratisation of knowledge eliminates the barriers to entry, enabling children such as Anvitha to build products that in the past could only have been built by a team of marketers and software engineers.

Democratised tools of production

In the old days, we needed staff, stock, factories, warehouses and other 'tools of production' to create a business. All that cost money and involved risk. Now, those tools of production have been

MAGONTO

democratised. For example, if you can work from home using your laptop to run an online fashion store and use dropship companies to deliver the product to the customer on demand, you don't need a retail premise, staff, overheads or capital to get started. The traditional barriers to entry are eliminated. You can just ... start.

Jane Lu from Showpo says, 'I didn't have to pay for my stock before selling it so that was a massive win as it took the risk out of setting up my first online store.'

Democratised software

In the old days, if you wanted access to powerful software and a website with grunt, you'd have to hire a developer to build it from scratch. That would cost a fortune and be out of reach for most startups. Now, due to open access, that software is affordable and accessible to most people. Online entrepreneurs rave about Magento, an e-commerce website platform built using open-source technology, as it provides the business owner with a flexible shopping cart system and significant control over how their online store looks and operates. It's also free for small businesses to download. With the power of Magento, a small online homewares site can compete with a traditional heavyweight such as Myer or David Jones without the hefty costs of paying for a custom-built software package.

Democratised capital

Money—or the lack of it—has traditionally been a big barrier to entry for many startups. But now, there are novel ways to source capital that did not exist a decade ago. Crowdfunding sites such as Pozible enable you to finance your movie, café or startup without borrowing a cent. Peer-to-peer lenders such as Society One mean you can bypass the banking system altogether. You can even use crowdfunding platforms such as Venture Crowd to get equity funding.

Social enterprise Who Gives A Crap was an early adopter of crowdfunding and used it to fund their first round of production. Here's what co-founder Simon Griffiths said:

> **We had to think differently. We had to get the capital behind us to make the product, so we ran a crowdfunding campaign to pre-sell the first $50 000 of toilet paper. To help things along, I agreed to sit on a toilet, with a live web feed transmitted out to the world until we hit our target.**

The video went viral and attracted worldwide media attention. As a result of that global attention, Simon and his team reached their target and the company has gone on to bigger and better things. Simon could have asked the bank for a loan but chose to use crowdfunding as his source of finance and in the process, was able to test his concept as well as pre-sell his first batch of toilet paper before outlaying big bucks.

These are the game-changing developments that enable crazy, and not so crazy, digital ideas to succeed like never before. And best of all, these open-access tools are available to anyone.

Have you checked the children?

If you've got children, take a moment to notice the apps and websites they use. It's worth noting because in the blink of an eye, those same children will become the next generation of cashed-up consumers, CEOs and entrepreneurs, more comfortable with technology than anyone over 50 will ever be.

They'll know how to instantly access information that will enable them to innovate and build world-class businesses from their bedrooms. If you have children, ask them what apps they are currently using at school. I asked my 11-year old and discovered he uses the very same apps the big disruptors use. Here's a summary of what he uses on a weekly basis:

- GarageBand—a music-making app
- Skitch—an annotation tool
- Book creator—a book-making app

- Trello—a planning and project management app
- Keynote—a slide-making program
- iMovie—video editing software
- Photoshop—image editing software
- Greenscreen—background for video
- Padlet—an ideas collation app
- Sphero—a coding app
- Hopscotch—a coding app
- Loop—a feedback app.

My point? If children like him are using sophisticated apps like this in Grade 5, imagine how clever they'll be when they reach Year 12?

On second thought, by the time they're 16, they probably won't even need to use their brains to think. They'll have microchips implanted in their skulls and the chip will do the thinking for them. I wish I was joking. I'm not.

Elon Musk recently launched Neuralink, a venture aimed at merging the human brain with artificial intelligence (AI).

WHAT IS NEURALINK?

Nueralink is a brain-computer interface venture centred 'on creating devices that can be implanted in the human brain, with the eventual purpose of helping human beings merge with software and keep pace with advancements in artificial intelligence.'[1]

With open access and the democratisation of knowledge, software and capital, the barriers to being brilliant have been well and truly eliminated. Is the market ready for a generation of disruptive smart children who use sophisticated technology as easily as we use mobile phones? Time will tell. Speaking of disruption, there's another development on the horizon that is causing many to feel excited and/or nervous about the future. Marketplaces.

Chapter 12

Marketplaces: Disrupting legacy industries

An online marketplace, such as eBay, Catch of the Day or Freelancer, is a platform that facilitates exchanges between buyers and sellers. They are hugely disruptive models and are both helping and hindering small businesses like never before. They're being used by startups and corporates to replace traditional ways of doing things. For example, corporations are increasingly recognising that marketplaces are the new models for finding a workforce. Some, like IKEA, are even partnering with recruitment marketplaces to reduce costs, increase services and harness the thousands of people working in the gig economy.

In short, marketplaces put pressure on traditional service providers to remain relevant, cut their prices and be more pliable.

For example, what does it mean for a carpenter if the building supervisor says, 'Cut your rate or I'll get a team from hipages [a trades marketplace] to do your work instead?' What's a graphic designer to do if the boss says, 'Work on a Saturday or I'll just get a freelancer from Upwork to finish the job instead.'

Here's how a few corporations have turned to marketplaces:

- IKEA Australia encourages customers to use hipages for installation services.

- GE's partnership and investment in Quirky, a community-led invention platform, means they don't have to invest so heavily in R and D and innovation anymore. They can turn to Quirky's community of inventors who are ready and willing to share their invention with anyone who can help them get it made.

- In 2013, US-based home improvement giant, Home Depot, enlisted Uber to deliver its Christmas trees to customers in lieu of couriers.

Marketplaces are a threat to legacy industries. Here's a snapshot of how three marketplaces are upending the 'natural order' of how things have traditionally been done in those industries.

Education marketplaces

Having been a lecturer in marketing for more than 25 years at numerous universities, I have been privy to what universities used to offer, and what they offer now. We've all seen the photos of empty classrooms, taken by lecturers despairing at the lack of attendance. That just reinforces what we already know. The current university model is broken and unsustainable. Education marketplaces such as Coursera, Fedora and Khan Academy offer free online courses that provide superior content to what some universities charge $50 000 for. How long before someone declares the (university) emperor has no clothes on?

Financial services marketplaces

The fintech disruption is well underway, with the big banks being kicked around by peer-to-peer lenders such as Betterment, LendingHome and Square. Crowdfunding marketplaces are also providing sources of startup funding that were once the province of the banks.

Construction services marketplaces

Have you ever seen a big forklift or digger lying idle on a construction site after the tradies knock off at 3 pm? Do you ever think, 'That's a lot of expensive machinery sitting around, not doing much?' I know I have. So, imagine if you could unlock that equipment in its down time, and offer it to someone to use for a fee. That's where marketplaces such as Getable come in.

San Francisco-based Getable was founded in 2010 to make it easier to connect contractors with the equipment they needed to get a job done. Getable helps construction companies access equipment via the on-demand market and provides an easy-to-use app that simplifies the process of renting construction equipment and keeping track of its equipment when in use.

Startups such as Mobilise are offering a similar service in Australia.

Who wins from marketplaces?

There are clear winners and losers here.

The winners? Consumers and established players who capitalise on the early opportunities presented by these services; and those who can afford to own the marketplace for their industry.

The losers? Small business owners who watch their clients turn to marketplaces to source cheaper services.

WHAT IS AMAZON SERVICES?

If you're a tradie or home handyman, you should know about Amazon Services. It will be a game-changer. Find out more at https://services.amazon.com/selling-services/home.htm.

There are marketplaces for everything now. There's even a website for marketplace software called Marketplacer. It's sort of like the Uber of Marketplaces. 'The Uber of … ' is fast entering the lexicon as a way to redefine how products and services now get delivered: The Uber of Vets (Vets on Call); The Uber of Lotteries (Lottoland); The Uber of legal services (LawPath).

What's the marketplace for your industry? Is there one? If not, maybe that's an opportunity worth exploring. Just saying.

***

If you're going to build an online business, you're going to have to know a little about the range of online tools and technologies available to you. That's what the next chapter is all about.

To fast track your success, I've done the heavy lifting and discovered what award-winning disruptors use to build *their* businesses. By using the software, systems and strategies they use, you'll save yourself a lot of time and effort—and a heckuva lot of money.

Want to set up a marketplace of your own?

Marketplacer, originally launched as BikeExchange, is a fully hosted 'plug and play' platform that allows clients to create their own customised niche marketplaces where they can bring together buyers and sellers. Co-founder Jason Wyatt told the Australian Financial Review:

'We saw a genuine need for people who wanted to create marketplaces. They don't have to be technologists, they need to be community managers. So we wanted to de-risk people investing into marketplaces.'

Chapter 13

Software hacks every startup should know about

Let's get this clear from the get-go: I am not a technical person in any way, shape or form; neither are many of the entrepreneurs I interviewed. And when I say I am not techy, I mean it. I don't enjoy 'playing around' with technology, nor do I enjoy finding out 'how something works'.

What I am and have been, however, is a judge for numerous online entrepreneurial awards. As a result, I get to read the award applications from leading online business owners. I get to peek 'under the hood' so to speak: to see the inner workings of their businesses. And in those applications they share all the good stuff: what web platforms they use, the email automation software they prefer, the user experience tools that help them calibrate their sites, the metrics they track, the best practice for shipping and returns, how they personalise their marketing campaigns, and the best tools to test and measure the success of those campaigns. For the record, I haven't breached an confidentiality agreements by sharing these tech tips with you. Most successful operators use them and you would have discovered these tools eventually. I've just saved you the effort of having to find them.

If you've ever wondered what software tools the experts use to build their online businesses, this is the chapter for you.

What software will you use to build your online business?

If you don't have the tech background to understand the backend of your site, the tools I am about to show you will give you the confidence to have more robust conversations with your web-development and marketing teams.

IT'S WHAT YOU LEARN AFTER YOU KNOW IT ALL THAT COUNTS

Choosing the right software to solve your business problem can be hit and miss because you can't be sure it will work until you use it. One way to reduce the risk is to watch the free 'how-to' videos that demonstrate how the software works. Not only will you learn more about the software, you'll also get an instant masterclass in the topic.

This is my 'little black book' of the go-to software products that leading online entrepreneurs use. Many use the same software, which is social proof that they must work. Why waste time trying new products if you can use what the experts use?

The tech tools listed here are tailored for e-commerce sites, but any online business would benefit from using some, or all, of them.

Website builder software

Many of the entrepreneurs I interviewed use 'out of the box' website platforms and customise them to suit their needs. Here are some platforms that many business owners use to build their websites:

- Magento
- Neto
- BigCommerce
- Volusion
- BlueHost + Woocommerce
- 3D Cart
- Shopify
- Weebly
- Wix
- Joomla
- Drupal
- Blogger
- Squarespace
- WordPress.

User-testing software

Entrepreneurs spend a lot of time thinking about how a person experiences their site. To see how people are experiencing your site, you can use a process called 'user testing'.

User testing is the process of watching people engage with your site. You're testing to see how useful and intuitive the site is. You can use companies such as www.usertesting.com or, as Jane Lu from Showpo suggests, you can keep it simple.

> **You don't have to get complicated about it. Just ask a friend to view your site on their mobile device. Watch what they do, see where they look, and notice what buttons they click on and what pages they go to. That will tell you as much as you need to know at those early stages.**

How to hack your own user testing experience

You can use your own family or friends to user test your site. It's quite simple to do. Let's assume you own an online electronics retailer site (www.xyz.com) and the user who is testing your site is your elderly mother who would not intuitively know how to navigate your website. You have the site open, and you sit behind her watching her every move. You ask your mother to speak all her thoughts and feelings out loud as she is using your site: what she is thinking, wishing, liking, not liking.

Here are the instructions you would give your mother:

Step 1: 'In this test, you're going to shop for gifts on my site, www.xyz.com.'

Step 2: 'Think of a gift you want to buy for someone. Try to find that gift on the site.'

Step 3: 'Find something else you need, and add it to your shopping cart.'

(You can ask more questions, but this is a starting point.)

That's it! That's how to hack a user test!

Afterwards, you can ask:

- 'What frustrated you most about this site?'
- 'If you had a magic wand, how would you improve this site?'
- 'What did you like about the site?'
- 'How likely are you to recommend this site to a friend or colleague?'

This information is invaluable in determining how people interact with your site. There may be obvious gaps, such as the pricing button not being easy to find or the refund policies are missing. User testing reveals those gaps.

Customer-service software

Most successful online entrepreneurs are obsessed with customer service and put the customer at the forefront of every decision they make. There's a choice of software you can use that will help you become more customer-centric.

For example, heat maps test and measure user experience and identify trends in user behaviour. These maps enable content to be better placed throughout the site and identify issues that may prevent customers from completing their purchase.

Examples of popular heat-map software products are Hotjar and Crazy Egg.

Software that allows the customer to contact the company quickly is also popular. These include:

- *Live Chat*—allows immediate access to a team, reducing customer emails and decreasing response time for simple enquiries
- *Zendesk*—great for setting up customer-service tickets
- *Feefo*—helps customers provide ratings and reviews after they receive their order
- *SurveyMonkey*—great for sending out surveys.

Recommendation engine software

How does Netflix predict with such accuracy that if I liked the movie *Trainwreck* I will like *Meet the Millers*? How does Facebook automatically suggest tagging friends in pictures? The answer is recommendation engines: algorithms that filter data from large pools of information and then, based on that data, recommend relevant and accurate items to the user. Successful online entrepreneurs harness the power of smart recommendation engines by digging into the past behaviour of their users and then recommending or suggesting potential products for them to buy.

Successful online entrepreneurs build intelligent recommendation engines by studying the past behaviour of their users. This enables them to provide relevant recommendations. They are an essential element in the toolkit of an online business as they go a long way to increasing average order value, have a massive impact on conversion rates and reduce site and cart abandonment. They are particularly useful for websites that offer a wide range of products as they help the consumer find what they want more quickly.

HOW DO I PERSONALISE THE USER EXPERIENCE?

If you delve deeper into recommendation engines, it quickly becomes the province of data science, sophisticated data sets and vector equations that would have John Nash scratching his head. Don't try nutting this out yourself. There are programs you can use that will do this for you, and do it well. Here are some to consider:

- SoftCube
- Barilliance
- Strands
- Monetate
- Nosto.

Marketing automation software

Based on the data they collect, recommendation engines enable the entrepreneur to create a series of personalised communication pieces that target that person's exact needs. This facilitates the creation of:

- personalised emails
- SMS and 'push' notifications
- customised navigation assets, banners and badges
- behavioural pop-ups.

If you have thousands of customers, you'll definitely need to have a customer relationship management (CRM) software package to help you manage the complexity of all that data.

Here are a few suggestions:

- Mailchimp
- Mandrill
- Infusionsoft
- Salesforce
- Emarsys

A/B or split testing software

Wondering which offer will be most effective with your customer? A/B or split testing software allows you to easily test multiple versions of on offer and discover which one works best. Here is some software to help you do it:

- Visual Website Optimizer (VWO)
- Google Optimize

Payment processing software

Online business owners know that cart abandonment often happens at the checkout stage. Buyer remorse, uncertainty or a poorly-designed checkout process are often the culprits. After all that work to get customers to this moment of purchase, there are a few tools you can use to fast track their payment process:

- Addressify is great for quick address validation in the checkout phase, making for a smooth customer experience and ensuring a reduction in incorrectly completed address fields.
- Braintree offers a frictionless checkout.
- Stripe is great for payment processing.

QUICK TIP

A single-page checkout with no header or footer increases the completion rate.

Surprise and delight

When it comes to wrapping goods for shipment, little things matter. Handwritten notes and gift cards that can be personalised add that extra touch customers care about.

Kate Morris from Adore Beauty adds a Tim Tam chocolate biscuit in each package and says it consistently rates as something people remember.

Sandy Abram from Wholesome Hub includes sample tea sachets, snack bars and some stickers as a way of 'doing something remarkable'. Small things can make a big difference. She adds:

> I never lose sight of the fact that a person, a human being, will open up this package in their home and I want them to have a wonderful experience when they do. It's easy to get lost in the day-to-day of running a business, but that end touch point is what it's all about and we need to pay attention to that moment.

Andre Eikmeier from Vinomofo went one further. In a bid to reactivate high-value customers who hadn't purchased for a while, he personally contacted each one to have a conversation with them to find out why they hadn't been back.

> It was a fantastic exercise on so many levels. You can forget that you're dealing with real people with busy lives. I learnt that some people hadn't come back because they had lost a job or got sick so there were lots of reasons why people hadn't bought. It gave me the chance to connect with my

customers. I loved it and they got a kick out of getting a call from the CEO. I followed that phonecall up by sending them a complimentary bottle of wine, a T-shirt and a nice note. The results were extraordinary as well. Sixty per cent of those people were reactivated.

Knowing the tech tools the experts use will help you fast track your website build and put the control and measurement of your marketing back into your hands. In the early days, you'll probably be unable to afford a team to do this for you so you will need to self-educate and/ or hire a specialist freelancer to assist you.

Depending on the product and company policy, best practice for fulfilment can include:

- same-day shipping
- free postage or free postage on orders over a certain amount
- click-and-collect options, parcel tracking and SMS notifications as standard offerings
- free returns with no time limit, a 365-day change-your-mind policy or lifetime guarantees (one company I know of sells lingerie with an unconditional lifetime guarantee).

QUICK TIP

Serious players relocate their warehouse to co-locate with their carriers, eliminating the time required to deliver the product to customers and allowing same-day fulfilment.

Chapter 14

How to build an information-based business

One of the benefits of selling information-based products, as opposed to tangible products, is that you can literally create a product out of thin air. It also means you can build a product that doesn't cost much, other than some time and effort. This is great for those who sell knowledge (such as accountants and coaches) and want to add a passive income product to their suite of services.

To prove it's possible, I'm going to outline the exact steps you need to take to build an information-based business using the tools of disruption we've already talked about — cloud, data, social and mobile, free or low-cost software and much more. There are some assumptions made, you may need some technical help and there will be some costs, but overall, you'll find that it's possible to build an online business without spending much money.

13 steps to creating your online business

We will create three information-based products:

- an eBook
- an MP3 audio file
- a video.

Google keyword plan

Our time starts now!

1. Set up the business

To begin, you need to get the basics sorted out:

- register a business name (www.asic.gov.au)
- register an ABN (you won't need to register for GST until you're earning more than $75 000).

2. Build a free (or low-cost) website

Here's a simple, step-by-step guide to building a website from scratch.

- Register a domain (www.crazydomains.com.au).
- Get a logo or site design (www.99designs.com.au).
- Build a site for free (www.wix.com; or www.wordpress.com if you need more than just a brochure site).
- Host your site (with www.siteground.com; or aws.amazon. com).
- Create template forms for customer surveys, online payment or customer lead forms (www.wufoo.com gives you three forms for free).
- Create page templates such as thank-you pages, lead generation forms and Call To Action pages (leadpages.net offers a free trial).
- Write the copy yourself or find a freelance writer on www. freelancer.com.

3. Research a popular topic that has a viable market

You can research a trending topic on any of these sites:

- Twitter (free app) or Google Keyword Planner (free)
- Google Trends (free)
- Buzzsumo.

4. Find a subject-matter expert to interview

Experts are easy to find. You can start here:

- *professional speaker bureau sites* — experts are often open to providing interviews and advice in exchange for promotional coverage
- *meetups* — meet experts in person by attending the meetup. com of your choice in your local area
- *LinkedIn* — let your fingers do the walking and find an expert online.

5. Schedule a convenient time to talk to the expert

Use the www.doodle.com interview scheduler (free for individuals) and save all that mucking around with finding a common time.

ARE YOU AN INVENTOR?

If so, you'll love these resources.

YouTube: The New Inventions

Discover the latest technology, inventions and gadgets from all over the world on this dedicated YouTube channel for inventors.

Georgia Tech Library's Quick Guide: Inventor Resources for Patents

This is a must-visit website for those with an invention and no idea how to get it off the ground. It's got links to sites about the all-important patents, intellectual property and the legal side of things too.

IPWatchdog.com

If you're worried about someone stealing your ideas or need to know more about patent law, copyrights or trademarks, this site is for you.

6. Create the information-based product

There are three easy steps to creating your product.

1. Create the MP3 audio file and video files by:

    -   interviewing your expert using the Skype.com app (free)
    -   recording the interview using the Skype MP3 recorder at mp3skyperecorder.com (free)
    -   turning on the video camera (free app) on your phone while recording the call and capturing video of the speaker
    -   editing the recording using Audacity (free from www. sourceforge.net)
    -   overlaying it with music using www.ccmixer.org (free)
    -   adding overlays to the video using Google Images or Creative Commons (free; or use Flickr's facility to search for free photos)
    -   touching up the images using Photoshop (free trial).

2. Create the eBook by converting the audio into text by sending the file to a transcribing service such as www.gotranscript. com (cost: about $1 per minute).

3. Tidy up the text and make it look great by sending it to a graphic designer at www.fiverr.com.

7. Promote your information-based product

Here are some ways to promote your product.

-   Advertise it to your niche community on Facebook.
-   Hire a micro blogger social influencer from TRIBE to promote your product to their network.
-   Put a snippet of the video on YouTube to drive traffic back to your website.
-   Promote the MP3 audio file in an AdWords campaign as a 'trial' product in exchange for the consumer's email or social details.

- Use Mailchimp to capture customer data and to build your database (free trial).

- Write a promotional email and send it to those who subscribed from the AdWords campaign.

- Upload the eBook for sale on Amazon.

- Post blogs on Facebook that educate your customers about the product.

8. Collect testimonials

Collecting testimonials and reviews is important because people will only buy from sites they trust.

- Email friends and others and ask them to leave a review for your product on Amazon (free).

- List your business on directory and review sites (Yelp, TrueLocal, Yellow Pages, and so on).

- Send a message to your Facebook and LinkedIn contacts about your new product and ask them to write a recommendation (free).

- Use those testimonials on your website to build credibility (free).

- Ask a strategic partner with a big network to promote it to their network for you and split the revenue you generate (use www.commissionfactory.com).

9. Run an off-line event to generate buzz

Next you'll want to do some off-line promoting.

- Launch the product at a respectable venue to 'borrow' credibility (high credibility venues such as universities, hospitals and banks often have function rooms for hire).

- Invite the subject-matter expert to speak about the topic.

- Use www.trybooking.com to take bookings for the event (small fee).

10. Process payments and seek feedback

Once your product starts to sell, you can:

- process payments for free or a small fee (PayPal, POLI, Bitcoin)
- conduct after-sales surveys and polls for free (SurveyMonkey).

11. Use on-demand staff to provide customer service

Here are a couple of options for servicing your customers.

- Handle enquiries from prospects and provide customer service without employing staff (free trial with www.zendesk.com).
- Use Live Chat to handle online queries.

12. Find investors

Need more money to grow? You'll need investors.

- Find bigger brains than yours to help you grow (attend a pitch night at www.fishburners.org).
- Hold meetings with potential investors at free workspaces (libraries, hotel lobbies).
- Network with others at co-working space events (www.hubaustralia.com.au).

13. Test and measure

Use data to track your progress:

- Get your site indexed by Google and track data to check the search terms being used to find you (free with Google Analytics).
- Check your email 'open rates' to see how many people are reading your emails.
- Check which blogs on Facebook are most popular and write more blogs on those topics.

How to turn your expertise into an online product

If you decide to build an information-based product to sell, what topic will you choose to talk about? It's an important decision. Here are three guidelines for choosing a topic that will increase your chances of creating a successful product. This is adapted from the Hedgehog Concept made famous by Jim Collins in his book *Good to Great*.

- **What are you great at doing?** Do you have a system or process that helps people solve a problem?
- **What are you passionate about?** You'll live and breathe this content for years to come so you'll need to love the topic.
- **Will people pay money for that content?** How much? Is that enough to justify your efforts?

What you find in the middle of those three guidelines is what you should talk about for your information-based product.

Getting started is always the most difficult aspect, so it helps to have a roadmap for what to do first and how to gain that all-important momentum. These 13 steps are not the definitive guide to building an information-based business, but they provide enough helpful 'pointers' to get you going.

Let's recap

So there you have it. The top tech tools, resources, questions and guidelines you need to move your business idea forward and build momentum.

Takeaways:

- What do you sell? What is the business model? How will you make money? Until you've worked out when and how people pay you and what you give in return, you will struggle to make money.

- Is your business information-based, product-based or a blend? Information-based businesses can scale quickly and become massively disruptive. Be aware of the differences.

- Don't reinvent the wheel. Use the tech tools the award-winning entrepreneurs use and save yourself a lot of hassles and a lot of money.

- Most of the software products have great demonstration videos. Even if you don't use the software, watch them anyway. They are masterclasses in marketing.

- Measurement is the name of the game. There are loads of free tools that help you work out which marketing messages are working and which ones aren't.

Coming up ...

Step 4 of the book is all about marketing. If you've ever built a website and had it sit there languishing, wondering where all the traffic went, you'll love this section: it's very practical in nature with lots of tips and tools on how to create content, how to access low-cost social influencers with large networks, how to write optimised copy for Google, and much more.

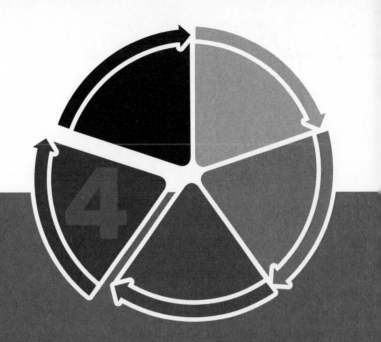

Marketing

How to get found, get traffic and get sales

Your website's up, and what with all that dosh that's about to come flooding into your bank account, you're ready to slap down that deposit on the Sydney oceanfront apartment. But you check your account the day after your website launch and the balance is...zero; not one customer; not one brass razoo.

What went wrong? Like those cartoon images, 'Omigod, I forgot to have children!', it's 'Omigod, I forgot to market my business!'

The chapters that follow provide practical, easy-to-follow steps on how you can manage the most challenging aspects of owning an online business: getting found, getting read and—most importantly—getting sales.

To kick things off let's dispense with one big fat myth. There's a widespread belief that just because we can create cheap websites, create even cheaper advertising on Facebook and post videos on YouTube for free, we will find customers. Fake news! Not true!

You need to work it and market your website, big time! The people I interviewed live and breathe the marketing of their sites. You'll need to as well.

Marketing has changed

For many reasons marketing an online business is harder than it used to be. Yes, you've got access to cheap technology to create your site and cheap advertising on social media, both of which make *setting up* the business easier than it used to be. But for every development that makes it easier, there's a counter-trend making it harder to succeed. For example:

- You're competing with thousands of other businesses.
- If you're not high up on Google's page rank, you'll struggle to get your site noticed.

- If you don't 'pay to play' on social media, your posts may not get seen.
- People are savvier and can research products themselves; they're not fooled by glossy advertising.
- People are less trusting so they need more information before making a buying decision.

For these reasons, it's more difficult than ever to market a business, and it's no secret why people tire of it. Marketing requires relentless application, focus, skill and knowledge, particularly if you're doing it on a budget. In short, it can be exhausting.

Google killed the salesperson

Where once a salesperson's role was to set out the difference between two or more products, and help guide the buyer to the right choice, now customers can just look up a peer-to-peer review on Google and make up their own minds. You can't just 'sell' anything to anyone now. Google has seen to that.

As a result, the sales process has changed and it's become more about *educating* the client, rather than *selling to* the client.

So, if a salesperson can't *sell* their product to a customer, what can they do? That's where 'influencing' the customer comes into play. For example, I may not be able to *sell* you something, but with the right information and approach, I could possibly *influence* you to buy something.

This shift from sales to influencing is what's known as 'influencer marketing' and it has dramatically changed the face of marketing.

Two popular forms of influencer marketing are Content Marketing and Social Influencer Marketing, both of which I'll detail in chapters 15 to 16. In chapter 15 I will also do a deep dive into how to make content such as podcasts and webinars. And then an even deeper dive into how to write headlines that get your content read. I'll finish off with some search optimisation tips on how you can get your website found on Google.

Chapter 15
Content marketing

What's made marketing so complex and expensive now is that *another* step in the buying process has been added. It's called 'content marketing'. Content creators *love* this new development because they get paid to make the content. Brands *don't love* this development as they have to pay the content creators to make the content.

Content is king.

There are only two rules for the creation of content:

- it must be useful
- it must be entertaining.

Ideally it's both.

Content marketing enables a consumer to get educated about their product before they buy. It can take many forms. Here are just a few examples:

- eBook
- brochure
- video
- infographic
- webinar

- slide deck
- podcast
- whitepaper
- case study
- photos

The days of 'hard core' selling are over. Yes, mass media is still a vital cog in creating awareness, but content marketing has become increasingly important. From initial research and consideration to conversion and post-purchase engagement, content plays a critical role in educating, guiding and influencing prospects.

The 3-step content creation process

Feeding the hungry 'content' beast that is Google can be time-consuming and expensive. But it doesn't have to be. The following strategies will help you create content quickly without exhausting yourself or blowing the budget. Irrespective of what you sell—be it product or services—content is king, and you'll need a lot of it, which is why this chapter will be helpful.

Here's a three-step guide to creating and making content work for you.

1. Decide what the content needs to do

Does your content need to build awareness, inspire purchase or something else? What pieces of content should you create? The type of content you need to create will be driven by what you'd like it to achieve. For example:

- if you want to generate *awareness* of your products or services, you should be creating analyst reports, eBooks, whitepapers and research papers
- if your prospects are in the *decision-making* stage of the buying process, you should be providing case studies, product comparison sheets and trial downloads

- if they're ready to buy, you should be providing *training videos* on how to use the product.

Figure 15.1 gives an overview of a typical buyer journey and the types of content they need to see at that specific stage that will help them make a buying decision.

Figure 15.1: what content should you create? Offer the right content at the right time to help move your prospect from 'awareness' to 'decision'.

Awareness *stage* — CONTENT

Your prospect has a problem they need to solve but don't know how to solve it.

They are looking for information and broad answers.

Analyst reports
Research reports
eBooks
Editorial content
Expert content
Whitepapers
Educational content

Consideration *stage* — CONTENT

Your prospect is closer to buying something and is tossing up between different providers.

Expert guides
Live interactions
Webcasts
Podcasts
Videos
Comparison whitepapers

Decision *stage* — CONTENT

Your prospect is ready to buy now and needs good, solid reasons to choose one provider over another.

Vendor comparisons
Product comparisons
Case studies
Trial downloads
Product literature
Live demos

Here's an example of how successful the right content can be.

The million-dollar whitepaper

Belinda Moore, co-founder of Strategic Membership Solutions (SMS) wrote a whitepaper on a topic relevant to her association and not-for-profit clients called 'Membership is Dead?' and the paper spread like wildfire. She says:

'It was terrifically successful. It was picked up by a number of publications from around the world and resulted in a huge volume of speaking and work enquiries. I still receive an enquiry a week from it now. Because of the way I structured it, with clear headings and involving headlines, it was easy to skim quickly. This meant it often got used as a board briefing paper. That whitepaper has been directly responsible for over a million dollars in revenue.'

Beware, great content can be a potent marketing tool, but it must be well-written or it will do you more harm than good.

2. Choose your topic

Obviously, the content needs to be connected to what your business offers, but having said that, you would be amazed how often people choose the wrong topic for their content creation. They sell shoes, for example, but create content around meditation, simply because they're interested in it. Being interested or even passionate about a topic does not qualify it to become a topic for your content. I like sleeping, but it doesn't mean I create a podcast on it.

Belinda Moore thought long and hard about the topic of her whitepaper. 'It was popular because it addressed a massive issue being experienced by the sector that no-one was talking about. A number of people said it got them to shift their perspective and address the issue more effectively.'

How to use Facebook to research hot blog topics

Digital marketer Meri Harli uses Facebook to find relevant topics.

'I had a consulting client who wanted to know what topic he should write on. To find what topic best resonated, we wrote seven industry-specific blog articles, posted them on Facebook and tracked their organic [unpaid] performance. One of the articles had a massive lead over the others with a great click-through [rate] to the website and high engagement levels. Based on that, we organised a paid campaign around that topic to increase their likes, grow their Facebook presence and drive more traffic to the website.'

---

3. Choose your sources of content

How you source your content will be determined by many things including how much time, money and effort you want to put in, and how high the quality of content needs to be. For example, one of my clients is a national research director for a property company. She has a PhD in the topic, so if she puts out a research paper it has to be well-written, meticulously fact-checked and typo free. If, however, you sell novelty chocolates to fund-raising organisations, your content may not need to be of such a high quality.

Here are three easy ways to source raw material for your content.

Frequently asked questions (FAQs)

Make a list of all the questions you've ever had from clients or customers and then answer them. It's as simple as that.

These questions can form the basis of a whole raft of content for your business as they address the key needs and wants of your audience. The questions being asked are obviously of interest to the audience so it makes sense to use those questions as the basis for your content.

Hunting for George, a homewares company, used this strategy and achieved a remarkable result. I asked co-founder Lucy Glade-Wright how they did it.

Bernadette: What content did you create?

Lucy: We came up with an educational, fun video series that would be presented with a Hunting for George personality. The first video ran for two minutes and it covered off a key problem we knew people had: how to fold a fitted sheet.

Bernadette: What was the result?

Lucy: The video trended on YouTube, racked up over 100 000 views in one week and had over 100 000 views on a single Facebook Post. To date this video has been viewed more than 500 000 times. The video was shared by *Lifehacker* and ended up on the 'trending' page of YouTube. This exposed our brand to a huge audience around the world. The viral and social nature of this video on Facebook incited huge engagement with comments and shares. With over 1000 likes and 150 shares this Facebook video quickly become a talking point around our current fans and customers, virally expanding our reach and audience.

Bernadette: Why do you think it worked?

Lucy: The video is not offensive to anyone and can also help people which gives it a sharable factor; all elements that give a video a chance of going viral.

Bernadette: What was the cost?

Lucy: The video was produced wholly in-house. The total expense was $150 in-studio hire for half a day.

Not a bad rate of return.

Product reviews

List all the products and tools used in your industry and by your customers and review them.

Creating product reviews and guides is not only useful but can be lucrative too. They're also brilliant for service providers such as lawyers and personal trainers who struggle to stamp their personality on their offering.

To add value to the product guide, simply add a cheat sheet or a quick-start guide and you've turned it into a workbook that people will pay for. You'll not only educate yourself in the process but it will help position you as a thought leader in your industry.

Expert interviews

List all of the subject-matter experts in your business and interview them.

This is a remarkably easy way to source content and can be a brilliant way to build your database quickly. Ideally, you'll choose a thought leader with a high profile (and an even higher social media reach) so that once the content is created, they'll also send it to their networks. In one fell swoop you've exponentially increased your reach.

Aim to interview the most famous people in your industry and work down from there. They're all findable on LinkedIn and you'll be surprised who might say 'yes'.

You can interview them via video, webinar or podcast. Each medium has its drawbacks and merits.

- *Video:* You'll need a video camera and a crew and you'll need to meet up in person. It will also need to be edited. This gets complicated and expensive quickly. Or you can keep it simple and use your mobile phone camera to do the filming.
- *Webinar:* GoToWebinar, Zoom and local outfit Redback Conference all offer low-cost webinar technology that is perfect for creating video and audio content.
- *Podcasts:* These are popular because they're cheap and easy to make and they can be distributed widely using low-cost, readily available technology.

> ## WHAT IS A PODCAST?
>
> Podcasts are like a radio show but they are available on demand via iTunes and other podcast sites. With the right equipment, you have the power to be a one-person radio station. You can access most podcasts for free by downloading them from the internet. They can be a few minutes in duration or as along as an hour. Most are free to download. Popular podcasts include *This American Life*, *The Moth*, *Serial* and *Hamish and Andy*.

Podcasts are the new black and they are very cost-effective ways of creating content that's valuable and interesting to an audience.

3 steps to creating a successful podcast

Don't know how to make a podcast? Neither did I when I started out, so I did a bit of basic research and discovered a few handy tools that I'll share with you here. I created a podcast as a companion piece for this book so you can see exactly what I created in the process.

You can listen to my podcast here: www.bernadetteschwerdt. com.au/podcast.

Here's three things you need to know.

1. Record it with...

I used a fabulous piece of free software called MP3 Skype Recorder. It enables you to record Skype calls from your computer using a normal pair of cheap Logitech headphones. No fancy microphone is needed as you can use the built-in microphone on the headphones. The sound quality is almost as good as a professional recording studio. Audacity is also great (and free); or use GarageBand for Mac.

2. Edit it with...

You can edit the audio track using Audacity. Add some free music from GarageBand or low-cost music from AudioBlocks and before you know it, you're sounding like a pro.

3. Upload it with...

Disclosure time! I did need some technical help with this bit. Thanks to the gig economy, I was able to find Lyndal Harris, a specialist podcast virtual assistant (VA), and she took care of the technical details. Sure, I could have learned how to do it, but it would have taken me forever and I may have abandoned the project altogether if or when it got too hard. I incurred a cost in hiring Lyndal, but it freed me up to do what I wanted to do, which was record the interview and get the content out to my audience.

LISTEN UP

Put the podcast on your website and make it free. If the point of the podcast is to drive traffic to your website, it makes sense to drive people to your website first. If they like it and want more, they can then subscribe to your podcast from iTunes or Google Play.

PS: Don't forget those with Android devices: while 65 per cent of listenership of podcasts is through Apple podcasts, submitting to websites such as Stitcher will provide a platform for people with non-Apple devices to subscribe and listen.

Like most technical things, you either have to learn it yourself or pay someone to do it. If you know the former won't happen, then you need to bite the bullet and do the latter. My podcast virtual assistant was worth her weight in gold.

How to promote your podcast

These are Lyndal's five tips for helping you market your podcast to the wider world:

1. Have a very clear objective/purpose for your podcast and know your target audience.

2. Write a brief description of the podcast. This will be used in various accounts, such as Apple Podcasts and Stitcher, to summarise your podcast.

3. When creating the podcast cover art, be sure to create something that will really 'pop' as most consumers will see a small version of it on their phone.

4. Create a hosting account because you'll want a specific podcast host separate from your website. Whooshkaa, Libsyn and Omny Studio are great options.

5. Marketing and promotion needs to be commenced in advance. You can't just post your episode the day it goes live; you need to have a distribution plan and promote each episode more than once.

How to create instant content — without writing a word!

Unless you hire a copywriter to write content for you, you will need to create your own content — and lots of it. If you can't write, don't have the time to write or just don't know what to write, you'll love this next tip.

James Tuckerman — founder of entrepreneurial online magazine *Anthill Online* — has an ingenious method for creating content on the run. He shared with me this amazing nugget of wisdom that will have you creating content in a jiffy — without even picking up a pen! The simplicity — yet sheer efficiency — of it is so impressive.

Here's what James does.

- He interviews a subject-matter expert.
- He records the conversation on his smartphone using the 'voice memo' function (you can download it from the App Store for free).
- He sends the recording to get transcribed (thank you gig economy!) and that transcription becomes a series of blogs.
  - ⇒ The blogs become 'cheat sheets'.
  - ⇒ The 'cheat sheets' become infographics.
  - ⇒ The blogs and infographics become an eBook.
  - ⇒ The eBook becomes an online mini-course.
  - ⇒ The online mini-course becomes a webinar series.
  - ⇒ The webinar series gets put on iTunes as a podcast.

Just slice and dice! What an awesome way to create great content instantly!

***

Let's recap. You've got great content and plenty of it. Check. It's been loaded to your site and looks amazing. Check. There's only one thing missing. Readers! Who's going to see it and read it? How are they going to find it? What will make them want to read it?

That's where social influencers and search engine optimisation (SEO) come into play. Let's start with social influencers and how they can help you get your content in the hands of prospects.

Chapter 16
Social influencer marketing

Can you really build a business using social influencers only?

That's what entrepreneurs Nik Mirkovic and Alex Tomic asked when they set up HiSmile, their teeth-whitening dentistry startup. After generating $10 million turnover in just 18 months you could say they have something to smile about.

They credit the glowing results from their teeth-whitening business to just one thing: social-media influencers.

How one Instagram image launched a thousand sales

When Nik Mirkovic and Alex Tomic launched HiSmile in 2014, their initial approach to social media was broad and unfocused. After lacklustre results, they carefully refined their filters and started aiming for the big names with big teeth and an even broader reach. They used Instagram to help them do it.

Instagram has been the game-changer platform for many startups. The right image of the right person with the right product at the right time can be the difference between success and failure.

When Kylie Jenner, part of the Kardashian clan, posted a photo of herself with a HiSmile box to her Instagram account with 76 million followers, the results were immediate.

(continued)

How one Instagram image launched a thousand sales *(cont'd)*

The post, which includes the hashtag #ad, attracted 1.6 million likes and more than a quarter of a million comments from adoring fans.

'It's really just putting your product or your brand where the attention of your target market is,' Nik says.

He wouldn't disclose how much Jenner was paid for the endorsement, but says the campaign was a success and his company will continue to use social media influencers.

Engaging a massive superstar like Kylie Jenner can have an immediate impact on the business and drive awareness through the roof. But it takes big bucks and guts to commit that much money to just one channel. The ultimate task is to turn those likes into sales.

How did HiSmile get started?

Nik, 21, and Alex, 23, bootstrapped HiSmile using $20 000 of their personal savings. Much of this was spent sending their $79.99 home whitening kits to influencers, convinced it was the best way to reach their demographic of 15- to 24-year-old women.

They were clear about their target market from the outset, 'It's important for us and our marketing team to understand who the 15- to 24-year-old female is looking up to and looking at for inspiration—who are they looking at for their look,' Nik explains.

'We don't believe in forcing a product down people's throats and saying, "You must buy this!" We're not trying to sell as such. We're selling a lifestyle.'

Nik predicts his company will turn over an additional $40 million by the end of 2018. They're using celebrities to increase awareness quickly and doing well with it.

Transparency and trust — the new currency of marketing

Marketing is different now. Consumers are savvier and have instant access to peer reviews, comparison sites, celebrities and CEOs. The claims advertisers make have never been under greater scrutiny. The dreams that the Mad Men of advertising spun have far less power than they used to. In the not-so-recent past, we believed their claims that 'this face cream will make you look younger'; 'this dress will make you look slimmer'; 'this car will make you feel sexier'.

We bought those products but they didn't deliver on the promise. We didn't look younger, slimmer or sexier but we didn't have an outlet to complain. Now we do. It's called social media. It gave the 'little people' a voice. Social media also gave power to those with large social networks: people who blogged about products and told their followers what products they liked and what products they didn't. These bloggers now have enormous power and, with one post or tweet, can make or break a company.

After all, if our favourite blogger, one we love and trust, tells us that the hotel they stayed in is terrible, are we going to believe them or the glossy commercial we see on TV telling us otherwise?

Those bloggers have become 'influencers' and they are turning the advertising industry on its head; any brand worth its salt knows they must engage with the key influencers in their industry.

You don't need millions of followers to be an influencer either. Having an audience of 3000 engaged and devoted followers can be far more powerful than having 300000 disinterested or fake fans. This rise of 'micro bloggers' — people with small but engaged fans — enables smaller brands with smaller budgets to get their word out to the world very cost-effectively.

The rise of the micro blogger

As A-list influencers are increasingly co-opted by the big end of the commercial world, the centre-of-influencer gravity is shifting towards micro bloggers. This is where we find people such as photography blogger Darren Rowse, baking blogger Lucy Mathieson and travel blogger Anna Whitehouse. The non-celebrity social influencers. Real people who express genuine joy, actual outrage and authentic vulnerability. And, happily for the brands, they come at a lower cost and with a more engaged audience.

These micro bloggers are foundational to how the social influencer movement began.

Real people. Real opinions

Anna Whitehouse, founder of Mother Pukka, the parenting lifestyle brand with 141 000 followers on Instagram, believes this change in approach is being driven by a desire for real experiences. She says, 'Ten years ago, when I was sent on a press trip as a journalist, I would write about the place in terms of function—rooms, food, view, friendliness. Now I write and vlog [which is like a blog, but on video] about hotels and travel experiences in a more personal way.'

By using social media to show not just a glossy image but, instead, a warts-and-all diary of travel, Whitehouse is forging more emotional connections with consumers. She explains that there was a shift from simply answering the question, 'What does this destination offer?' to 'How do I feel here?'

'Travel companies we've worked for want to know about our experience instead of getting an obvious puff piece that sells the place,' she says. 'On a recent trip to Martinhal Resort, a Boomerang video of my daughter beaming as she's chucked in the air by my husband in the swimming pool made them more bookings than a lengthier blog post "selling" the facilities.'

WHAT'S A BOOMERANG VIDEO?

Boomerang is a video app from Instagram. It takes a burst of photos and stitches them together into a high-quality mini video that plays forwards and backwards.

Making big from baking

Lucy Mathieson is a baking blogger from Victoria who has turned a passion for cooking yummy things into a profitable business. Her blog, Bake Play Smile has only been in operation for four years and yet she has over 110 000 followers on Facebook and counts Tip Top, San Remo and Tefal as clients. The blog generates an income of over $100 000 per year which means she's been able to quit her job as a primary school teacher and can focus on building the business.

'It took about a year for it to take off and I didn't really make any money from it until then,' Mathieson says. 'It's all about trust. Brands trust me, and they know I understand what my audience wants. Having said that, I need to maintain the integrity of my blog, so I am selective with the campaigns I choose.'

You need only engage Mathieson if you want the truth. She only accepts campaigns that she knows will be a great fit and that she can talk positively about. If she loves a product or a brand, she'll happily tell her audience all about it, but if it's not something she believes in, you won't see it on her website. That's the honesty her followers rely on and it is the reason why the market for micro bloggers has exploded.

Social influencer platforms

The rise of social platforms such as TRIBE and Srunch means consumers can directly connect with their celebrity, mini celebrity or micro blogger of choice. That was unheard of before. Likewise, the brand can also connect directly with their consumer. That was also unheard of before. When I worked for impresario Harry M. Miller as a celebrity manager, our cache—in fact, our reason for existence—was we had the 'ear' of the celebrity. No-one got access to the celebrities unless Harry said so and certainly no-one got that celebrity's endorsement without paying big dollars. This brokerage model, of course, is not new. All forms of gatekeepers use it: actor agents, model bookers, real-estate agents, stockbrokers.

What's changed on the celebrity front is that we can now get direct access to these celebrities through their social media account and personal brand websites. Everyone is accessible—heck, I can tweet the President of the United States. The very idea of a gatekeeper seems quaint now, almost laughable.

So, in other words, we're moving away from the traditional sales approach where we got force-fed a steady stream of manufactured concepts designed to sell us the dream. And we're moving towards the role of real people writing real opinions about a product they really use. It's this new wave of influencers that is powering this shift from sales to influencing.

The marketplace as gatekeeper

The gatekeeper's role has returned in the form of the marketplace. Companies such as TRIBE move in, formalising the influencer arrangement and helping broker the deals between the influencer and the brand.

How startups can access social influencers (without the hefty price tag)

TRIBE is the brainchild of former TV and radio star Jules Lund. It is an online marketplace connecting brands with influencers. It's a much quicker way to formalise the influencer arrangement, and brands can take advantage of all the systems and processes that TRIBE has already put in place.

TRIBE launched in Australia in early 2016 and has connected 5000 brands with 30 000 influencers. They've expanded to the UK and brands such as Moët Hennessy, Selfridges and Burt's Bees helped them launch.

How much do influencers get paid?

'Let's say a brand spends $10 000 on a campaign with TRIBE,' says Jules. 'TRIBE takes 20 per cent of that ($2000) and the rest goes to the influencer. Tribe also brings in additional revenue through content licensing fees when brands buy the content created by influencers. We've paid out over $4.5 million to these influencers along the way. It's great for the influencer as many haven't capitalised or don't know how to monetise on their followings.'

How does it work?

Jules is quick to point out they're not a talent agency representing influencers and social media superstars, but a technology platform that connects brands that want coverage and influencers who can give it to them via their network.

Unless you're a top-tier marketing agency, trying to co-ordinate, book and manage an influencer campaign can be time-consuming and expensive. TRIBE harnesses Other People's Stuff (in this case, their networks and databases) to help brands find customers.

How small businesses can use influencers

Influencer marketing is perfect for big brands wanting instant content, but it's great for small brands that are starting out, have no database or can't afford AdWords and other traditional forms of advertising.

Jules Lund says genuine engagement with followers is the top priority for brands searching for effective influencers.

> **For us, it's all about engagement—getting those important comments, likes and shares. It's also about ensuring that the content our influencers create is original, unique and of the highest quality. Whilst we know big businesses appreciate what an influencer can do for them, we are increasingly seeing smaller businesses engage with social media influencers because it enables them to reach new audiences cost effectively. Micro influencers charge less than celebrities because they don't yet have the audience, or the broader public awareness outside of their online tribes.**

How one mention can make a difference

One mention from a respected influencer can make a massive difference. For Matt Barrie that came in the form of a passing comment by the Tom Friedman, the Pulitzer Prize winning journalist and author of *The World is Flat*. Friedman gave a commencement speech for a leading university on how technology enabled things to get done more quickly and in that speech and subsequent interviews, mentioned how it was now possible to get a prototype made in China, have it manufactured in Vietnam, and you could then engage Amazon to distribute it and use Freelancer to get the logo done. Barrie said that the mere mention of Freelancer by this luminary figure caused the blogosphere to 'light up' and put Freelancer on the map.

All or nothing? What works best

HiSmile founder Nik Mirkovic says, 'We're spending money in different places rather than limiting it to just the one platform, like Instagram. So, we're really trying to go hard on all the platforms that we think suit our target market, so for us it's Snapchat, YouTube and Musical.ly.'

Marketing expert Adam Franklin from Bluewire Media warns social media marketing isn't a one-size-fits-all solution for small businesses.

'Social media marketing is important and it's valuable to a lot of businesses but it should not be portrayed as a magic pill that will instantly transform a poorly performing company," he says.

Social media may be the best way to reach a young demographic, but Franklin insists it isn't the only way.

Be careful before pouring all your marketing spend into social media as you may find it just fills the coffers of Google and Facebook and has no impact at all on your sales. The best solution is to integrate social media with other media choices and ensure your website is the mothership that all roads lead back to.

Radio is still going strong and flying along according to Daryl Mitchell, head of sales at Melbourne radio station Light FM.

Social is important but when combined with radio, it's absolutely potent. We use our Facebook page to complement our clients' radio spend so the client gets two bangs for their buck: they get a radio advertisement and we also promote their offer on our Facebook page. So clients are loving how we've been able to blend those two mediums so effectively.

Social influencers are a new and exciting tool in a startup's arsenal of ammunition and can provide access to a new source of prospects quickly and cost-effectively. Once those new prospects hit your website they'll need to be dazzled and delighted with what you have to offer. The words you use on your website will go a long way to helping you do that. Coming up are some tips on how you can write powerful headlines for your website, blogs, social posts and other content.

Chapter 17

How to write great headlines that get results

If you can write good copy, you can sell anything. Take a look at the advertisement in figure 17.1, which the great explorer Ernest Shackleton purportedly wrote when he needed to find brave men to accompany him on his Antarctic journey.

Figure 17.1: if you can write good copy, you can get people to do anything—even risk their lives!

> Men wanted for hazardous journey. Low wages, bitter cold, long hours of complete darkness. Safe return doubtful. Honour and recognition in event of success.

Despite the caveat that they would all probably die, the trek was oversubscribed. Nice copy Ernie!

***

We've established who the key players in your startup need to be: the Hacker, the Hustler and the Expert. There's one other very important person you'll want to engage as an employee or freelancer: a copywriter. Why are they important? Because they determine whether your startup thrives and flies or falls and dies. Really. They're that important.

WHAT'S THE DIFFERENCE BETWEEN A CONTENT CREATOR AND A COPYWRITER?

Not much. Copywriters write the words for all forms of content. Content creators do the same, but they may have extra skill sets that may include graphic design, image editing and video production editing.

The ability to write persuasive copy is one of the most important skills an entrepreneur can acquire. It's not a stretch to say that if you can write well, you can sell anything. Never forget: great things can come to those who write.

What do copywriters do?

Copywriters write the words for your content pieces. 'Content' is anything you create that's designed to sell your product or service. For example:

- websites
- blogs
- videos
- email newsletters

- social media posts
- brochures
- banner advertisements
- AdWords text

By the way, copy is not just the written word either, it's the verbal words you use in your sales pitch, phone calls to clients, meetings and all the other words you use when you're talking to stakeholders. Words matter! Just ask Donald Trump, who sailed into the top job using four simple words: 'Make America Great Again'.

In short, copywriters write words that sell—words that make people want to buy something: a product, a service, a concept, a set of behaviours.

If your words fail to make that impact and therefore fail to cause a transaction between the company and the buyer, your copywriting has failed and along with it, your startup dreams. It's a harsh reality, but it's true. Your words have got to convert.

How to write great headlines

A good headline tells readers what a story is about; it induces them to read the story: it's the ad for the ad!

The headline is without doubt the most important element in any piece of copy, so here are some formulas you can use to come up with one quickly. All professional copywriters use formulas. They don't have time to wait for inspiration or for that 'creative spark' to hit. They have to write a lot, quickly, and it has to get a result. Formulas have been tried and tested and they work.

The top 3 formulas for creating successful headlines

A reader should be able to scan down your page, quickly digest your headlines and figure out what you're offering. Once the prospect knows you have something they're interested in, they will take more time to read your entire letter, ad or web page. Most people read headlines first, so concentrate on getting the headline right and everything else will follow.

There are dozens of formulas, but here are three that get used a lot.

1. 'How to' headlines
2. Question headlines
3. Number headlines

1. 'How to' headlines

Okay, you wanted to know how to write headlines that get attention. Well this is it.

This is quite structural and you may think you're having a grammar lesson, but you're not. It just helps to understand how language is being used so you can manipulate it for your own purposes.

This technique works well because you can create a generic headline for a blog or web page that appeals to a wide range of people. But if you want to then niche the headline down and target a very specific market, you can do so easily without rewriting the whole piece again. Stick with me. This will make sense in a moment.

Creating headlines is easy—all you have to do is establish the problem you're solving and then whack a formula in front of it. The more specific the problem, the more niche your headline becomes.

For example: you can choose how 'niche' you'd like to go. If you were a Snapchat marketing consultant, you could use this broad range of headlines to attract a variety of people with different needs:

- How to master Snapchat
- How to master Snapchat *marketing*
- How to master Snapchat marketing *in 10 days*
- How to master Snapchat marketing in 10 days—*even if you've never used it before.*

Here's why this is so powerful...

Niching your content down makes it really easy to advertise to micro targets. And with Facebook you can find these audiences very quickly and advertise to them very cheaply. Using this technique helps you create a relevant and powerful headline for that audience.

Now you need to write the rest of the piece, but that's the topic of another book (or visit my website copyschool.com and get the low-down on how to write copy like a professional. Notice the nice little 'how to' headline I just threw in there!).

Even just adding the word 'how' in front of a headline gives it an additional appeal.

Compare these two examples:

- A strange experience saved me from bankruptcy
- How a strange experience saved me from bankruptcy

See the difference? Most people say the second headline is more powerful. The first one can be used, but it won't be as effective.

Here's a nifty technique for using formulas to write 'how to' headlines.

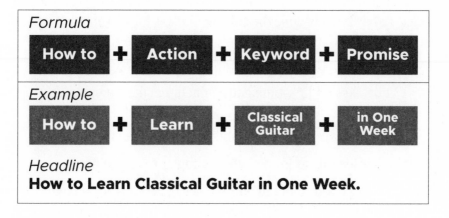

Easy, isn't it?

2. Question headlines

Question headlines are based on the premise that our brains are answer-seeking devices and that if asked a question, the brain cannot *not* answer it. A question headline forces the reader to answer the question in their mind. This style of headline automatically gets the prospect involved in your message.

Many people will read further into your letter, advertisement or website copy just to find out what answer or solution you provide.

This headline formula taps into the prospect's problems and your headline is the magic pill that fixes that problem. Again, make sure the question focuses on the reader's interest, not yours. So, pick a good question that reflects the problem that your target market has. For example:

- Do you make these 3 mistakes when choosing a web developer?
- How long should your email newsletter be? Find out here.
- Is work stressing you out? Here's 3 weird but practical ways to help you relax.

3. Number headlines

Number headlines work because they are based on the premise that someone has already done the culling of ideas for you and that what's left is the pick of the bunch. Here's some examples:

- 7 quick and easy ways to build your testimonial file
- 3 mistakes all first-time entrepreneurs make when building a website
- 5 clever ways to use your podcast to generate new leads.

There are three tips to follow when using numbers in headlines:

- Try to use a zero in the number—10, 20, 30—or an odd number—3, 7, 9, 101. Don't ask me why—it just works better than even numbers. I'm sure there's a thesis on this somewhere. (And by the way, 3 and 7 are the best numbers to use for short lists.)
- Use digits rather than words—'10 ways to …' works better than 'Ten ways to …'
- Place the number at the head of the sentence: '5 ways to reduce anxiety and stress' works better than 'How to reduce anxiety and stress in 5 ways'.

Here's a helpful technique for using formulas to write number headlines.

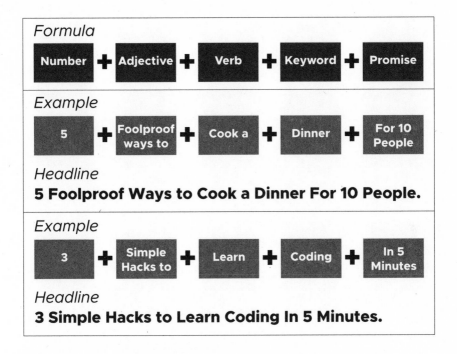

Formula
| Number | + | Adjective | + | Verb | + | Keyword | + | Promise |

Example
| 5 | + | Foolproof ways to | + | Cook a | + | Dinner | + | For 10 People |

Headline
5 Foolproof Ways to Cook a Dinner For 10 People.

Example
| 3 | + | Simple Hacks to | + | Learn | + | Coding | + | In 5 Minutes |

Headline
3 Simple Hacks to Learn Coding In 5 Minutes.

Let's recap. You've got great content and plenty of it. Check.

You now know where to find social influencers who can help you get your content out to the world. Check.

You know how to write headlines for your blogs and website that will get noticed and acted upon. Check.

What's missing? Ah yes, your site is not showing up on Google. Maybe it's because you haven't 'optimised' your content for Google? Optimised? What does that mean? I'm glad you asked. The art and science of search engine optimisation (SEO) will help your site land on page one of Google and that's coming up next.

Chapter 18

How to get on page one of Google

Aside from North Korea's nuclear missile deployment, the Myanmar crisis and the sinking of the Kiribati islands, getting found online is one of the greatest challenges of our time—a first-world problem perhaps, but for businesses trying to make a go of it, a very real problem. And it's the first problem they need to address if they are to hold their own in the online world.

Where's the best place to hide a dead body?

On page two of Google.

So you've got your website up and running. Great! There's only one problem. No-one can find it. Your site, that is, and all that lovely content you spent months crafting lies there languishing, unseen and unread. It's like you're standing in the middle of the freeway, waving your hands but there's no cars driving by. 'Where's all my traffic?!' you cry.

There are two main ways you can be found on search engines:

1. organically (your site shows up on page one without you paying to be there)
2. on Google's paid advertising platform, which is AdWords.

Matt Barrie, founder of Freelancer, knows a thing or two about websites and this is his tip for getting online traffic:

On a normal day, two billion people spend most of the time punching little words into Google and getting blue links spat back at them. So, if you can figure out a way to use Google effectively through either search engine optimisation or search engine marketing then that can be effective for some businesses.

Getting listed higher on Google is the art of search engine optimisation (SEO) and it is the holy grail for any business owner serious about making their website work. Why? Because it means more traffic to your site; without traffic, you may as well pack up and go home. But with Google regularly changing the 'rules' (or the algorithm) to prevent any one company from dominating the landscape, it can be tricky to create a clear-cut plan on how to get found on Google and get that all-important traffic.

QUICK TIP

Write copy that engages your customer first, and then write for Google.

However, there are strategic things you can do regularly that will give your site a greater chance of being seen on page one of Google for your preferred search terms. SEO can get complex quickly, but I'll give you enough information here to be a little bit dangerous and to get some easy wins.

'But I don't want to get technical!' you cry. 'Why should I have to learn all this stuff? Why can't I just put my site up and make moneeeeeey?'

Do you like eating? Do you like putting petrol in your car? Do you enjoy having a roof over your head? Well then you have to get a handle on SEO. There is no other option.

> ## WHO IS IN CHARGE OF SEO? THE WEB DEVELOPER OR THE COPYWRITER?
>
> Jim Stewart from StewArt Media had this to say.
>
> 'A builder builds the house but they still need the sparky and the plumber to make it work. The same is true of SEO. Both copywriters and developers have a role to play. A web developer's role in SEO is to make sure the site is structured properly and functions well. A copywriter's job is to help build the SEO content, the audience and the brand.'

The business owner should also have a good understanding of SEO to make sure they hire the right SEO consultants.

Where do you rank on Google?

The best way to start any SEO work is to find out where you rank on Google. It's worth taking a moment to find this out because if you can't find yourself on Google, chances are your prospects can't either.

If you don't know how to go about finding yourself on Google, your best bet is to ask, 'What words would the average person type into Google if they wanted to find my business? (These words are called 'keywords'.)

This is where it gets interesting because in order to do this, you need to crawl inside your prospect's head and start thinking like they do. This is easier said than done because people will search for your service using words that would never have occurred to you.

To work out what those keywords are you first need to put yourself in the shoes of your customer. What words would they use to find you on Google? What phrases would they use to find a product/service like yours?

Let's make some assumptions to demonstrate the principle. Let's assume:

- you're a lawyer specialising in workers compensation law
- the person seeking your services lives in Melbourne and has never had to contact a lawyer before.

Here's what that person might type into Google to find you:

- 'Lawyer, Melbourne'
- 'Solicitor, Melbourne'
- 'Workers Compensation'
- 'Workers Comp Lawyer'
- 'Workers Compensation Lawyer, Melbourne'.

> **QUICK TIP**
>
> Keywords don't just refer to 'words' but to 'phrases' as well. For example, 'Lawyers in Melbourne' is a keyword, even though it's a phrase.

All those search terms (or keywords) will bring up different search results, so it's worth trying out a few different combinations to see if it makes any difference to where you rank.

Where does your site show up? Page one? Well done. Page four? You've got work to do. Don't despair. With some clever SEOing, you can move up the ranks surprisingly quickly. Whatever the result, take comfort in the fact that at least you now know where you rank on Google.

Table 18.1 lists some sites you can access to find out how you rank on Google.

Table 18.1: helpful sites to see how you rank on Google

Term	Explanation	Tool
Domain authority	Find your authority score (1–100)	www.moz.com
Traffic rank	Find your rank at Alexa	www.alexa.com

And don't forget to get Google Analytics attached to your site so you can start to look at how much traffic you're getting, where it's coming from and what phrases are being used to locate your site—all valuable data that will help you move up the ranking.

And by the way, try doing a search on computers that aren't yours, such as at a library or on a friend's device, as your computer remembers your searches and is influenced by your past search history.

WANT TO SEARCH INCOGNITO?

Google allows you to search 'incognito' on your own computer. This helps you work out how other people are seeing your site and where it ranks. Look up Google's 'incognito mode' for more information on how to access it.

Where do your competitors rank?

This exercise begs the question: if you're not on page one of Google, who is? This is the perfect opportunity to work out where your competitors rank.

Take note of who the high rankers are and take a virtual stroll through their website to see what they're up to. You can find out what competitors are using as their keywords by tapping on 'Control + U' (also known as 'View Page Source' on your computer when you're on their website). That will bring up the coding on the backend. This feels like you're accessing their hidden data and to some degree you are: you're getting a bird's eye view into how their page has been constructed and what text they've used to get ranked. It's a very powerful little trick and it will save you hours in working out what SEO content you should use.

> ## HOW TO HACK YOUR WAY TO PAGE ONE ON GOOGLE
>
> Checking out the code on competitors' sites will show you the description tags and the title tags they use, and from there you can adapt those tags for yourself. This is the cheat's guide to SEO 101, also known as 'how to hack your way to page one on Google'. Why reinvent the wheel by coming up with new SEO phrases for your site when you can look at the high-ranking competitors and use their SEO keywords as inspiration? Don't copy and paste it wholesale. Just see what they're doing and adapt it for your business. It's perfectly legal.

Where is your audience hanging out?

Meri Harli, founder of digital marketing consultancy Fat Cake Media, says you've got to know who your audience is and what platforms they're on.

A few years ago, you could build a website, optimise it, pay a bit for AdWords and watch the sales roll in. That was the modus operandi for most businesses. That is not going to cut it any more. You need to be on multiple channels. For example, if you sell skin care, you're most likely going to find women in their early 20s hanging out on social channels like Instagram and/or Snapchat. And for slightly older women in their late 20s and up, you're going to want to have a strong presence on Facebook. These days you need to find out where your target audience is hanging out and create content for those channels.

You've got to work really hard to get organically found because most people trust organic listings over paid listings. However, if you can't get organic traffic or you need more than what organic traffic can deliver you, then you'll need to pay for AdWords. Google offers lots of free guides to get you started, but that's like putting Dracula in charge of the blood bank. If you choose to use AdWords, be careful! It can be horrendously expensive and in the hands of inexperienced players, it can hoover up your monthly marketing budget in a day. Sandy Abram from Wholesome Hub has this to say:

We made a big mistake with AdWords. We had a consultant do it for us and they really didn't know what they were doing. It cost us a fortune and we did not get the results we were expecting. You really need to understand the platform before you use it or you'll waste a lot of money very quickly.

QUICK TIP

If you don't know how to write an AdWords campaign or you don't know how to measure whether it's working or not, don't use it. Your best option is to do a short course in how to write AdWords or at least do some research on how to use it effectively before you start spending money.

Also, if you're going to spend money on AdWords, make sure your website is the best it can be and that the offers you use on the landing pages have been tested and are working well. There's no point sending paid-for prospects to a landing page that has a lousy conversion rate.

How to improve your Google page rank

There are dozens of factors that influence your SEO rank. Many of them are in your control. Here's the top seven 'on-page' SEO ranking factors that you can influence at little or no cost.

1. *Quality:* Does the website feature a lot of content and is that content well-written?
2. *Research:* Have you researched the keywords people may use to find your content?
3. *Words:* Do your headlines, images and links feature those keywords and phrases?
4. *Engagement:* Do visitors spend time reading or 'bounce' away quickly?

blog?

5. *Freshness:* Do you add content to your site regularly and is that content relevant to your main business?

6. *Titles:* Do the title tags contain keywords relevant to page topics?

7. *Descriptions:* Do the description tags describe what the pages are about?

TO BLOG OR NOT TO BLOG?

Blogging serves many purposes.

- It educates your clients on who you are and what you do.
- It builds trust in your expertise and shows you know your topic.
- It shows Google that your site is regularly maintained so it will rank you higher.
- It adds fresh content and keywords to your site, which helps you get found more easily.

As mentioned, SEO can get complex, but there are some easy wins to be had and that starts with doing a Keyword Analysis. It's the first thing you should do when embarking on an SEO campaign. Google's Keyword Planner is a great place to start. On a really simple level, you can use Google's predictive menu to get you up and running.

What should you blog about?

Let's say you have a craft/knitting blog and you can't work out what topic to blog about. Google's predictive menu will automatically drop down the most popular searches in recent times on your computer. When you type in 'how to knit...' it will show you what people have recently searched for. For example, it might say:

- how to knit...beanies
- how to knit...scarves
- how to knit...for dogs.

That tells you which topics people are searching for. Maybe one of those should be your next topic?

SHOULD I PAY FOR TRAFFIC?

Meri Harli, digital marketer and founder of Fat Cake Media says:

'Paying for traffic is the same as renting versus buying your own home. If you do your SEO right, your organic [free] traffic should grow to the point where you shouldn't even need to pay for AdWords. Or you may want to run a small-budget AdWords campaign just to glean the keyword intelligence that you can then use in your SEO.'

Choosing an SEO consultant to help you rank higher on Google may be an investment worth considering. If so, there's some questions you need to ask to ascertain which consultant is right for you.

How to eliminate unwanted traffic

Meri Harli of Fat Cake Media tells how she used SEO techniques to find more of the traffic she wanted and to deter the traffic she didn't want.

'A client offered a luxury, high-end drug and alcohol rehabilitation retreat. The problem was almost all of their incoming enquiries were from desperate people who couldn't afford their level of service. It was heartbreaking for them to turn away so many people on a daily basis. To alleviate this, we used carefully chosen SEO words to ensure that it was clear that the service was a very high-end offering. This eliminated most of the unwanted traffic and phonecalls and saved everyone time and stress.'

5 questions to ask an SEO consultant before hiring one

Jim Stewart of StewArt Media has this advice for those seeking to hire an SEO consultant. Here's what you should ask them.

1. Can I speak with current/former clients?
2. What are the goals of this campaign?
3. How long will it take to see results?
4. How do you measure results?
5. Have you had success with a website like mine before?

You can pay people to help you with your SEO, but those consultants can be expensive and you may not get the results you hope for. If you do engage a consultant, don't sign any long-term contracts until they demonstrate their worth. In any event, you should educate yourself on the topic so you can either do it yourself or at least hold your consultants to account.

5 questions to ask a web developer before hiring one

Most people struggle to find a great web developer. Jim Stewart suggests you ask these questions.

1. Have you built a website like mine before? Choose the developer who best matches your budget and industry.
2. Who owns the final code and what warranty do you offer?
3. What are the ongoing costs for maintenance updates?
4. Will they handle hosting? If so, is it fast and secure?
5. How often is it backed up and how easy is it to restore from backup after a disaster?

Hiring a web developer is like taking on a business partner so choose wisely.

Top 8 free Australian business directory listings

If your site languishes on page five of Google, hopping on these directories and review sites will potentially 'piggy-back' you onto page one. It's an easy win and because lots of businesses don't understand how powerful these sites are and how they can help you 'leap-frog' onto page one, they don't bother listing. You should bother.

1. Pure Local—www.purelocal.com.au
2. Yelp Australia—www.yelp.com.au
3. Hot Frog Australia—www.hotfrog.com.au
4. Start Local—www.startlocal.com.au
5. Womo—www.womo.com.au
6. Aussie Web—www.aussieweb.com.au
7. True Local—www.truelocal.com.au
8. Local Business Guide—www.localbusinessguide.com.au

So how do you get online reviews?

It's simple. You ask for them. I know that asking for reviews is really confronting, but my theory is one minute of discomfort in asking can result in a lifetime of having a wonderful testimonial about your business. Here's the text you need to use in your request.

'Hi Paul, I'm trying to build some Facebook reviews and wondered if you'd be happy to write one for me. If so, here's a link to my page ...'

You can do the same for Yelp and other review sites as well.

That small, two-sentence request can generate reviews to you that will live on for the entirety of your business.

One last tip: treat your website as the mothership

Not everyone agrees with this, and it will depend on the type of business you have, but it's wise to treat your website as the 'mothership' and use the other platforms to drive traffic to your site. Yes, social media is super important, but don't overlook your own website in favour of social media. Your website is an asset you own. Other than the hosting or domain company, few can take down your site without your permission. We've all heard the horror stories of Instagram queens having their accounts deleted overnight due to an erroneous posting or inadvertently breaking the rules. *Bam!* The business is gone. You're left with nothing. Spread the risk, look after all your sites and treat your website as the mothership.

Let's recap

Marketing is a blend of art and science and it does take a bit of work to get your head around the best strategies to use. But if you just focus on getting the basics right—creating useful, entertaining content; harnessing the power of social media and influencers; writing keyword-rich headlines; and using basic SEO strategies—your marketing activities will start to pay off.

Takeaways:

- Social influencers are great for small businesses that want to get their word out to the world cost-effectively.
- Headlines are key to getting your copy read, so spend time getting them right. If they're not compelling, no-one will read the rest of your copy.
- Use formulas to help you create headlines more quickly and get better results.
- Start small and don't get overwhelmed with SEO. Do a keyword analysis for just one page and go from there.
- Don't use AdWords unless you know what you're doing. It's a licence to burn money.
- Select your web developer and SEO consultants carefully. It's like a marriage. Easy to get into; harder to get out of.
- Treat your website as the 'mothership' and have all sources of traffic leading back to it.

Coming up ...

You've got your crazy idea, you've built your MVP and you've got your website up and running. You've got the tips and strategies for marketing and you're being found online and getting great results. But what are you doing 'offline' to help your business succeed? What relationships are you building with the media, your strategic alliances, your investors and your staff? What personal qualities, skill sets and stories are needed to inspire others to do business with you? All that and more is coming up.

Motivation

How to pitch, persuade and influence others to do business with you

Dwight D. Eisenhower, the 34th President of the United States said, 'Leadership is the art of getting others to do something you want done because they want to do it.' What he's really talking about is the power of influence, the ability to motivate others to see our point of view and the art of inspiring people to be as excited about our ideas as we are. We all know people who embody these qualities — Richard Branson, Anthony Robbins and Oprah Winfrey come to mind. They earn millions because they inspire others to believe that anything is possible. What a great skill to have. Can it be learnt? It depends. If you call what they have 'charisma' or 'magnetism', then that's pretty hard to replicate. But if you reframe those qualities as being 'influential', then it suddenly becomes a skill that can be learnt.

In the chapters that follow, I'll outline how some of Australia's top entrepreneurs have used their persuasive abilities to land lucrative contracts with broadcasting organisations, gain extensive media coverage, dominate the speaker circuit, snare top staffing talent and attract truckloads of customers.

They do it by firstly being exceedingly savvy about how the media works and how to leverage it to attract favourable media attention. They also do it by carefully cultivating their communication skills and public speaking abilities so that when the media does come calling, or they are invited to speak in front of investors, customers and stakeholders, they are capable of delivering a compelling message that inspires people.

Chapter 19

How to source media coverage for your startup

When it comes to getting media coverage, there are three options open to you:

- *DIY*: you can learn how to 'do it yourself' and take responsibility for writing your own media releases, sending them out and contacting journalists
- *DIFM*: you can hire a publicist to 'do it for me' or hire a talent manager who will find you media opportunities
- *DIY + DIFM*: this blend of both is proving popular for those who don't have the time to do it themselves but don't have the budget to hire a professional.

Let's start with learning how to DIY. For those starting out or on a budget, these tips will be invaluable.

DIY (do-it-yourself) PR

The 24/7 media cycle has created a 'hungry beast' that needs feeding—and that's a great thing for entrepreneurs. Why? Because it means your business has a higher chance of getting media coverage and nothing builds brand and awareness faster than favourable media coverage.

What's more, with dwindling staff numbers at media organisations, journalists are increasingly relying on companies to write their content for them. They don't have the time to work out the story or tease out the angle; they need it done for them. That's good news if you're looking to promote your startup or brand because if you can write a punchy media release you have a higher chance of having your story show up in the paper exactly as you want it to appear.

Creating the right content for media outlets can lead to exposure that's both immediate and immense. But what is the right content, what should you include and where should you send it? In short, where do you begin?

Someone who knows more than most about PR is Jocelyne Simpson, the founder of a do-it-yourself PR service called I Do My Own PR (www.idomyownpr.com). She headed up the PR accounts for some of the world's best-known brands, such as Coca-Cola, Disney, American Express and LEGO. She knows how expensive it can be to hire a publicist. That's why she created a DIY PR kit for entrepreneurs.

I asked Jocelyne for her tips on how to get media coverage.

Jocelyne: Getting your story right is probably the most crucial part of the process. No-one cares that you have a new product or service. They do care, however, about the problem it solves and how it changes people's lives, so straight up you need to focus on this first and your product second. With this in mind, you can start developing your story.

Bernadette: **How do you build a strong story?**

Jocelyne: There's a company called Baxter Blue. They make a fashionable range of glasses that filter out the harmful blue light from digital devices and alleviate the symptoms of digital eyestrain.

Bernadette: **How did they engage with you?**

Jocelyne: They used our DIY PR kit to launch to business media. It's a process anyone can follow. We liken it to baking a cake. Follow the recipe, and you'll get a result.

Bernadette: **What results did they get?**

Jocelyne: Fairfax published the story across its metro newspapers online including *The Age, The Sydney Morning Herald, The Brisbane Times* and others, reaching millions of potential new customers.

Bernadette: What are the ingredients in the cake (see figure 19.1)?

Jocelyne: You need your 'base story'. This is the essence of your product or service and the problem that it solves. This is the reason you launched, it's what gets you out of bed every day, and it's also why and how you started the business. Your personal backstory and the sometimes bumpy road to launch can be an interesting talking point.

Figure 19.1: how to write a media release—it's like baking a cake

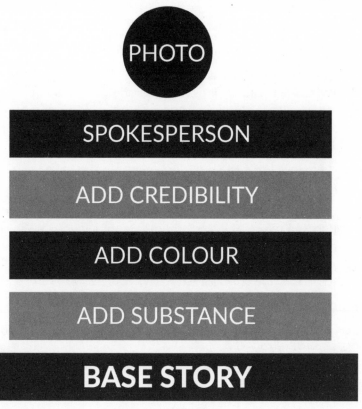

©2017 I Do My Own PR

Bernadette: What's the angle for Baxter Blue?

Jocelyne: The story here is the launch of the glasses; however, the more interesting addition to the story is the issue of digital eyestrain as it potentially affects everyone.

Bernadette: **What's the next ingredient in the cake?**

Jocelyne: Add substance. Research and statistics, make your story believable and help a journalist craft an article rooted in fact rather than just opinion.

Bernadette: **How can you do that?**

Jocelyne: You can reference statistics from existing reports and published studies so long as you credit the source. You can also do your own research and release the findings as part of your story; however, the number of people you survey must be substantial in order for the study to carry any weight — a survey of three people won't work.

Bernadette: **What did Baxter Blue do?**

Jocelyne: They had a wealth of existing stats and data at their fingertips. Scientists, including the World Economic Forum and Harvard Medical School, were investigating the issue and had started releasing their findings, so they had the chance to jump onto this hot topic.

Bernadette: **What's the next ingredient in the cake?**

Jocelyne: You need to add credibility. An expert opinion that is not your own is gold! It gives the journalist an independent person to talk to and makes the story more rounded. If you can save the journalist the job of having to find an independent expert, someone who can talk about the problem you're solving in general, it's another tick on the checklist to getting your story to run.

Bernadette: **Who did Baxter Blue put forward?**

Jocelyne: They put forward Dr Kristy Goodwin, the author of *Raising Your Child in a Digital World*, who recommends Baxter Blue glasses for children with sleep issues.

Bernadette: **How do you get people to care about the topic?**

Jocelyne: You need to add colour. The success of building a strong story is based on making the issue personal to as many people as possible. How do you show people that your product or service will make their lives better, easier, happier, more streamlined? If your statistics and evidence don't already do this, then you can put a spotlight on someone who has experienced the problem. We call this person a case study.

Bernadette: Who did Baxter Blue use?

Jocelyne: The founders used their own experience and talked about how they personally suffered from eyestrain from sitting in front of a computer all day and that's what drove them to create the solution.

Bernadette: How important is it to supply photos and images?

Jocelyne: For print and online publications, the photo that goes with the story is almost as important as the content of the story. This is usually the founders with their product in action, but try to think of how you can make this more interesting than simply two people wearing a branded polo T-shirt.

Bernadette: How did the story run?

Jocelyne: The story ran with the headline, 'Are you in front of a computer all day? Maybe you need glasses'. The piece included the data they provided, their key messaging about digital eye strain and why people should be wearing blue lens glasses to protect their eyes. It also included the founders' backstory, some anecdotes on their journey to launch and it referenced their independent expert.

Bernadette: What happened as a result of the coverage?

Jocelyne: The sales calls started coming in at 5.34 am the morning the story was published; their web traffic went through the roof; it gave them a sales boost and it gave them that all-important credibility they were after. It also helped them to close a deal with an international distributor.

To read the full media release used by Baxter Blue, visit www.bernadetteschwerdt.com.au/book.

DIFM (do-it for-me) PR

Professional publicists can be expensive, but if you need to get serious media coverage quickly and have the budget, they can be worth their weight in gold. Their job is to be constantly on the lookout for opportunities to get you noticed and will manage all aspects of the process for you.

The right media exposure enables entrepreneurs to become superstar personalities virtually overnight. Just look at how the profiles of *Shark Tank* judges Naomi Simson and Janine Allis have soared since the show began; and Mark Bouris experienced that same effect after his stint on *Celebrity Apprentice*. Those media appearances can translate into millions of dollars of free publicity, which of course can translate into sales.

If you want to seriously increase your media profile, getting on TV or radio either as a commentator, panelist, judge or host is one of the fastest ways to do it.

But how do you land a highly sought-after gig in mainstream media? One person who knows more than most about what media executives look for is Karen Eck.

How to get a gig on TV

Karen Eck is the founder of PR agency eckfactor.com and co-founder of talent agency Plus One. She's worked with Oprah Winfrey, Mark Burnett, Cesar Millan and Tony Robbins. She also represents local entrepreneurs and puts them forward for potential media opportunities. When media producers are looking for new on-air business 'talent' they turn to people like Karen for suggestions. Karen is highly selective about who she manages so I asked her what she looks for when taking on entrepreneurs as clients. Here's her list.

- Is the spokesperson 'good talent', or do they have potential to be good with the right media training?
- Do they have an existing profile in the media? Is it positive?
- Do the entrepreneur and their business align with my values?
- Will they be good to deal with?
- What does my gut tell me?

High profile publicists like Karen may not take you on at the start of your entrepreneurial journey but never forget that television networks and media outlets are always on the look out for up and coming talent and you might be just the person they are looking for. Visit their websites to see what casting calls, shows or productions are in development and see if there may be a role for you. You've got to be in to win it!

HOW DO I GET MEDIA MOMENTUM?

If you don't have an existing media profile, here are Karen's suggestions for getting some media momentum.

- *Do a brand stocktake:* Get your house in order with the right branding and PR materials.
- *Create a following:* Start to build your social following and embrace new platforms quickly.
- *Create content:* Post engaging and relevant content to your fans on platforms where they are watching and listening.
- *Don't wait for perfection before starting:* Just do it to the best of your ability and keep moving forward.
- If you're not willing to work hard, forget it.

DIY + DIFM (do-it-yourself + do-it-for-me) PR

As you can see from Jocelyn's tips, trying to get a journalist to cover your story can be hard work. They're busy, hard to get in front of and your story may not be of interest to them. If you think doing it all yourself is just too hard and you can't see it happening, there is one other way of getting noticed. This is the blending of DIY with DIFM that I mentioned earlier. For example, if you'd like help crafting and putting that pitch in front of the right journalists, without the hefty price tag of a publicist, you need to know about people like Nic Hayes.

Connecting the media with entrepreneurs

Nic Hayes runs Media Stable, a platform that connects the media with entrepreneurs and other subject-matter experts. The media is always looking for talent and a new way for content to be delivered to them. Media Stable has filled these gaps. He says:

'One appearance on a morning TV program like *Sunrise* or *Today* can instantly lead to brand and financial success. Many of our experts go on to become regular contributors on radio, television, newspapers and online. This exposure has a direct impact on the number of speaking events they get, the sales they generate or the books they sell.'

Nic's model is subscription-based and an entrepreneur pays a modest yearly fee to be on their books.

So there you have it. You can either source media coverage yourself, you can hire a publicist to do it for you (or engage a talent manager to find you opportunities), or you can use a blend of both models and use a platform such as Media Stable to connect you up with the journalists who matter.

***

Media coverage can be a massive boom to your business, but if the media land on your doorstep, you need to know how to manage them.

That's where being a confident public speaker comes into play.

Chapter 20

How to pitch, present and persuade

Here's a phrase I hear all the time—not: 'I love public speaking'. It will come as no surprise that many of the entrepreneurs I interviewed hate speaking in public.

They loathe it for the same reasons most people do: it's nerve wracking, stressful and all-consuming. Never forget, one wrong move in front of the media can have a negative impact on your reputation and business. If you court the media, you have to be ready for the media.

SPEAK UP! IT'S GOOD FOR BUSINESS

In my personal experience, more women than men shy away from public speaking. This is a mistake. We women need to have our voices heard on stage, on panels and in public. If we give away these opportunities to others, we surrender our power and the potential to influence. If you get the chance to speak in public, take it. Practice makes perfect. Don't wait for the nerves to go away either before you give it a go. They won't. You just learn how to manage them more effectively.

Woe betide any entrepreneur who can't hold their own on stage, at a media conference or at an impromptu door-stop. But that fear of getting it wrong shouldn't stop you from trying to learn how to become a better public speaker.

Jane Lu from Showpo has the right attitude.

> **I hate public speaking. I get so nervous I feel sick. But I do it because I like to overcome my fear. I want to conquer it and not let that fear define me. As an entrepreneur I get asked to speak a lot so I figure I may as well learn how to do it while the stakes are low so that when a big opportunity comes, I am ready for it and I have learnt my lessons.**

Even the most experienced entrepreneurs can put a foot wrong. Elon Musk delivered a presentation at an Adelaide event on SpaceX about how his rocket will be able to reach any destination on earth in under an hour. Whether it was jet lag, nerves, the Adelaide water—who knows—but his performance was hesitant, awkward and disjointed. Here's a word-for-word extract from early in the presentation.

> **...well we we're sort of...searching for the right name, but the code name at least is BFR*.**

It gets better:

> **Um...and...I...the...probably the most important thing that I want to convey in, uh, in this presentation is that I think we have figured out how to pay for it.**

*Big F***ing Rocket—his words not mine.

The stammering delivery got noticed, and not in a good way. These were some of the media headlines:

- 'Was Elon Musk's weird SpaceX presentation the mark of an awkward genius?'[1]
- 'Elon Musk Fails Public Speaking 101.'[2]

Interestingly, his speech also endeared him to many. Here's what a few tweets said:

- 'Anyone else wanna just give Elon a big hug?'
- 'He seems so proud that he's about to burst into tears.'
- 'He's completely authentic.'

Being off kilter and stammering may work for Elon. He's got a few wins on the board, which allows him to be eccentric. For startup entrepreneurs trying to get investors on board or attract world-class talent, that hesitancy may not be as endearing. Clearly Elon speaks in public because he has to, not because he wants to. Why else would someone who is so clearly uncomfortable on the stage do it? But he knows what all successful entrepreneurs know: being a competent public speaker is an essential component in the marketing toolkit of a world-class entrepreneur.

Why being a good public speaker is good for business

For sheer efficiency, nothing beats public speaking for getting the word out about your business. What's a better use of your time? A one-to-one meeting for one hour with 50 different people, or delivering a one-hour keynote to a group of 50 people?

Public speaking is not just about efficiency either. It's about credibility building. If you're delivering an opening keynote at an industry conference, by morning tea time, you'll be known to all and sundry. You won't need to introduce yourself or hand out business cards; people will be thrusting their business cards at you, hoping to get your attention, wanting to 'have a quick word'. If you do a good job on stage, you'll be a minor celebrity off stage and that exposure will kick-start a series of business relationships that simply couldn't have happened without that keynote opportunity.

QUICK TIP

The best way to get in the 'speaking' door is usually by securing panel spots during breakout sessions at various conferences.

Someone who knows a lot about putting business speakers on the stage is Phil Leahy (www.retailglobal.com.au). He heads up a global retail conference company that regularly engages world-class entrepreneurs to be his keynote speakers. Here's what he looks for when booking his speakers:

The speaker needs to have a proven track record in the subject matter and the ability to deliver a clear and concise message so the audience can benefit from the advice with great take-aways.

The keynote stage is reserved for those who have successfully graduated from panels and breakout presentations.

My advice for those wanting to speak would be to seek professional guidance by attending speaker training classes to refine your delivery. Attend speaker nights and learn from others. Join relevant meetups in your local area. Contribute to industry blogs and build a following, and most importantly, attend the conferences you hope to speak at in the future.

How a lack of preparation can cost you

Elon Musk can get away with having a bad day on stage. Most can't. I once saw a high-profile fashion entrepreneur being interviewed by a journalist at an investor briefing. For the purposes of this case study, I'll call the entrepreneur 'Shannon' to protect her privacy. There were more than 1000 people present at the briefing and they were hungry to hear why their investment in her company had taken a nosedive. Here's what happened.

What not to do when being grilled by a journalist

Unfortunately for Shannon, an unflattering story concerning the financials at her company was released on the morning of the briefing. The journalist's first question was, 'Are you bankrupt?'

He proceeded to grill her relentlessly on what the true financial state of her company was, inferring the investors should be getting out of her business. This briefing was her perfect opportunity to set the record straight and reassure investors all was on track. For some reason — either through fear, or lack of preparation — she was unable to rebuff any of the questions or even provide her side of the story. She allowed the journalist to take control of the conversation, was reactive in her answers and failed to reassure her investors that all was on track. To cap it off, she was sweating heavily and her face, beamed onto a big screen behind her, showed every bead of it.

The upshot? Investors came away from that session wondering if this was the right company to be investing in and indeed, if this was the woman they wanted in charge of their investment.

That's a media event she would rather forget.

Do I have sympathy for Shannon? Of course. Was she jet-lagged from a punishing long-haul trip from the United Kingdom? Probably. Could she have done more to reassure investors? Yes.

Any public speaker of any note has been in hot water on stage. To be fair, I've never been grilled as ferociously as she was, but I've certainly had my fair share of on-stage calamities. I'll tell you more about those a bit later on.

So how could Shannon have handled that grilling more effectively?

Quite simply, she could have predicted what the questions were going to be and prepared her responses accordingly. That's where the Preparation Pyramid will come in handy.

Chapter 21

How to prepare a great presentation

A one-to-one meeting with a serious investor can be every bit as nerve wracking as delivering a TED talk beamed live to millions. It's not the number of people at the presentation that makes it nerve wracking; it's about what's at stake, and sometimes the stakes are high and all that's standing between you and catastrophic failure is your ability to influence.

If you've read Richard Branson's autobiography *Losing My Virginity*, you'll recall a story he tells about the early days of his business. He owed a lot of people a lot of money and Mike Oldfield, the singer, was due to be paid his royalty for his smash hit, *Tubular Bells*. But Branson didn't have the money and knew that if Oldfield called in the payment, he would go broke. That phone call asking Oldfield to hold off was perhaps the most important phone call of Branson's life and he needed to summon every ounce of persuasion to convince Oldfield to concede. Branson did convince him to hold off, and the rest, as they say, is history.

It's moments like these where you wish you had a fool-proof system for creating a persuasive pitch. That's what the Preparation Pyramid is for.

Welcome to the Preparation Pyramid, the fast-track solution to creating presentations that rock.

The Preparation Pyramid: A 3-step formula for pitching and persuading

Just as hope is not a marketing strategy, 'winging it' is not a presentation skills strategy. I've rarely heard someone say after a presentation, 'You know, that lack of preparation really paid off.'

The formula I'll share with you here works for anyone for any topic, be it a wedding speech, a sales call or an investor pitch. It's called the Preparation Pyramid.

A presentation is like an iceberg. The audience only see what's 'above the water line' — the speech that gets seen on stage. But what supports the speech and makes it solid is the mass of ice (your preparation) that underpins it. The success or otherwise of a presentation always relates to how much preparation a speaker puts in. See figure 21.1 for a visual representation of the three core elements that make up the Preparation Pyramid.

Figure 21.1: the preparation pyramid

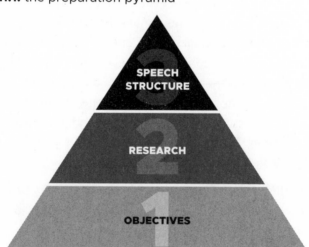

The first plank in the pyramid is the objectives.

1. Objectives

Before you write one word of your presentation, you must ask yourself two key questions: why are you presenting and what do you want to achieve? These questions are the foundation of any presentation and must be answered if the presentation has any hope of being a success.

There are two types of objectives to consider:

1. factual objectives
2. emotional objectives.

Factual objectives

What do you *physically* want your audience *to do* as a result of your presentation? It's vital you get clarity on this because once you establish it, the rest of the presentation will expand on why they need to take this action.

You'd be amazed at how few people actually think about this before they head into a meeting, which is why we often sit in presentations scratching our heads saying to no-one in particular, 'Why am I here?'

Your objective could be to get the audience to do any one of the following:

- buy your product
- book a meeting with you
- trial your service
- endorse your process
- implement an idea.

Notice each objective starts with a verb. That's a 'doing' word, in case you were wondering.

Using Shannon's media interview from chapter 20 as the real-world material for this exercise, here's what her factual objective could have been: *After this event, I want the audience to hold onto their shares in my company (and not sell them).*

Emotional objectives

Once you've got the factual objectives sorted out, you'll need to work out what your 'emotional' objectives are. In other words, what do you want your audience to *feel* after your presentation?

Do you want them to feel:

- calm
- delighted
- enthusiastic
- motivated
- shocked?

It stands to reason that if you want them to *feel* 'excited' then you, as a presenter, must *be* exciting. If you want them to *feel* 'shocked' then you, as a presenter, must *be*, *do* or *say* something shocking. So, whatever you want your audience to feel, you as the presenter must *be* that first.

For Shannon, knowing she was about to be grilled on that damning newspaper article, her emotional objectives could have been to:

- *soothe* their concerns about the newspaper article
- *inspire* them to hang in for the longer term
- *excite* them about her future plans.

YOU NEED TO BE BIGGER THAN YOU ARE

There's a big difference between sitting in a chair in an auditorium (that's called being a normal person) and stepping two metres onto the stage (that's called being a presenter). Suddenly you're in the hotspot and if you want to 'own' the stage, you will need to take on the persona of a much bigger version of you.

This requires you to put in a lot more energy and effort. Actors call it their 'performance energy'; your voice needs to be bigger; your gestures need to be bigger, your stance and body language need to be bigger.

2. Research

The second layer of the Preparation Pyramid is research. Most executives I've trained are very upfront about this stage of the process and declare indignantly, 'I don't have time to spend on this! I've got other more important things to do!' That's all well and good but when you're on stage, in front of 500 people at the annual company conference, you may wish you'd put in a bit more time and effort. It reminds me of a doctor who lectures on the importance of exercise in warding off illness: 'If you don't have time for health, you'll have to make time for sickness.'

From a presentation point of view, if you don't make time for research, you'll need to make time for failure.

Before you speak, you need to walk a mile in the shoes of your audience and really imagine what it's like for them to be hearing you speak.

Here are a few questions you need to ask before you start writing your presentation:

- Who is in the audience, and what are their job titles or roles?
- How many people will be there and do they know each other already? Do they like each other or is there rivalry and/or animosity?
- What do they already know about this topic?
- What are their feelings about your topic and how much of it would they agree/disagree with?
- Why would they believe what you have to say?
- Why wouldn't they believe you?
- What unspoken questions would they have about your topic that you should address?

… and there would be many more questions to consider.

If you are to deliver a thought-provoking, impactful presentation, you must know everything you can about your audience.

Shannon, our entrepreneur mentioned earlier—knowing she was about to be grilled on that damning article—should have known her audience would have had questions such as:

- Why has the company performance been lacklustre?
- What is she going to do about it?
- Was the newspaper report accurate or did it leave out important facts?
- What are her future plans that will turn the balance sheet around?

Knowing what your audience is thinking and feeling will help you create the right content for your speech and identify the right stories to tell.

What business stories should you tell?

Let's talk about Kevin.

Kevin is a successful startup entrepreneur. He's been asked to give a keynote speech at a university graduation event. He loves these jobs because they supplement his startup income, which is pretty patchy. He's been booked for four consecutive events — 'rinse and repeat' as they're known in the business. The first event takes place. Kevin thinks it has gone well. The university begs to differ. They ring the speaker bureau and complain that Kevin 'has missed the mark; he's not connecting with the audience'. I was asked to help coach him on how to revise his presentation.

I spoke with Kevin and asked him that first basic question: who's in the audience?

'I'm not sure,' he said.

I asked, 'Is it just students from the university? Their parents? Future employers? And if it's all three, who is the main focus?' Kevin didn't know who was in the audience. He hadn't taken the time to find out. If he had known, he would have known what stories to tell. That's why he missed the mark: the stories he used didn't connect.

For example, if the primary focus is on the:

- *students*: Then the keynote stories should be around 'Congratulations *students*! You've got through, you're on your way, you've got an exciting future ahead of you and here's some tips I can share from my own journey that will help you succeed'

(continued)

215

What business stories should you tell? (*cont'd*)

- *parents*: Then the stories should be around 'Congratulations *parents*! Your child is on their way! Well done on shepherding them through this time in their lives and here's some ways you can help your children get graduate jobs...'

- *employers:* Then the stories should be around 'Congratulations *employers*! You are in the presence of the next generation of leaders. You have access to the smartest, most innovative talent in the country and here's why these young people should be considered as future employees...'

Three different audiences require three different story approaches and if you have to accommodate all three, you tell stories for each. Kevin failed to ask this simple question — Who's in the audience? — and that tripped him up and caused him to lose the trust of his client.

Moral of the story: Know your audience.

Check the weather app

This story is about Ted and the sweat marks — and no, that's not a band from the 60s. Ted is a man I worked with in my advertising agency days. I've never forgotten him. After this story, you won't either.

The scenario:

Month: February

Time: 2 pm

Location: Miller St, North Sydney, Australia

Scene: Advertising agency boardroom

Present:
- Ted, the advertising agency boss
- me, the account director
- five other agency staff (copywriters, art director, and so on)
- the prospective client and three of their team.

Purpose of meeting:

We're pitching for a new account. It's in the fast-food industry and a multimillion-dollar piece of business. We've been working on the pitch for months. Today's the big day.

Background:

It is a hot, muggy day. As on all pitch days, we have been frantically pulling the pieces together. We are frazzled and tetchy.

The client arrives. Pleasantries are exchanged. 'Nice to see you', 'We're really looking forward to working with you', and other little white lies like that. Ted stands up to speak. With a theatrical Houdini-esque flourish, he takes off his linen jacket to signal 'we mean business'. As he throws down his jacket, the clients gasp.

Ted is hot. Not as in the good-looking, 'phwaaaaah' sense, but in the over-heated sense. We know this because under Ted's arms are sweat marks the size of dinner plates; and on his baby-blue coloured shirt, the sweat stains are impossible to miss.

We lost the pitch. Was it because of Ted and his big, blue sweat stains, or was it something else? We'll never know, but what I do know is, check the weather app before you get dressed for a big presentation.

Moral of the story: Do your research and prepare for all contingencies.

3. Speech structure

Let's recap. You know the objectives of your presentation. You've done your research. Now you need to start writing the actual content.

So, where do you start? I've developed a 5-step speech-structure template (see table 21.1) that I use to fast-track the creation of my speech content. I highly encourage you to use this template because it will cut hours off your preparation phase and give you a solid foundation to follow every time.

Table 21.1: the structure of a presentation (duration: 30 minutes)

Step	Content	Timing
1	**Opening statement**	**2 minutes**
2	**Factual objective**	**2 minutes**
3	**Content** Feature/Benefit Feature/Benefit Feature/Benefit Feature/Benefit	**22 minutes**
4	**Summary**	**2 minutes**
5	**Conclusion + call back**	**2 minutes**

1. Opening statement

The first step in building a presentation is to create an 'opening statement'. For a 30-minute speech, this should not run for more than one or two minutes maximum.

The opening statement needs to be three things:

1. *succinct*—short, sharp and punchy
2. *focused and relevant to the audience*—it must connect to why the audience is there
3. *memorised*—you should know this opening word for word.

There are lots of ways to open a presentation, but the main focus should be to get people's attention. You can get their attention with:

- props
- statistics
- launch statements.

Props

Props can be a whiteboard, a flip chart, product samples or anything tangible that people can see and feel. For example, it could be:

- *a book*: I once saw a CEO use the popular book *The Decision Book* as a prop to open his presentation. He used it to focus the conversation on the decisions that were being made by his company. He held the book aloft in his hand as he spoke. This is what he said: 'I read this book over the weekend and it struck me that we as an organisation are making some poor decisions about the way we invest our money and time. This is costing us and it has to change. I have photocopied a few pages from the book for you to read and I want you to come back to me by next Monday with three ways in which we can improve our decision-making processes.'

  Result? He got the attention of his team instantly, they knew what the topic was and they knew how it related to them. Using props like this catches the eye and provides a point of focus for the audience.

- *a bell*: a real-estate auctioneer I know uses a big, brass bell to fire up the auction crowd before he starts the bidding.

  Result? This real-estate agent has become known for this bell and he uses it in his marketing collateral as a branding device. It gets people's attention very quickly. Simple but effective.

I've seen all sorts of items used as props: tennis balls, yoyos, food, hats, whips. Remember when Pauline Hanson wore a burqa to Parliament? That's a provocative prop and boy, did that get attention.

Statistics

Statistics can be used to create an effective opening. You can find a statistic to support most points of view and they help persuade audience members who value facts above emotion.

Here's how a police spokesperson on road traffic accidents used statistics to create shock and awe in his audience of 500 noisy teenagers.

I'd like you to look at the person next to you. And then I'd like you to look at the person on the other side of you. Take a good look at them because, statistically speaking, in three years' time one of you will be dead from a road accident. I'm from the road traffic authority and I'm here today to talk to you about how wearing a seat belt can reduce the likelihood of you or a friend dying in a car accident.

You could have heard a pin drop.

---

3 QUESTIONS A PUBLIC SPEAKER SHOULD *NEVER* USE TO OPEN A PRESENTATION

1. How do I turn this microphone on?

2. Is it on?

3. Can everyone hear me?

Launch statements

Aside from these little 'stunts' and props, you can use pre-written phrases as powerful attention-grabbers.

One of my skill sets is copywriting. My job is to use the written word to grab people's attention. Now, I could wait for inspiration to hit me and then write, but if I'm on a deadline I need to use tried and tested openings that are guaranteed to work. That's why I use these launch statements. Launch statements are used by most professional copywriters to write captivating headlines for advertisements but they can also be used to kick-start verbal presentations. I highly recommend you use some of them to start your speeches. Here's four of the best.

1. It's no secret that...
2. Believe it or not...
3. The results are in...
4. If you're like most people, you probably...

Here's how Shannon could have used these launch statements at her panel session to get her out of hot water.

Let's assume that Shannon's Factual Objective is to convince investors to hold onto their shares. To 'kick-start' her opening statement, she could use any one of these four launch statements. Let's also assume her emotional objective is to 'reassure' her audience that all is on track and that she can be trusted:

Interviewer: So, Shannon, are you bankrupt?

1. *'It's no secret that...*all startups are under pressure right now. The dollar has fallen sharply and investor confidence has taken a hit since the election.'
2. *'Believe it or not...*you can't believe everything you read in the newspaper.' [Add a smile and a twinkly laugh—never let on how nervous you are.]
3. *'The results are in...*and I agree, they're not looking good.'
4. *'If you're like most people...*you probably check how your investments are performing on a weekly or even daily basis.'

Each one of those kicks off the conversation with a strong start that puts her in the box seat. She has:

- acknowledged the issue
- stated a truism that no-one can dispute (this builds rapport with her investors)
- connected her topic to her audience.

These launch statements let her steer the conversation to suit her needs and focus on topics that suit her, not the journalist, giving her control over the conversation, and a platform to establish her Factual Objective. She can now elaborate on what she plans to do to with the company:

1. *It's no secret that...* all startups are under pressure right now. The dollar has fallen sharply and investor confidence has taken a hit since the election. (*To 'convince them' she now adds:* 'That has hurt us in the short term but we have plans in place to counteract the fall of the dollar and restore our share price to its previously high level. I'll share with you the top three things we're doing right now that will achieve that.')

2. *Believe it or not...* you can't believe everything you read in the newspaper. [Add a smile and a twinkly laugh.] (*To 'convince them' she now adds:* 'What the article didn't say was that we just built a new factory in China, which slashed our profit for this year, and that will set us up for massive growth over the next five years.')

3. *The results are in...* and I agree, they're not looking good. (*To 'convince them' she now adds:* 'As a result, we have restructured the team, cut costs, refinanced our debt and really pulled in our belts. This has enabled us to get back to what we do best and we feel confident our best days are ahead of us.')

4. *If you're like most people...* you probably check how your investments are performing on a weekly or even daily basis. (*To 'convince them' she now adds:* 'What's important to remember is that the share price changes on a daily basis and that it should never be judged or seen in isolation in a snapshot moment.')

What Shannon has done here is address the issue (the share price has plunged) and then got back on track by focusing on the topics that strengthen her position. She has taken back control over the conversation and given the investors confidence that she knows what she's doing and that they can have faith in her.

She could choose any one of these launch statements to start her presentation. Now let's move onto Step 2. This is where you introduce the Factual Objective for your speech, that is, you tell your audience what you want them to do.

2. Factual objective

This is the factual objective that you decided on earlier in your planning process. For Shannon, her Factual Objective is to 'convince' the investors to hold on to their shares, so everything she says throughout the speech must give them reasons why they should do so.

3. Content: Features and benefits

We're at the point where we create content for the rest of the presentation. This will make up the bulk of the presentation. For example, if your speech runs for 30 minutes, this section would run for about 22 minutes. This helps you work out how much content you need to create. Everything that gets mentioned here must support your Factual Objective. Let's recap.

You know your factual objective.

You've got your opening statement and you've used a prop or a launch statement to kick-start the presentation with a bang.

This is where you bring out your big guns: the reasons why people should do business with you; why they should agree to follow your factual objective.

This is where you detail the features and benefits of your product. All good marketers know that features and benefits are the essential building blocks of any piece of marketing collateral, be it a website, a flier, or an email newsletter, and your presentation is no different.

When you are presenting to an audience there are two questions that are going through their minds:

1. So what?
2. Who cares?

It sounds harsh, but it's the truth. Most people sitting in your session are running the 'so-what-who-cares' filter over everything you say to assess what's in it for them.

'So what … that you've been in business since 1929.'

'So what … that you have the largest widget in the Southern Hemisphere.'

'Who cares … that you won an Entrepreneur of the Year award.'

'Who cares … that you have 1000 staff in 100 countries and that you turn over 100 billion dollars.'

All the audience is thinking about is, 'What's in it for me?' So we need to tell them what's in it for them.

As presenters, we need to work hard to get their attention. We need to sell the sizzle, not the sausage, so to speak.

Take this quiz (see figure 21.2).

Can you guess what product this is?

Figure 21.2: list of terms

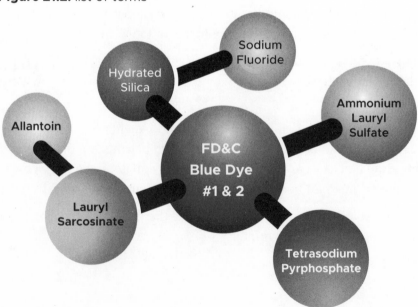

Answer: toothpaste.

Here's the thing. Do you ever see these ingredients featured in the advertising for toothpaste? No, of course not. If they were, we'd never buy it again. After all, what sane person would put those toxic chemicals in their mouth? That's why they don't promote the features. What they do promote are the benefits made possible by those chemicals. Benefits such as:

- fresh breath
- a healthy, radiant smile
- confidence and sex appeal.

Moral of the story: Sell the benefits, not the features.

What's in it for me?

I'm a signage junkie. I read every billboard, bus sign and instruction notice that comes into view. Weird, I know, but to me signage is like the haiku of advertising; the essence of a story condensed into just a few lines.

Most signage is written without thinking through why the reader would be inclined to comply, which is why most people ignore signs like 'No exit' or 'Wet paint'. Here's an example of a poorly-written sign, and of a revised version showing how they could have written it better. If we want to persuade people to do something, we need to tell them 'what's in it for them.'

Give people a reason to do something

I used to live in an apartment in North Melbourne. I was working at Melbourne University so I rode my bike to work most days.

Upon my return to my apartment, I'd park my bike in the foyer and lock it to the stair rail. Within a week or so, other people started doing the same thing and before long, the foyer looked like a bike shop. The body corporate sprang into action. The first sign appeared:

(continued)

225

Give people a reason to do something (*cont'd*)

Don't leave your bike in the foyer.

The bikes remained where they were. The sign had minimal impact. It didn't really give a good reason why anyone should change their behaviour and so people just ignored it.

A new sign appeared:

PLEASE don't leave your bike in the foyer. THANKYOU.

...as if some upper cases and a few courteous pleasantries could induce a change of behaviour.

It didn't work. The bikes remained. A new sign appeared:

Please don't leave your bike in the foyer. Three bikes were stolen from here last night. Lock it in the bike cage to prevent theft.

Boom! Those bikes vanished quicker than a toupee in a hurricane.

But one bike remained: a rusty, crumpled old bike that had seen better days. Clearly the owner had bought their bike from Crime Converters...I mean, Cash Converters. They'd rather take the risk of it being stolen than put in the effort to lug it down to the bike cage.

So what sort of reason would have to be given to inspire this recalcitrant resident to change their behaviour?

A new sign appeared:

Please don't leave your bike in the foyer. If someone trips over it and hurts themselves you could be sued. It's happened before. Store it in the bike cage. Thank you.

And just like that, the bike disappeared. The recalcitrant resident may or may not have been me. I'll plead the fifth on that one.

The moral of the story? Give people a reason to do something; tell them what's in it for them and you'll get compliance from even the most hard-hearted, sociopathic narcissists.

4. Summary

This bit is easy. The summary sums up all the points you've just made. Don't be afraid to repeat the key ideas in your summary. Remember, you've heard these ideas before, but your audience hasn't so you won't be boring them by repeating the key points.

It can be as simple as saying, 'In summary ...' and then repeating the main points again without the detail.

5. Conclusion + call back

The conclusion reiterates the factual objective and brings the speech to an end. If you can manage it, try to reference your opening statement so that you give the audience a satisfying conclusion.

Let's hook back in with Shannon, our entrepreneur, to see how she could have concluded her conversation.

Conclusion:

'In conclusion, I encourage you to hold onto your shares and have faith in the company and in me. This newspaper report is just a blip on the radar and we have plans in place to take the company to the next level.'

...+ call back (to reference the newspaper article that the journalist mentioned at the start):

'There will always be newspaper articles offering financial 'snapshots' of startups like mine. It's just that: a snapshot. I'm glad I had the chance today to give you the full facts.'

Postscript

So there you have it. The 5-step speech structure for creating content for a presentation. It takes practice but once you use the template a few times, I guarantee that you'll find it really helpful and you'll use it as your go-to structure for all future presentations.

Okay, I promised I would share a public-speaking clanger I've made.

What not to say...

I was facilitating a panel in Adelaide, South Australia for an event on disruptive entrepreneurship. There were some heavy hitters in the room including the heads of Uber and Vinomofo, government head honchos and the like.

After the panel was over, we gave the audience a chance to ask questions. The auditorium was dark, so it was hard to make out individuals in the audience. I saw a man's hand go up at the back of the room. Wanting to offer him the opportunity to promote his business, I said, 'Sir, could you please stand up and tell us where you're from?'

An eerie hush fell over the room. Out of the silence, a lady's voice rang out from the back of the room.

'He's in a wheelchair.'

Yep. True story. No amount of rehearsal could have prevented that embarrassing situation from occurring. But one thing I definitely won't do in future is ask audience members to stand up.

Being a confident public speaker is about commanding attention and motivating people to see your point of view. But how do you cut through the clutter and get your message through? How do you connect when everyone is so busy? That's where great storytelling comes in. If you'd like to learn how to create stories that people remember, the next chapter is for you.

Chapter 22

The art and science of business storytelling

In today's busy world it's said we're exposed to more than 3000 messages daily—emails, billboards, radio, Google advertisements, street signage, parking signs, brochures. We're bombarded with stimulus.

As a result of this 'white noise', our brain is overwhelmed and has to determine what to pay attention to and what to ignore. Sadly, most of what it ignores is the carefully crafted, meticulously thought-out advertising messages I showed you how to create earlier. Sad but true. The good news is, there's a way to cut through the clutter. We do it by telling 'stories'. Stories help us get our message out to the world. This chapter will help you identify the right story to tell, provide you with a template to craft a story that connects with your audience on an emotional level, and show you how to link the story to your business objectives.

So, what's your story?

As an entrepreneur, you will often be called upon to 'tell your story'. Investors will want to know how and why you got started; award judges will ask about your entrepreneurial 'backstory'; the media will almost certainly want to know your 'hard luck' story and how you overcame those challenges to succeed; family and friends will want to know why you've given up your plum job at the bank to give this 'thing' (also known as 'your business') a go.

All the top entrepreneurs understand the power of a well-told story and work hard at crafting a story that will help them achieve their business objectives. What many may not know, however, is that there is an art to telling a good story—and it all begins with following a prescribed structure.

Without this storytelling structure, the stories most people tell aren't stories; they're just boring facts delivered with passion.

Wouldn't it be good to know what this structure is so that when you have to tell a story, you can use this 'scaffolding' to turn boring facts into compelling stories? That's what this chapter is all about.

To get started, let me tell you a story that demonstrates how this structure works. This is a true story that happened to me. Read it carefully as I'll pose some questions at the end to see how much you remember. I'll then reveal the structure that underpins that story.

Once upon a time ...

Ladies and gentlemen, this is the story of the Christmas Day Fire. I'm telling you this because it could save the life of you and your family.

Here's what happened.

It's 11:30 am Christmas Day. I'm in my home in Melbourne. I'm cooking lunch for my family. There's 18 people on the backyard deck, drinking champagne and eating nibbles.

I'm in the kitchen cooking the lunch. I'm preparing the roast potatoes. I like my potatoes really crispy so here's how I cook them. First up, I parboil them in the microwave for five minutes, I drain them, pat them dry and then I place them in a big fry pan filled with hot oil. The oil is really hot, smoking hot. As I put the potatoes in the pan, the water on the potatoes hits the oil, and it creates a spot flame. On most occasions, that flame flares up really quickly and then it fades out.

On this day, however, maybe because the oil was so hot, the flame doesn't calm down. In fact, the flame gets bigger, and bigger, and bigger. It gets so big the flame licks the top of the rangehood. Within seconds, the rangehood catches fire. From there, the fire spreads rapidly. The timber cupboard on the right of the stove catches fire; the timber cupboard to the left catches fire. I panic. The fire's getting bigger.

I grab the tea towel and start to whip the flames, hopelessly outgunned by the fierce flames that have taken over. I step back and realise with horror that my kitchen is on fire and there's nothing I can do about it.

I can't move. I can barely speak. All I can do is muster a croaky cry for help: 'Fire! Fire!'

Phil, my husband, runs in, miraculously knows somehow that we have a fire extinguisher in the pantry, grabs it, unclips the lid, sprays the entire wall with the white foam and extinguishes the fire. We stagger back against the opposite wall, survey the destruction in front of us and breathe a sigh of relief. The fire is out. The house, and our lives, have been saved.

I look at my husband and say, 'Thank goodness we had a fire extinguisher…and thank goodness you knew how to use it. I didn't even know we had one!'

The moral of the story, dear reader, is this: every household needs a working fire extinguisher and everyone in the family needs to know where it's located and how to use it.

So please, check that you have a fire extinguisher, and that you know how to use it.

It could save your life and that of your family.

That's the end of the story. Now if I were to quiz you on that story, how much of it would you remember?

- What day is it?
- What suburb are we in?
- How many people are on the deck?
- What are we drinking?
- What am I cooking in the kitchen?
- What's my husband's name?
- What is the moral of the story?

How much do you recall? A little or a lot? When I tell this story at my workshops, it's remarkable how many facts and details people remember.

They remember everything: the time of day, my husband's name, how I like the potatoes cooked, what caught fire and in what order, and so on. Perhaps most importantly, they remember the moral of the story, which is ... 'check you have a fire extinguisher and that you know how to use it'.

If I was trying to convince you to take fire safety more seriously but just told you to 'check you have a fire extinguisher' — without the dramatic story to reinforce the point — how compelling or memorable would that request be? Chances are, that request would be like 'white noise' to you — it would go in one ear and out the other and be instantly forgotten. It's just a dry, boring, unremarkable request. But if I take that same request — 'check if you have a fire extinguisher' — and tell you a memorable story to convey the importance of it, you're more likely to act on it.

Facts tell, stories sell

Good storytellers wrap their 'moral' or 'instruction' in a juicy, emotionally engaging story. The story enables people to see the situation — to imagine themselves in the scenario and to reflect on what they would do in the same circumstances. They connect with the story, and by extension, they remember the moral of the story too. Stories help people remember—remember your instructions, remember your business, remember *you*. That's why we tell stories.

How to structure a powerful story

There's an art to telling a good story, and underpinning that art is a storytelling template known as 'The Hero's Journey'. Here's a quick overview of how that template came to be and the backstory of the person who created it.

Joseph Campbell, an American psychologist and mythologist was interested in understanding why some stories and myths were passed down through the ages, and why other stories fell by the wayside. Why did some stories thrive, while other stories died? Campbell made it his life's work to study all the myths, fables, folklore and fairytales to see if there was a pattern or system that all the successful stories followed.

He found a pattern and was so enamoured with it, he gave it a name: 'The Hero's Journey'. This 'journey' describes the 12 'plot points' by which the protagonist (the main character) moves through their fictional world.

That research formed the basis of his famous book, *The Hero with a Thousand Faces*. It's still in print and very popular. It was made even more popular when movie-makers George Lucas and Steven Spielberg decided to use 'The Hero's Journey' as the basis for their movie scripts. They used the process to write blockbuster movies such as *Jaws, Raiders of the Lost Ark, ET* and *Star Wars*—all of which follow 'The Hero's Journey' to the letter. (You'll find films such as *Black Swan, Lord of the Rings, Harry Potter* and almost every Pixar film follow the same pattern.)

We too can use that same process to help us tell memorable business stories that cut through the clutter. I've condensed the 12-step process into six steps to make it easier to use. This process will enable you to craft compelling stories that will have your audiences, hopefully, eating out of your hand—or at least not fleeing the room crying for mercy from the bone-crushing boredom you're inflicting on them.

Before I launch into the storytelling template, we need to cover off one more important storytelling element and that's the 'moral of the story'.

And the moral of the story is...?

Remember how most fairytales finish? 'And the moral of the story is…' They then offer a salutary life lesson that our parents hoped would keep us on the straight and narrow: 'Be good to others'; 'Don't steal'; 'Don't talk to strangers'.

Every story—be it a fairytale or a business story—needs a moral. The moral of the story you choose for your presentation should be connected to the factual objective of your presentation, as we saw earlier. You'll see how the 'moral of the story' fits in a bit later.

The 6-step storytelling process

As you can see in figure 22.1, the six-step story structure consists of:

1. **C**ontext
2. **C**hallenge/hindrance
3. **A**ction
4. **R**esult
5. **L**esson
6. **S**uggested actions.

To demonstrate how the process works, I'll overlay the six-step structure on the Christmas Day fire story I told earlier.

Figure 22.1: the CCARLS storytelling process

1. Context

Context sets the scene so we know what 'world' we are in. For example, are we in suburban Melbourne in the modern era, are we in New York in war time or are we in a dystopian ghetto in 2050? Times, dates, numbers and locations are needed to paint the picture clearly.

It's *Christmas Day.* I am at home in *Melbourne,* cooking in the kitchen. My family (*18 of them*) are on the *deck, drinking champagne and eating nibbles.* (Notice how I have used details to paint the picture—this helps set the scene.)

2. Challenge/hindrance

What goes wrong? What prevents the main character (the 'hero') from going about their daily life? What causes the upset?

The potatoes in the frying pan catch fire. The cupboards next to the rangehood catch fire. I can't put the fire out. The house is in danger of being burned down. Disaster is upon us.

3. Action

What happens as a result of the challenge?

I call out to my husband: 'Fire!' He rushes to the pantry, picks up the fire extinguisher and sprays the fire with the foam. The fire is extinguished.

4. Results

What happens as a result of the action? What disaster is averted? How do their lives change?

Through Phil's actions, he saves the house from burning down and saves the lives of his family. Life returns to normal, but we are better for the experience and have learned something new.

5. Lesson

What can we learn from this story? What is the 'moral of the story'?

Always have a fire extinguisher in the house and know how to use it! (And don't get me to cook Christmas lunch. I told you on page one I didn't like cooking!)

6. Suggested actions

What actions should others take as a result of hearing this story?

Go home and check whether you have a fire extinguisher and test it to make sure you know how to use it.

How long should a story run for?

A story can last for 30 seconds or, if you're Martin Scorsese, it can last for three hours. The structure works irrespective of how long the story is.

Who should the story be about?

Here's another quiz.

If you were the sub-editor of a tabloid newspaper, and you had to choose between these two headlines, which would attract more attention?

- *3000 people under 30 died last year in road accidents in Queensland*

or

- *29-year-old mother-of-two dies in Toowoomba car crash*

Any editor worth their salt would choose option B. Why? Because that headline is more evocative and emotional, but more importantly because it focuses on the 'one' versus 'the many'. It's a little-known fact that we are more likely to connect emotionally with stories about one person than we are with stories about 3000 people.

Let's deconstruct it to find out exactly why this principle of the 'one versus the many' works.

The first headline was about '3000 people' who died: 3000 anonymous, faceless people.

The second was about one person, a '29-year-old mother-of-two'. Mmm. That image sparks a memory, a thought: 'How tragic. A mother of two. How awful. How sad for her family ... Hey, I know a 29-year-old mother of two in Toowoomba. Jane just moved up there. It couldn't be her could it? Gosh, I'd better call her to see if she's okay.' Suddenly, you're involved; you can picture real people, real situations — in other words, you care.

Newspaper editors know the power of an image to tell a story. Do you recall the heart-rending images in our newspapers of Syrian refugees fleeing their country—thousands of people walking on the road with nothing to their name but the clothes on their backs?

As distressing as those images were, did those images change public opinion or government policy on immigration? For the most part, no, they did not.

Now, fast forward to the tragic image of Alan Kurdi, a three-year old Syrian toddler, whose lifeless body, found washed up on a deserted beach, was cradled in the arms of a distressed Turkish paramilitary police officer. That picture became a symbol of the Syrian refugee crisis; that picture did change public opinion and it changed government policy too. In fact, based on that one image Germany's Chancellor, Angela Merkel, amended their refugee policy to allow an unprecedented one million immigrants into the country. What was the difference between the two images? One was of thousands of faceless, anonymous people. One was of a small, lifeless boy. The one versus the many.

Stories about the 'one' will always be more memorable than stories about the 'many'. When it comes to telling your business stories, choose ones that reflect one person's story, not those of a team or of the company.

What's the 'moral' of your story?

What story you should tell depends on what your factual objective is (we discussed that earlier in the section on the Preparation Pyramid). From there you can work out the moral of the story and therefore the right stories to tell.

This is why the research you do at the start of your preparation is so important. It dictates everything that comes next within your presentation.

The 'moral' reflects what you're trying to say to your audience. There are well-worn morals such as 'bigger is better', or conversely, 'good things come in small packages'. It could be 'good things take time' versus 'he who hesitates is lost'.

When choosing the moral of your story, it's instructive to look at the famous fairytales that have been passed on through the years. Each had a very clear 'moral to the story'. For example:

What's the moral of the story of 'Little Red Riding Hood'? From a child's point of view the moral would be 'don't talk to strangers'. Adapting it for a business perspective, the moral might be 'don't deal with people you don't know'.

Three little pigs? For kids the moral could be 'don't take shortcuts'. For business? 'Don't use inferior materials or dodgy suppliers.'

Snow White and the Seven Dwarfs? Mmm, not sure what the moral of that one is. I never could work that one out. 'Keep your options open?' Who knows.

What kinds of stories can you tell?

Let's recap. You have to give a presentation. You've done your research using the Preparation Pyramid. You know what you want the presentation to achieve (your factual objective) and you know what the 'moral of the story' is. So what 'wrapping' are we going to use to convey that 'moral of the story'? What story will you use to cut through that 'white noise' so that your key message becomes memorable? There's a raft of storylines you can choose from. Here are three popular themes and some prompts you can use to get your story started.

1. 'Founder' stories

Founder stories are great for startup entrepreneurs as the media loves a 'how I overcame adversity to build my successful business' hard-luck story. Here are a few prompts to help you decide what the starting point for your Founder story will be:

- Can you recall an event or experience that has profoundly influenced or shaped who you are today?
- Share with me that moment when you just knew that you had to give up what you were doing to pursue the business/career you have today.
- What inspired you to start your own business?

2. 'What we stand for' stories

This story prompt is great for established leaders seeking to tell an inspiring story about values and culture.

- What situation or event have you experienced that led to you having the values that you have today?
- Elaborate on a time in your life when you became very clear about what is essential to your ethical well-being.
- Could you share with me a time when a principle that is important to you became not-negotiable?

3. 'What we do' stories

This story prompt is for those who want to communicate their 'purpose' for being in business.

- Share with me a time when you were deeply impacted by a person or situation, and how did this influence you?
- What is the personal legacy you believe you are leaving behind through the work that you do?
- Tell me about a time when you realised you cared deeply about the work that you do?

Startup entrepreneurs often use the 'Founder' storyline as it closely follows the Hero's Journey template we looked at earlier.

To demonstrate, let's take a fictional startup entrepreneur ('Wendy') and use the CCARLS six-step structure to come up with a great story she can use in her presentations to get the media interested.

How to use the storytelling structure to tell your startup 'Founder' story

Here's a 'Founder' story using the six-step story structure.

1. Context (sets the scene)

Wendy came to Australia in 1974. She arrived from Vietnam on a refugee boat with her mum and dad when she was just four years old. After suffering great hardship and deprivation on the boat journey, the family survived and settled in Sydney. Her parents didn't speak English so the only work they could get was in a factory. Wendy studied hard to please her parents, got great marks at school and pursued a career in banking so she could make money and help her parents live a better life. She got a job in the city, earned a six-figure salary and seemed to be successful. But she's not happy. She hates her job and the work is stifling. She wants out. She has a great idea for a business but she can't afford to give up her well-paying job as she uses those funds to help pay her parents' mortgage. She is stuck.

2. Challenge/hindrance (What goes wrong? What causes the upset?)

One day, on her way to work, Wendy gets a phone call. It's bad news. Her best friend has been killed in a car accident. She is devastated to lose such a close friend, but the accident causes her to re-assess her priorities. 'That could happen to me,' says Wendy. 'I could die tomorrow and I'd have wasted all the potential I have simply because I'm too fearful to step outside my comfort zone. I have to make a change.'

(continued)

How to use the storytelling structure to tell your startup 'Founder' story (*cont'd*)

3. Action (What happens as a result of the hindrance?)

Driven by her new-found passion to get the most out of life, she quits her job and decides to follow her dreams to become a fashion designer. To get started, she sells her hand-made silk scarves and shirts at the local market each weekend. Her parents pressure her to return to banking but she assures them the business will succeed. But the business is flailing. Sales are slow, competitors abound and she's struggling to pay her bills. On a whim, she applies for a business award. This is her last shot. If she doesn't win the award, and the prize money that goes with it, she has to return to banking.

4. Results (What disaster is averted?)

She wins the award. The prize money enables her to build a website. The media coverage from the award attracts new buyers. The website orders come rolling in. Investors take an interest in her business and offer her funding so she can expand. Her site grows and grows and within a few years, she's turning over millions, employing a team of 20 and has become a mentor to other young, female entrepreneurs. Her parents are proud of her and can see that her decision to take a gamble has paid off. She buys them a mansion by the water. Everyone is happy.

5. Lesson (What can we learn from this story?)

Wendy's story demonstrates that no matter where you come from or how little you have to start with, if you work hard, persist and believe in yourself, you can achieve anything.

6. Suggested actions (What actions should the audience take to learn from this?)

Follow your dreams, take a risk, have a go, get started.

Wendy's story is fictional, but if you read the startup stories that feature in mainstream media, you can see that the Founder storyline is used regularly. You'll also notice that the six-step structure is used to create drama, intrigue and curiosity.

Most business owners have a Founder story—what's yours? Try using the six-step structure to craft your story and then practise telling it so that you get confident and comfortable with the material. If you become successful, you'll be called upon to tell it, so you may as well start practising now.

Let's recap

Takeaways:

Here's a few tips on how to go about becoming a better communicator and how to influence others:

- Take time to learn how to write a media release or hire a publicist to help you.
- If you court the media, you must be prepared when they call—one wrong move could cost you your reputation.
- Get clear on what you want your presentations to achieve.
- Research your audience and tailor your presentation for them.
- Being a confident public speaker takes practice, so accept all opportunities to speak in public—practice makes perfect.
- Don't 'wing' important presentations—schedule time to prepare and rehearse.
- Use the CCARLS six-step story structure to create compelling stories.

IN CLOSING

That brings us to the end of this story and in fact it brings us to the close of this book. You made it! You are one of the few who finish a business book so well done!

So, what's the moral of this story? It's simple. If you want to build an online business, you just need to get started. Fulfil the true meaning of the word 'entrepreneur' and make it happen, take a risk, give it a shot.

You now know it all begins with a crazy idea. From there you build your MVP, share it with the world, get feedback, build your site, test it, sell it to one person and then another and see where that takes you. Learn from the experts to fast track your success and seek out like-minded collaborators who can help you bring your idea to life faster.

Yes, it will be challenging; yes, there will be times you'll wish you'd stayed at the bank or wherever you worked; yes, you'll have long days and even longer sleepless nights. It won't be easy, but then nothing worthwhile ever is.

The ball's in your court. Take action today—do something, anything—just don't put this book down without making one decision that commits you to the next stage of building your business. Make a phonecall, send an email, post a blog.

Believe in yourself and follow your instincts—and never, ever listen to what others say if your gut says they're wrong. Trust yourself. Back yourself. And one last question before I go:

What's *your* pinch of salt?

Resources, templates and checklists to help you get started

I've got some resources for you that you'll find immensely helpful as you go about building your online business.

Here's just a sample of the templates you can download from my website:

- Web strategy planning template
- Web marketing report template
- Web marketing health check template
- Social media planning template
- SEO planning template
- Landing page design template
- Guest blogging strategy template
- Content marketing sales funnel
- Blog post planning template
- Top 20 headline formulas

… and much more.

To download these templates and to find out more about my courses on how to build an online business, digital marketing and public speaking, visit:

www.bernadetteschwerdt.com.au

If you'd like to enrol in any of my courses on copywriting, content creation and SEO copywriting, visit:

www.copyschool.com

A final note

Thank you for reading this far. Thank you for buying this book. Thank you for taking a risk on me, and investing precious hours of your life listening to my thoughts and reflections.

I wish you all the best. I hope you succeed beyond your wildest dreams and that you keep in touch and tell me all about it.

I can be contacted at info@copyschool.com.

Twitter: www.twitter.com/BernSchwerdt

Facebook: www.facebook.com/BernadetteSchwerdt

LinkedIn: www.linkedin.com/in/bernadetteschwerdt/

Goodbye and good luck!

REFERENCES

Chapter 1

1. https://www.fastcompany.com/3043761/6-ways-technology-is-breaking-barriers-to-social-change

Chapter 3

1. https://www.marketingmag.com.au/news-c/realestate-vr/

Chapter 11

1. https://www.theverge.com/2017/3/27/15077864/elon-musk-neuralink-brain-computer-interface-ai-cyborgs

Chapter 20

1. https://www.stuff.co.nz/business/opinion-analysis/97446167/was-elon-musks-weird-spacex-presentation-the-mark-of-an-awkward-genius
2. https://www.inc.com/minda-zetlin/elon-musk-fails-public-speaking-101-heres-why-we-hang-on-every-word-what-you-can-learn-from-him.html

INDEX